What the Moon Saw

a novel by

Laura Resau

DELACORTE PRESS

Published by Delacorte Press
an imprint of Random House Children's Books
a division of Random House, Inc.
New York

The song lyrics on pages 164 and 241 are excerpted from *"Te Doy Una Canción"* and on pages 110 and 133 from *"Canción del Elegido,"* both by Silvio Rodriguez. The song lyrics on page 180 are excerpted from Violeta Parra's *"Gracias a la Vida."* English translations by Laura Resau.

www.randomhouse.com/teens

Educators and librarians, for a variety of teaching tools, visit us at
www.randomhouse.com/teachers

Library of Congress Cataloging-in-Publication Data
Resau, Laura.
What the moon saw / Laura Resau. — 1st ed.
p. cm.
Summary: Fourteen-year-old Clara Luna spends the summer with her grandparents in the tiny, remote village of Yucuyoo, Mexico, learning about her grandmother's life as a healer, her father's decision to leave home for the United States, and her own place in the world.
ISBN-13: 978-0-385-73343-4 (trade hardcover) —
ISBN-13: 978-0-385-90360-8 (Gibraltar lib. bdg.)
ISBN-10: 0-385-73343-7 (trade hardcover) — ISBN-10: 0-385-90360-X (Gibraltar lib. bdg.)
[1. Self-perception—Fiction. 2. Grandparents—Fiction. 3. Healers—Fiction. 4. Rural life—Mexico—Fiction. 5. Racially mixed people—Fiction. 6. Mexico—Fiction.] I. Title.
PZ7.R2978Wha 2006
[Fic]—dc22
2006004571

The text of this book is set in 12-point Minion.

Book design by Angela Carlino

Printed in the United States of America

10 9 8 7 6 5 4 3 2

First Edition

ACKNOWLEDGMENTS

I couldn't have written this book without the friendship and warmth of several Oaxacan women who have treated me like a granddaughter, especially the healers Epifania García Diaz and the late María "Chiquita" López Martinez. *Muchísimas gracias* to friends who have shared their stories with me and commented on the manuscript: the Gallardo Martinez family, the López López family, the López Salazar family, Javier Guerrero García, Sergio Gutierrez, Eustaquio Morales Gonzáles, Mercedes Ortíz Gonzáles, Alex Rea, Verónica Vásquez Hernández, Gaby Velarde, and August Wagner.

Deep gratitude to the writers in my life—Peter Fendrick, Kim Lipker, Suellen May, and Leslie Patterson—for their enthusiastic feedback on draft after draft after draft; Debby Vetter for valuable revision help; and Sarah Ryan, Joan Schmid, Tracy Ekstrand, Teresa Funke, Jean Hanson, Kathy Hayes, Luana Heikes, Paul Miller, Karla Oceanak, Laura Pritchett, Greta Skau, Lauren Myracle, and Hazel Krantz for their encouragement. Thanks to my talented editor, Stephanie Lane, for believing in this book. And thanks to anyone who's ever asked me, "So, how's your book going?" . . . because that kept it going.

I am forever grateful to my husband, Ian, and my father, Jim, for their unwavering love and faith in me. This book would not exist without my mother, Chris, who has not only helped me every step of the way, but also has always made me feel that anything is possible, whether eating ice cream for breakfast, impulsively moving to Mexico, or writing a book.

Finally, in the words of the folk singer Violeta Parra, *Gracias a la Vida que me ha dado tanto.* Thanks to Life that has given me so much.

Para mis amigos en Oaxaca que han compartido
sus casas y sus corazones conmigo

For my friends in Oaxaca who have shared
their homes and their hearts with me

Prologue

The moonlight touches them both tonight, despite the thousands of miles between them.

In a village deep in southern Mexico, wind slips in and out of a house pieced together from wood, reed, and tin. Just outside the door stands a woman who has seen nearly a thousand full moons in her lifetime, yet still feels a thrill at each new one. Most nights, she simply stands there, soaking up the calm expanse of stars, listening to mountains whisper secrets, watching leaves gesture silent messages. But tonight she is restless, uneasily rubbing the ribbon in her braids. She's had another dream of the young girl whose eyes are nearly the same as her own.

A faint rustle comes from the corn plants. A large white bird she's never seen before emerges from the shadows of the stalks. The bird stands on tall legs, close enough that she can see it watching her, telling her something. Yes. It's time, she decides.

With bare feet she walks past the bird, through the cornfield, over three hills, to a shack even smaller than her own. The sleepy-eyed boy who answers the door listens closely to her whispers.

The moonlight is bright enough for him to sit on the doorstep, pencil in hand, and lean over his notebook as the woman dictates a brief letter to him. She looks over the five lines of circles and curves and folds up the paper carefully. Tomorrow she will walk half a day to the nearest post office and drop it off. The letter will take six weeks making the journey to the Baltimore suburbs, to the neighborhood of Walnut Hill.

●

The moonlight pierces the girl's open window and shines on her eyelids, keeping her awake. Other people in Walnut Hill close their blinds, shut their windows tight, and seal themselves in their air-conditioned worlds. But this girl wants the night to come into her room. She wants the expanse of sky to fill her.

She tiptoes downstairs, slips out the sliding glass door, and walks to the edge of the yard, surveying the stretch of identical houses as far as she can see. They look like flat cardboard cutouts, scenery for a play—the fake shutters that won't close, the carefully landscaped yards with perfectly rectangular bushes.

What is real? she wonders. There is something more real than this, something deeper. When she holds very still she feels it in the wind—a whisper, a song, a low drumbeat. Sometimes she wants to scream, to dance wildly, to run and run until she gets to the edge and takes a leap into what is real.

1

Clara

Moonlight is what started everything, what led me to the edge one May night. Yes, I know I sound like a lunatic, but it's fitting since Luna is my last name. Clara Luna. Clara Lunatic is what some boys at school call me. I turn red and roll my eyes when they say it, but Mom says this is the way eighth-grade boys flirt. I wish they knew what my name means in Spanish: Clear Moon. I didn't feel like a clear moon on the day my adventure began, though. More like a fuzzy moon, just a faint light through clouds.

It was the afternoon of my neighborhood's spring fair, and I was supposed to meet my best friend, Samantha, at one o'clock at the snowball stand, but she was late as usual. I was sweating and waiting in line for a raspberry snow cone when I noticed a miniature Walnut Hill set up on the table next to me. It was an exact replica of my neighborhood—every single house was there! There were little plastic people everywhere—smiling kids with helmets riding bikes on my street, women gardening, couples jogging, a teenager mowing the lawn, people barbecuing on their decks. It was kind of cool, but kind of creepy.

I found my family's house, and sure enough, the shutters were dark green, and the aluminum siding was tan, just like ours. For some reason I shivered, even though the sun was blazing and sweat was dripping down my neck. In the backyard of our house, under a tree, stood a girl who looked about my age, fourteen. Her skin was lighter than mine and her hair was only down to her shoulders, but still, looking at her gave me goose bumps. Of course, her hair was painted on, so I couldn't tell if she had the same streak of pumpkin orange underneath where I'd tested blond highlights the month before. She did have the same chubby cheeks, and the same way of standing awkwardly, as though she didn't know what to do with her hands.

I paid for the snow cone and stayed staring at the tiny neighborhood, licking the syrupy ice.

"Pretty neato, huh?" said one of the mothers at the table behind a sign that read WALNUT HILL NEIGHBORHOOD ASSOCIATION. "You see your own house there, hon?"

I pretended not to hear her, and she turned away to talk with another mother about a shoe sale at the mall. Then I did something crazy. I didn't know why, but I reached over and tried to pick up the plastic girl. She was glued down, and didn't budge. I reached my other hand over and held down the turf grass as I yanked her up. She came up, but only after half my snow cone had fallen into my miniature yard.

The mother glanced back at me as slush dripped off the tree, making a red puddle where the girl used to be.

Her mouth dropped open, and before she could say anything, I turned and ran.

●

Samantha walked up to me at the bike racks just as I was fumbling with my bike lock. I could tell she'd spent hours in the bathroom perfecting her makeup, which was probably what made her so late. She begged me to stay and hang out with her for a while. I did, but I made sure we stayed far away from the miniature neighborhood. The rest of the afternoon I didn't talk much. I felt like a hazy moon, all fogged up with questions that Samantha wouldn't understand. *I'm more than just a plastic doll, aren't I? Who am I, really? Who did I come from?*

On Dad's side, I had no idea. All I knew was that before I was born, Dad crossed the Mexican border into Arizona, illegally—probably the only time in his life he'd broken a law. He hiked through the desert for three days and two nights, thirsty all the time, careful to stay hidden from the border police. In the cool darkness of night he walked, and during the blazing days he rested in the shade of cacti. Over the next years he picked tomatoes in the Southwest, and apples in the Northwest, and then made his way to the East Coast, where he mowed lawns and fell in love with his English tutor—my mother. He married her and started his own landscaping business. Then I was born and then my little brother, Hector, and we all moved to Walnut Hill, suburban Maryland.

For all my fourteen years I'd never thought much about Mexico—at least not until those questions began taking over my mind like tangled weeds.

●

The night after I freed the plastic girl, I couldn't sleep. The moonlight through my window made me restless. I picked up the girl from my nightstand and felt her hard and smooth in my hand. I couldn't stop fiddling with her, the way I could never help wiggling a loose tooth with my tongue.

After a long time, I slipped the doll into the pocket of my nightgown and crept downstairs, opened the sliding glass doors, and balanced there on the metal edge in my bare feet. The air felt damp and warm for a May night. The grass smelled especially strong, and the trees seemed to be watching me.

I took the first step onto the cold concrete of the patio. There was the hum of the air-conditioning fan, and beyond that, songs of crickets and maybe frogs.

Another few steps. My feet touched the wet blades of grass. This shocked me, woke me up. I walked across a wide stretch of lawn, and the ground squished beneath me like a sponge. I didn't know where I was headed or why I was headed there.

Once I stepped past the edge of our yard, the grass didn't feel any different, but *I* did. On and on I went. Across the Morgans' lawn, along the Taylors' fence into the Sweeneys' yard, around their plastic-lined pond and down their driveway. I cut across the cul-de-sac, through more yards and streets. No cars moving. No people. Purple-blue shadows draped everything. I realized I was making a beeline for the patch of forest that marked the end of Walnut Hill.

I crossed the border between the last trimmed lawn and the tangle of wild grasses. I walked farther and farther into the shadows, weaving in and out of tree trunks, letting my hands run along their rough bark.

I missed this feeling. Until the year before, Samantha and I used to play in these woods together after school. Sometimes we were priestesses who could talk with animals in the Otherworld. Sometimes gypsy dancers living in treetops in the Black Forest. Sometimes scientists collecting insects in the Amazon. I'd always thought it was a magical place during the daytime, but in the moonlight it was more than magical; it was a different world.

I climbed over logs slick with moss, and ducked under low-hanging leaves that stroked my hair. Now I was really leaving Walnut Hill. I was dropping off the edge.

I reached the stream where Samantha and I used to try to catch minnows with paper cups, before she became more interested in looking at fashion magazines than fish. What would she say now if she saw me? What would anyone say? Just when I was thinking that I *was* a lunatic, that I should go home and be normal, something made me stop. There, at the water's edge, stood a white bird balanced on its long legs, its neck a graceful S. I moved closer. Slowly, it unfolded its wings, and with three great flaps, flew up to a high branch. I couldn't see it anymore, but I felt it there watching me.

Down on the muddy bank, I placed my feet over the bird's forked footprints. Slime oozed between my toes. Suddenly, I wanted to know how it felt to be under the water's surface, inside a world of hidden things. I wanted to be wrapped in cool, underwater mysteries. I pulled the nightgown over my head and tossed it over a fallen tree. Maybe I was a lunatic, but something was calling to me, and I was going to follow it. Farther and farther into the stream I walked, to the middle, where the water nearly reached my waist. I lowered myself. I gasped at its coldness, but kept going until I was lying entirely underwater, every last strand of hair soaking wet. All the cells in my body quivered, awake, alive. *Remember this feeling, Clara.*

Almost as soon as I was under, I leaped out, shivering, thrilled, and threw my nightgown back on before I'd even dried off. I started to leave, but then stopped. I pulled the plastic girl out of my pocket and tossed her into the water. The current caught her and carried her downstream, around a curve—to who-knows-where.

As I ran back, my limbs flailed around like the wings of a crazy bird just released from a cage. Back to the neighborhood, the yard, the patio, inside the sliding glass doors. I closed them carefully behind me and tiptoed upstairs to bed. The next morning I wondered if I should tell anyone. Maybe last year Samantha would have understood, but I could imagine what she'd do if I told her now. She would slouch against the lockers outside homeroom and lean her head back and raise her plucked eyebrows. Then she'd wrinkle her lip-glossed mouth into a smirk and look around to see if anyone had heard me, and whisper, "Clara, you are soooooo weird."

Just thinking about telling her nearly gave me a stomachache, so I decided to keep it my secret. After all, the only witnesses were the trees, the white bird, and the moon.

●

Mom and Dad didn't catch me sneaking out that first night, or the second time, but the third time, after the last day of school, I got careless. I thudded boldly down the stairs and noisily unlatched the sliding glass door.

When I came back to the edge of our yard with muddy feet and wet hair, I noticed that something was wrong. The lights were all on—the kitchen light, the living room lights, all the bedroom lights except Hector's.

My insides tightened. This was it. I wasn't worried so much that Mom and Dad would punish me, more that they'd feel betrayed and never trust me again. How could I explain what I'd done? I wasn't even sure of the reason myself. I wiped off my feet and slunk inside like a guilty dog.

Mom stood there in the kitchen, holding the phone between her chin and shoulder, popping her knuckles one by one. That was what she did when she was very, very nervous. Her eyes looked huge through her thick glasses. "She just came back," she said into the phone, letting out a long breath. "Yes, thank you."

She hung up and hugged me so tightly I couldn't breathe. My ribs nearly cracked, she squeezed so hard. Finally, she took a step back and ran her fingers through her hair, which shot out in all directions in a frizzy blond halo. She'd been twisting and tugging it, which was another thing she did when she was very, very nervous. Then came the questions like bullets, like a police interrogation.

No, I wasn't hurt, I told her. No, nothing bad had happened.

"But what were you thinking, Clara? What were you doing?" Mom demanded, sinking into a kitchen chair. At least she'd stopped cracking her knuckles, which had been knotting up my insides even more.

I pushed my bangs out of my eyes because I knew how much she hated my hair in my face. I looked around for an excuse, and for the first time I noticed Dad standing back in

9

the shadows of the hallway. His eyes were bloodshot and his face shiny with tears.

I froze for a few seconds, then spoke. My voice sounded strangely calm as I lied. "I was swimming in a pool a few streets over." That was something Samantha told me high schoolers like her older brother did—pool-hopping. Somehow that seemed more normal than what I had done, more like a typical teenage thing to do. My wildness in the woods seemed too weird to talk about.

"That was the police on the phone," Mom said, her voice wavering. "We didn't know if you'd run away, if someone took you, if you were coming back . . ." and on and on, as I lamely whispered "Sorry" during the pauses. She lectured me until the sun started to come up, while Dad stood there, so silent, almost invisible.

●

He didn't say a word until the next evening when the letter came. He walked right through the front door in his mud-caked work boots, and handed me the envelope. I knew it must be important since he'd tracked dirt right across the carpet. The letter was addressed to me, with a Mexican postmark and stamps, and a return address that said:

Familia Luna Estrada
Domicilio Conocido
Yucuyoo, Oaxaca, México

I opened the letter slowly, wishing Dad would stop staring at me. His eyes were still wet from the night before. Mom came in then, her keys and jewelry jingling, back from dropping Hector off at soccer practice. She saw right away that something big was happening. I handed her the torn envelope as I unfolded the letter. "From Mexico," I said.

Her eyes grew big. She sat cross-legged next to Dad and held his hand so tightly I could see the whites of her knuckles. The letter was written in Spanish, in neat cursive handwriting, but a little shaky, as though someone was trying very hard to do a good job. The paper had been ripped out of a small spiral notebook, and still had fringe on the side.

> *Querida Clara:*
> *La invitamos a nuestra casa por el verano.*
> *Vamos a esperarla el día de la luna llena, en*
> *junio, en el aeropuerto de Oaxaca.*
> *Con cariño,*
> *Sus abuelos*

My grandparents. A light, tingling feeling swept over my skin. I'd never seen them before, not even in pictures. Sometimes my friends asked me how I got to be fourteen years old without knowing anything about my grandparents. Well, Dad hardly ever talked about them. When I was younger, it never occurred to me to ask about his life before he crossed the border. He was just Dad, and in my little kid's mind, he hadn't existed before me. Once I got older I asked him about why he left home, what his life was like growing up, if he had brothers or sisters, if his parents were alive. He answered each question with just a few words.

This is all I found out: He was an only child. His parents were alive in a remote village in the mountains. We couldn't visit them; it was too far away, too much money, too much time. When I asked if he missed them, he said, after a long pause, "*Mira,* Clara, I knew I couldn't go forward in life if I

11

was always looking back. I had to learn English and work hard and save money. And now, look where I am. I can give a good life to my children. I look to my future, not to my past." He said this as though he'd rehearsed the words in his head so many times they sounded hollow. After that, I stopped asking him questions. Part of me was relieved. It made it easier to forget that Dad had come here illegally.

I put the letter on my lap and glanced up. "It's from my grandparents."

Dad's face looked serious—but not in the stony way it got when he was angry. It looked as though a protective out-side layer had been pulled back, like when you peel off a Band-Aid and find tender pink skin underneath.

Mom's face glowed, lit up, curious. She practically had to sit on her hands to keep from grabbing the letter and read-ing it herself. "What does it say, Clara?"

My neck pulse was beating hard and fast now. "They want me to come for the summer."

Mom's mouth dropped open with a little squeal. "That's *won*derful!" She was still in her superenthusiastic teacher mode. "It's about *time* you met them, Clara!" Then she gave Dad a sideways look and raised her eyebrows. Her smile had a little bit of "I-told-you-so" in it. She'd probably been trying for a while to convince Dad to have me meet my grandparents. Whenever I asked her about Dad's family, she sighed and said, "Ask your father." I figured either she didn't know or she'd promised not to talk about it.

"But there's no one to go with me, Mom. You teach sum-mer school and Dad'll be too busy with landscaping."

"You could go alone," Mom said. "After all, you're the one they invited."

"But they don't even give a date!" My cheeks were growing hot and flushed. I looked down at the letter again, hiding my face behind my hair. "They just say they'll meet me on the full moon in June at the airport in Oaxaca—"

"Wa-HA-ca," Dad interrupted in a hoarse voice. "It's pronounced Wa-HA-ca."

I pushed my bangs out of my face and looked up at him. The *first* time in my life I'd seen him crying had been the night before. Now his tears came again.

Seeing him cry made me feel like someone had reached inside me and rearranged my internal organs. I avoided his eyes, set the letter on the table, and left the room, stuffing my hands in my pockets to stop their shaking.

●

At dinner, I could tell from my parents' expressions that they'd already made a decision, but I tried to argue anyway. I'd been wanting a change from Walnut Hill, but what I'd had in mind was a beach vacation to a tropical island complete with howler monkeys and wild parrots.

"I can't go," I said. "What about hanging out with my friends?" I loved summers, long humid days drenched in sunshine. Riding bikes on the paths in the woods, water fights by the stream, the cool relief of tree shadows. But then, I could tell this summer would be different, since all Samantha wanted to do lately was wander around the mall for hours or sit in front of her computer instant-messaging boys. Last summer, Samantha and I had been completely wrapped up in our collection of dried pressed leaves from the woods, but once school had started she'd made me promise not to tell anyone about it. She'd even thrown out her half of the leaves.

I thought about doing the same, but since Dad was so excited about them I stuck them carefully in a drawer instead.

"Two months away from your friends won't kill you," Mom said.

"I'll miss out on all the summertime parties." Samantha had gotten invitations to three boy-girl pool parties already, and I was still hoping I'd get at least one.

"Parties?" Mom asked, curious.

I shrugged.

Hector sat calmly during all this, eating his noodles and chicken and green beans systematically. He sat there like a prince on his stack of phone books, with his T-shirt tucked in neatly, and socks that matched the light blue stripes on his belt.

"Clara," Mom said carefully. "We think you should go."

"But I don't even know them!"

"You'll get to know them, Clara. It'll be an adventure," Mom insisted.

Easy for her to say. She wouldn't be the one stuck with two old strangers in the middle of nowhere. "What do they *do* there anyway?"

"Farm," Dad said.

"What will *I* do there?"

"Well, you'll find out, won't you?" Mom's cheerfulness sounded a little strained.

"How did they even know our address?"

In a raspy voice, Dad said, "Sometimes I—" He cleared his throat. "Sometimes I send them letters."

"You do?" Mom and I said at the same time.

"A few times a year," he said. He had more secrets than I'd ever imagined.

"Well, Dad, do they speak English?"

"Of course not."

"But my Spanish isn't good enough—"

Dad interrupted sharply. *"Hablas muy bien español, Clara."* Your Spanish is very good.

I decided to try one last angle. "What if they're not there to meet me? What if—"

"If my mother"—and here he paused. Maybe the words sounded strange for him after so many years. "If my mother says she will be there, she will be there." He looked out the kitchen window for a few moments, squinting at something far away. For the first time I noticed a few lonely silver hairs in his mustache. "You think it was a coincidence this letter came right after you did this thing last night?" His voice shook. "My mother knows things. She *knows* things."

I wondered what that meant. Mom raised her eyebrows, gave him a questioning look.

I'd never seen him like this before, and suddenly I had the unsettling feeling that I didn't know my own dad. Sure, I knew that his favorite food was marshmallow brownies and that he always woke up before the sun, and that he was scared of little dogs. But there was a giant chunk of his life that I didn't know about. We sat in silence and I watched the dark circles under his eyes.

"Time for ice cream!" Hector announced. He sucked the last rice noodle off his fork, and flashed his toothless six-year-old grin. He was too young to notice Dad's strange expression.

"Okay, c'mon," Mom said, and led Hector into the kitchen. They clattered around with bowls and spoons as Dad and I stared at each other awkwardly.

I could refuse if I wanted to. They couldn't force me. I imagined myself kicking and screaming the whole way to the airport and handcuffing myself to the waiting-area seat. But deep down, I wanted to know more about my grandparents, about their world far away from Walnut Hill, even if it was in a tiny village in the mountains.

"¿*Qué decidiste, hija?*" Dad asked me softly. What did you decide, daughter?

I closed my eyes. I was balanced on the edge of a cliff, peering over.

"Fine," I said at last. "I'll go."

●

In my room later that night, I sat on the carpet by my open window, with the vent under my legs blowing cool air up and out into the muggy night. Balanced on my knees was my sketchbook. Instead of drawing maps of imaginary tropical islands like I usually did, I started a list of what I would take on the trip:

> *CDs? DVDs?*
> *Seashell swimsuit?*
> *Shiny black shoes with ribbons and purple skirt*
> *Fuzzy green sweater with holes?*
> *Two tubes of toothpaste?*
> *Art shirt*

There were question marks after nearly everything, because really, I had no idea what the weather would be like. Or if they'd have a DVD player. Or a swimming pool nearby. Did they even sell toothpaste there? My shiny black shoes I would definitely bring, even though they gave me blisters. When I wore them with the purple skirt with tiny mirrors along the hem I felt like a gypsy princess. And I knew I couldn't go anywhere without my paint-splattered art shirt, an old sweat-shirt that Dad had given me that I used as a smock in art class.

Through the air vent I heard my parents' voices—low whispers that grew louder and louder until they realized how loud they were getting, and began whispering until their voices grew loud again. Their voices were muffled, but I caught a few words, including my name.

I tiptoed to the landing of the stairs, and sat on a step, resting my gaze on a piece of light blue fuzz on the carpet. Now Dad's voice sounded clearer.

". . . I panicked . . . when we couldn't find her last night . . . going from room to room, searching all over the house . . . do you know what kept going through my head? . . . that she'd left us, forever. . . ."

Now I heard Mom's voice, soft and soothing as hand cream, but I couldn't make out what she was saying. It was getting harder to hear them over the dishes clanking against each other in the dishwasher.

Then Dad's voice: ". . . and I kept saying to myself, this is how my own parents felt when I left . . . this is what I made them suffer. . . ."

The noise of the dishwasher filling with water drowned out their voices, but I didn't want to listen anymore anyway. It was giving me a funny feeling in my stomach, the feeling that watching Dad cry gave me. I went to the bathroom to brush my teeth and looked in the mirror, wondering if one of my grandparents was to blame for my chubby cheeks.

●

As much as I complained to Mom, and stayed clear of Dad over the next two weeks (I really didn't want to see him cry again), secretly, my curiosity about his village grew. It was impossible to have a blank bubble in my mind about the future. I had to picture *something*. What I came up with was a little adobe house with red flowers in the window boxes and a neat fenced-in garden. I think the image came from a New Mexico postcard that used to hang on our refrigerator. I figured my grandparents probably couldn't afford a regular two-story house with a big yard, so everything would be smaller and older: a small, old car and a small, old TV and a small, old refrigerator. Their house would have Latino flair, like Mexican restaurants—the chairs painted bright blue with yellow sunflowers, the floor covered with earthy pink tiles. Clay moons and suns would smile from the walls. For dinner, we would eat nacho chips and spicy salsa and cheese-smothered enchiladas, with shredded iceberg lettuce and diced tomatoes and sour cream on the side, and then fried cinnamon ice cream for dessert.

I opened my new sketchbook and breathed in the fresh smell of paper and drew the house I saw in my head. All the while, a voice inside me was saying that really all I knew was this: The plastic me-doll in the stream was going somewhere, floating around the bend. And two weeks later on the plane, sipping my ginger ale nervously, watching clouds from above, I was between two worlds, drifting down the stream, letting the currents carry me, blindly trusting that I would end up in a good place.

2

Clara

Trees were what my grandparents made me think when I saw them at the airport. Brown tree trunks, worn by the wind and sun and rain, solid and tough, scarred and callused. Their skin looked rough as bark, and their feet, in sandals, as leathery as Dad's old boots.

The look in their eyes, though, was gentle. My grandmother's—Abuelita's—eyes were black, like shiny beans. And my grandfather's—Abuelo's—were like bits of wet sea glass, one brown and one green, I noticed, amazed. The way his face lit up when he spotted me reminded me of Hector, bouncing up and down on his phone books, excited for dessert.

"*Mucho gusto en conocerla, Clara,*" Abuelo said, beaming. Good to meet you. They must have known it was me, since I was the only fourteen-year-old girl looking lost and alone.

Abuelita took a step toward me and touched my hand softly—not a handshake, but something more gentle, like stroking a puppy. Her touch calmed the wild jumping in my stomach.

On the way to the airport in Baltimore, I'd made a deal with Mom and Dad that if my grandparents were weird or mean I could go home after two days instead of two months. But I could tell already they weren't weird or mean. Abuelita's smile was full of light, like the ocean early in the morning.

We waited for my bags to appear on the conveyor belt, and Abuelo whispered to Abuelita in Spanish, "How she looks like you, *m'hija!*" And a moment later, "Clara! How you look like your grandmother, *m'hija!*" I'm not sure why he called us both "my daughter," but it seemed nice, like how Mom called me and Dad sweet pea or sugar pie. I pushed my bangs behind my ears.

Then he burst out, "Your eyes! It's your eyes, *mi amor!*"

I hoped he wouldn't bring up our cheeks, because my guess had been right; my squirrel cheeks came from her. On my grandmother, the rosy round cheeks looked cheerful, but mine made people think I was still in elementary school.

Abuelita looked at me with the hint of a smile, as though we shared some secret. Meanwhile, Abuelo talked and talked—about how good my Spanish was, how sorry he was he spoke no English, about how it was rainy season and he hoped I'd brought plenty of warm clothes (I hadn't), about how sorry he was that the only phone in their village had been out of service for three months. "So you had better call your parents now, Clara," he said.

Why hadn't Dad warned me about the phone situation? Or about the rainy season? Maybe he thought I would have used them as excuses not to come. I would have.

Outside in the sunshine, we stopped at a bright blue phone booth. I dialed a whole string of calling card numbers, and then cradled the receiver and counted the rings. My grandparents watched me, Abuelita's face calm and curious, and Abuelo's straining with anticipation, like a little kid in line for a roller coaster ride. After six rings the voice mail came on and I heard my voice, sounding young and far away. I mumbled a quick message in English. "Well, I'm here. I'm fine. They seem nice." A lump began to form in my throat. "It might be a while before I can find a phone again," I added, forcing my voice to stay steady. Then, even though I was a little mad they hadn't been waiting by the phone for my call, I added, "Love you."

When I hung up, my grandparents looked crushed. "He didn't ask to talk to us?" Abuelo asked solemnly. So I explained voice mail, which they'd never heard of. Even after I cleared that up, they seemed disappointed. They'd wanted to hear Dad's voice as much as I had, I realized. It had been over twenty years since they'd heard his voice.

We carried my bags across the parking lot, toward the bus stop by a palm tree. As we waited in the shade, the sparkle came back into Abuelo's eyes. "And your hands, *m'hija*! How they look like your grandmother's!" I couldn't see anything our hands had in common. Hers were thick and huge, like a landscaper's, like Dad's. Mine were piano player's hands, Mom always said, even though I gave up the piano after four months of lessons. Long, slim fingers with the nails filed into proud ovals and painted blueberry.

I caught a whiff of a nice smell—soil, campfires, leather. It came from Abuelo. Then I noticed the smell that clung to Abuelita. She didn't smell like perfume counters in department stores the way other grandmothers did. She smelled like chiles roasting, chocolate melting, almonds toasting. And like herbs—the teas that Dad gave me when I was sick.

I must have been smiling just thinking about it, because Abuelo said, "And the same smiles!" He dropped my bags, and stood dramatically still, watching a grin spread over my face. Even though I tried to keep my mouth closed to hide my squirrel cheeks, I couldn't help laughing at how hyper my little grandfather was.

I snuck a closer look at Abuelita's dazzling smile. Did mine really look like that?

●

The first bus ride was a short one, from the airport on the outskirts of Oaxaca City to the bus station downtown. On the way, we passed shacks and fields and trees with big orange flowers that I'd never seen in Maryland, or anywhere else for that matter. The streets of the city were lined with pastel cement buildings, with store signs painted right on the walls. Tiny Volkswagens filled the streets, speeding and beeping and weaving crazily around each other, skidding between buses, through puffs of black exhaust.

At the bus station we boarded a bus headed outside the city, toward a smaller town. The view out the window made me thirsty—dry brownish hills spotted with tall cacti and shrubs with sharp leaves bursting out in all directions like fireworks. Villages speckled the landscape, each with its own giant cathedral and cluster of small houses. They weren't the cute houses I'd imagined. Most looked haphazardly thrown together from unpainted concrete blocks and sheets of scrap metal. Heaps of sandbags and construction materials littered the dirt yards, and laundry flapped on barbed wire fences. The nervous ball in my stomach was growing bigger. I told myself not to worry, that my grandparents' house would match my picture.

After two hours on the second bus, we switched to a third bus. *Another bus?* I nearly groaned. I felt like stomping my foot and whining, *Why aren't we there yet?* When Abuelo saw the look on my face, he said, "Don't worry, *m'hija,* only one more bus after this! And what a beautiful ride! You will see!"

Even though it was early evening, the heat felt heavy. This third bus wasn't air-conditioned. I unstuck my thighs from the ripped vinyl seats and crossed my legs the other way. My body felt stiff as old spaghetti from so much sitting. My grandparents were dozing now. In front of us sat a woman with three chickens in her lap, their legs tied together with frayed twine. Every time the bus hit a bump, the chickens bounced up, flapping their wings and squawking. The bus held a strange mix of smells—animals, sweat, ripe fruit, raw meat. I pushed open the window and a fresh breeze blew in, rattling the panes and rippling through the torn curtains.

Now the hills were growing green and shady, thick with pines and flowering trees. Along the roadside, two boys my age strutted along without shirts. They looked tough, with faded red bandannas wrapped around their heads. They were laughing and casually swinging machetes as long as their arms. I wondered what they used the machetes for—hacking through jungles, maybe? An old barefoot woman passed by, leading a sheep tied to a piece of rope. The boys stopped swinging their machetes and stepped politely out of her way. A little farther on, three girls in too-small dresses and plastic flip-flops giggled and tried to keep their goats out of the path of our bus.

When we reached a town of low buildings painted sherbet colors, the bus lurched to a stop, clanking and rattling. It sounded like a bowling ball was rolling around in the engine. We were in front of what looked like a big garage full of blue plastic seats. TERMINAL DE AUTOBUS was stenciled on the wall with orange paint. The bus station. We gathered our bags, shuffled off the bus, and waited on the plastic seats, which turned out to be as uncomfortable as they looked.

At the curb, a three-legged dog was sniffing for scraps near a food stand with a torn cardboard sign. Tacos with head and tongue, I translated silently. My stomach was already beginning to turn. Tongue of what?

"Are you hungry, *mi amor*?" Abuelita asked.

"Not really," I said, imagining the whole head and tongue of some animal wrapped up in a tortilla. Were the eyes in there, too?

A boy walked by waving ice pops in the air and carrying a cooler streaked with mud.

"Would you like an ice pop?" Abuelita asked.

I nodded. The ice pops looked safe enough in sealed packages. Anyway, I was almost too hungry to care. At the airport, when it was too late to change my mind, Mom had given me a long list of things not to do: Don't drink unboiled water; don't eat street food; don't eat raw fruits or vegetables; don't eat without washing your hands for thirty seconds first. The last thing I'd eaten was the lasagna I'd nibbled at nervously on the plane.

Abuelita called to the ice pop boy.

I liked watching my grandmother. Her braids were woven with an orange ribbon and tied together at the ends. Her hair reached down to the small of her back, and it looked like she'd never cut it in her life. And another thing about her—even though she was shorter than me, she *seemed* tall. The way she held her neck long and her head high reminded me of a cat I had years ago. There was something catlike and graceful in the way she moved, even though she was so sturdy.

She gave three coins to the boy, and he handed her an orange ice pop.

His hands were filthy. The plastic wrapper dripped muddy water as Abuelita passed it to me.

"Here, Clara," she said, and settled back down in the seat.

I wiped the wrapper off on my shirt while she wasn't looking. The ice pop turned out to be mango-flavored and good. I licked it and tried not to worry about germs. I hadn't even been able to wash my hands after I'd peed behind a cactus at our last stop. I didn't see any sign of a bathroom at this stop, either. I wondered if I'd get Montezuma's revenge. That's what Samantha's cousin got when she went to Cancún and had ice cubes in her Coke. She spent the whole vacation in the bathroom.

Abuelo bought the tickets for our last bus, which would head toward the coast. The coast! Just when I started imagining a beach complete with snorkeling and palm trees, he said we would get off hours before the ocean, probably at around dawn.

What? A whole night of traveling? This was unbelievable.

Abuelo showed me the route on a map hanging on the wall by the ticket counter.

"It can't be that far," I said, looking at the key, wondering if I'd entered a land where time and space worked inside a different set of rules.

"Oh, but it is all narrow mountain roads," he said. "The bus must crawl slowly around the curves. Like a snake." He moved his hand like a snake and laughed.

I laughed back to be polite, but I didn't like the idea of any winding mountain roads. It sounded dangerous.

A half hour later, at sunset, when the sky was streaked with pink and orange, we boarded the bus. It started up after a few tries and made its way up the twisted road, snorting and wheezing as though it had a terrible cold. The houses along the side of the road were patched together from scraps of metal and plastic. We swerved suddenly around a little girl riding a rusted bike with a toddler in a diaper on the handlebars. I hung on to the seat in front of me. Chickens flew up, squawking wildly. I noticed they belonged to the same old lady who had been on our last bus. I wished I were back in Maryland in Mom's new Toyota with AC and airbags, riding along a wide, straight highway lined with clean rest stops and fast-food places. I wouldn't even complain about the talk radio she always made us listen to.

Abuelita rested her hand over mine. My fingers were still sticky from the ice pop, but she didn't seem to mind. The weight of her hand calmed me. It felt comfortable, like a winter blanket.

●

After darkness fell, drops of rain began to splatter the windows. The chicken lady's chickens settled down into her lap. I liked how peaceful they looked sleeping, all breathing together in a pile. Abuelo snored lightly. The rain pounded the windows harder by the second, and soon I could barely see through the sheets of water.

"What's out there?" I whispered to Abuelita.

"Jungles, mountains," she replied. Her voice was soft. "Banana trees, a tree called *huele de noche*. It smells lovely, you see, but only in darkness."

Huele de noche. Smells at night. Or, smells *like the* night. I remembered how the night smelled in the Maryland woods at three a.m. "And what else is there?"

"Oh, streams and rocks." She looked out into the darkness and cocked her head, as though she were listening very carefully to something. "A jaguar."

"A jaguar?" I didn't know whether to be scared or impressed. "Really?"

She nodded. "I feel it there," she said after a pause. "I feel it."

I strained to look out the window through the rain. No streetlights. Only the winding road, and next to it, a steep drop-off. Past that, darkness.

"What's below the cliff?" I asked.

"A big river, wild and high. It is the time of the rains, you see. Every afternoon, the storms come out from the caves. Like feathered snakes, they move across the sky. They move over the trees, over the fields, and bring us water."

Her voice sounded cozy. The way her words came in waves reminded me of how Dad used to tell me bedtime stories. As I began drifting off, she wrapped her shawl around me. It smelled like wool sweaters and fireplaces. In and out of sleep I swam, while the bus jerked this way and that, and the brakes slammed at the sharp curves. I dreamed that I dove deep underneath the ocean's surface, into the currents that move in the dark.

Sometime later my eyes flew open. It took me a few seconds to remember where I was. My eyes rested on my grandmother next to me. She was sitting straight up, her eyes wide open, staring at the driver. Her hand was squeezing mine tightly.

"What's wrong?" I whispered.

"Hold my hand, *mi amor*. You have nothing to fear."

What was she talking about? I looked past her, through the window, and saw rain streaming down the plastic pane. I couldn't see much through the watery darkness, only the edge of the road that dropped off at a cliff. Everyone else on the bus seemed to be asleep, wrapped up in shawls and blankets with their chins nodded off to the side. No one but Abuelita seemed worried. The bus twisted around the curves, jerking us from side to side while Abuelita kept her firm grip on my hand.

Suddenly, the bus skidded sideways with a screech. The bus lurched and my body slammed into the seat in front of us. Now the bus was tilting on its side, and I braced myself for it to fall all the way over. But it seemed to settle there in the mud. The floor of the bus was slanted down like a ramp toward the windows on our side, which were facing downward. The chickens were crying out and flying up in a confusion of feathers. People were starting to wake up, murmuring and dazed.

I rubbed my shoulder and peered out the window. Instead of seeing the ground, I saw something reflecting light. It was the river way down below, at the bottom of the cliff. It was churning and spitting up foam. It took me a moment to understand what was happening, and that was when my confusion turned into real, cold fear.

Our bus is clinging to the edge of the cliff.

My grandparents and I were sitting on the right-hand side—the low side—the side that would crash down into the river first. All kinds of thoughts flooded my head. *Will I ever see Mom and Dad and Hector again? Why did I even come here? I can't die now. I still haven't ever kissed a boy or painted a masterpiece.*

Abuelo was awake now. This was the first time I'd seen him without any trace of a smile on his face. He pulled down the window and stuck his head out into the rain, holding his hat. He craned his head to look ahead to the patch of light from the headlights; then he tilted his head up and down and moved it back inside. Water dripped off the rim of his hat, and underneath, his eyebrows furrowed together. "We must leave the bus," he said. "Before it slips down more."

Most people on the bus didn't seem to know what was happening. They yawned and stretched and sighed as though we were just stuck in traffic. Abuelo stumbled to the front of the bus.

"We must move people off the bus," he told the driver.

The driver just sat there in a daze, pressing the gas pedal, switching gears. He tugged at his mustache and muttered, "Don't worry, don't worry."

Abuelo moved past him and tried to open the door. He pressed his body against it, but it wouldn't budge. It must have been stuck in the mud of the embankment. Anyway, it would have only opened to the cliff's muddy edge.

Soon other people began to realize we were trapped. Their voices grew louder, as though someone were turning up the

29

volume with a remote control. Still, the driver insisted, "No problem." He pressed the gas and the engine revved while the wheels just spun in place.

Without warning, the bus skidded a little farther down and threw us all sideways. That set children screaming, babies crying, an old man praying, a piglet squealing.

Abuelo and Abuelita said a few things to each other in a language I didn't understand, then quickly gathered our bags and moved over to an empty seat on the other side of the bus, where the windows pointed high up.

Abuelita unlatched the window and slid it to the side. "Now," she said to Abuelo.

He climbed out the window until he was grasping the edge with his hands. Abuelita took his hands in hers and leaned out the window, lowering him down slowly. Abuelita's strength was unbelievable! When she let go, Abuelo landed on his feet in the mud below with a splat.

Next was me. I climbed to the window frame and squatted, holding my breath. The sharp metal edge of the window frame dug into my bare feet. I remembered over a month ago, balancing in my bare feet on the metal edge of our sliding glass door in Walnut Hill.

I turned around until I was facing inside the bus, looking at Abuelita.

"Let your legs out, *mi amor*," she told me. Her face looked strong and shiny with rain or maybe sweat.

I froze. I wanted to close my eyes and click my heels three times and be home.

"Clara!" Abuelo called up. "I will catch you!"

I didn't move. How far was the fall? I couldn't tell. What if I broke my leg jumping out? Or worse?

Abuelita looked at me calmly. "You can do this, Clara."

I let my breath out slowly and lowered my body outside so that I was pressed against the cold metal side of the bus and hanging by my hands. The edge dug into my fingers and I felt myself slipping. But Abuelita had a firm grasp on my wrists. She bent over, out the window, and lowered me slowly. My feet dangled in the space between the bottom of the tilted bus and the ground. The rain was drenching me and pounding the metal bus so loudly it filled my head. Exhaust fumes from the bus mixed with the smell of wet trees and something sweet—maybe *huele de noche*.

"Now!" yelled Abuelo, and I felt Abuelita let go of my wrists.

I closed my eyes and slid down the slick metal. As I fell, time slowed down and I saw things, heard things. The jaguar, sleek and spotted. The white bird high in the branches. Both of them watching us from the forest. I saw the little plastic doll and the plastic houses and plastic trees sucked under the rushing water. I heard the rain drumming out a deep, low song. It was the rhythm that had pulled me past the edge of Walnut Hill. It was the deep song that seemed to come from underground, or maybe from somewhere inside myself.

And boom, I landed in Abuelo's arms. He staggered, then stood still, holding me. I felt his heartbeat, strong at my shoulder.

When he put me down and the cold mud oozed between my toes, I remembered I was barefoot. My sandals were lying, forgotten, under the seat on the bus.

Abuelita tossed down our bags and Abuelo caught them. I expected her to follow, but no, she lowered the chicken lady, and after that, the three chickens in an uproar, dangling from the string. My grandparents seemed to be the only ones with clear heads. Soon the bus driver and the other passengers followed their lead. Within moments, at every window people were lowering babies and children, old women and men, and animals, until finally everyone was out, including Abuelita.

We stood together in the rain, goose-bumped, shivering, watching the bus barely holding on to the edge.

●

"No problem," the bus driver said, shielding his eyes from the rain and smoothing his dripping mustache. "In one hour the sun will rise and another bus will come. Don't worry." All of us passengers huddled together under damp blankets underneath the trees. The chicken lady sat on one side of me, and Abuelita on the other, with Abuelo on the other side of her. It felt kind of cozy, and I didn't mind the smell of wet wool and chickens.

I dozed until the rain let up and the sky turned lilac. People were starting to stand up and stretch, ready for the next bus. I dug my shiny black shoes out of my suitcase. I slipped them on and tied the ribbons carefully around my ankles. I hoped they wouldn't get too muddy.

The chicken lady looked at my shoes and smiled. She seemed to like them. She pulled a bunch of little reddish purple bananas out of her sack and offered some to me and my grandparents. When I said *gracias*—thank you—Abuelita translated into another language so that the lady could understand—*nku ta'a vini*. It sounded nothing like Spanish— more like Chinese. The words were choppy, some high-toned, some low. Abuelo explained that Mixteco was the language people here spoke before the Spanish explorers arrived, hundreds of years ago.

I tried to repeat. *"Nku ta'a vini,"* I said slowly, a little embarrassed.

The chicken lady threw back her head and laughed. She patted my shoulder and offered me another banana.

I took it. These red bananas tasted better than regular bananas. Or maybe I was just very hungry. *"Nku ta'a vini,"* I repeated. My mouth was full of banana mush.

She shrieked with joy and piled banana after banana onto my lap, while I smiled and chewed and wondered what other things I would encounter—besides the Mixteco language and red bananas—that I'd never imagined existed.

The next bus came along about an hour after sunrise. I had to leave my sandals behind in the other bus, since it was still stuck in the mud, waiting for a tow truck to pull it out. I climbed into the next bus in my ribboned shoes, which were giving me blisters on my heels after only a few minutes. Passengers already filled the seats, but they let people from our bus stand in the aisles. At the curves I shifted from one foot to the other, trying to keep my balance as people fell against me. My feet ached.

After an hour on that bus, the chicken lady got off. I was sad to see her go. Abuelo grew talkative, explaining the names of the villages we passed. The Hill That Flew. The Land of Hornets. The Place of Glowworms. Finally, with a huge grin, he announced, "We have reached Yucuyoo! The Hill of the Moon!"

It *could* have been the moon, for all I knew. There was nothing that looked like a town. Not a single house. Only hills thick with trees, and patches of fields and meadows in the distance. We were smack in the middle of a huge valley of light that fell through millions of moving leaves. Sounds of birds and insects nearly drowned out the bus engine's rumble. On all sides, green mountains surrounded us, and far above, at the peaks, clouds drifted slowly. It was like a dream that leaves you breathless but makes your heart pound once you realize there's nothing familiar to hang on to.

I swallowed hard. "Where is it?"

"We must walk a bit," Abuelo said brightly. He slung his bag over his shoulder and jumped up.

I hoped we wouldn't have to walk far. I wished I'd brought my tennis shoes. I'd been able to fit only one extra pair of shoes in my bags (since there were CDs and DVDs and other things that I was beginning to doubt I'd get to use). The ribboned gypsy shoes had won over the tennis shoes and hiking boots. And now the gypsy shoes were the only ones left.

As soon as we stepped off the bus, it chugged away around the curve, leaving us at the roadside, surrounded by my bags. For a minute I had an urge to run after it.

I picked up a suitcase and started walking along beside my grandparents, limping a little from the blisters. After about four steps, Abuelita stopped, slid off her sandals, and handed them to me. "Here, *mi amor*. You don't want to ruin your nice city shoes."

"But what about your feet?"

"Mine are already tough," she said. "Like a jaguar's."

"Not even a thorn could enter your grandmother's paws." Abuelo laughed. He skimmed his hand over her back.

Her sandals were well-worn leather with some kind of animal hair still clinging to it. The soles seemed to be cut from pieces of tire and attached to the leather with small nails. They fit me lengthwise but were too wide. I was glad she'd made me wear them, though, because we had to walk on a muddy path dotted with sharp rocks. For a while we walked through woods, through light that swam and flashed between leaf shadows. Soon we entered a clearing, a stretch of hilly meadows. My legs fell into a rhythm. Each step made it harder to go back to the bus stop, take a string of buses to the airport, and fly home to Walnut Hill.

We reached a small stream, and Abuelo slipped off his sandals. He rolled up his pants and waded right in. "It's only knee-deep, *m'hija,*" he said. "Easy to cross."

I took off the sandals and stepped into the cool water. It wasn't easy to hold my suitcase above the surface. Halfway across, I shifted the bag to my other hand and looked back at the hills we'd walked over.

Abuelita paused next to me, balancing the heavy duffel bag on her head, one hand steadying its weight. Her other hand rested at my back, urging me forward. "We have almost arrived, Clara."

I'd never seen an eighty-year-old with this much strength. When we stepped onto the opposite bank, her hand brushed a branch of small white flowers which leaped up at her touch. But they weren't flowers after all! They were butterflies, and as they rose, they seemed to emerge from her hand, one for each finger, flying up like magic.

●

A few minutes later, after we had turned a sharp bend in the trail, Abuelo set down the bags and pointed to the cluster of wooden and bamboo shacks that had just come into view. "This is our home!" he said. "And your home!"

One shack was the kitchen, Abuelo told me as we drew closer, one the bathroom, one the bedroom, one a living room with a little bedroom attached. They looked like run-down toolsheds. They were old and small, but that was about all they had in common with my imagined house. I peered into the living room to see if there was a DVD player. Not even close. Only three wooden chairs and a table. Not even a TV, not even a sofa or rug or armchair. None of the things that made a living room a living room. My stomach sank.

The farthest shack was the tiniest, just a few boards pieced together, with a torn sheet hanging over one open side. That was the bathroom.

I tried to say something but couldn't find any words.

"There is a market every Saturday at the next village over," Abuelo said. "If we leave at dawn, we arrive before the heat. Two hours walking." His voice was hopeful, trying to please me, but now I barely noticed his effort.

I said nothing. Two hours?

"But what a pretty walk it is," he added. He glanced nervously at Abuelita, who watched us in silence.

He motioned to a field of green stalks with big leaves moving in the breeze. "Our cornfields," he said. "We grow beans and squash, too. And in the woods, coffee plants."

I hardly heard his words. All I could think was, *How can I live here for two months without suffocating from boredom? How can I live in a place without even a sofa?*

They led me through a patch of weeds to a wooden shack with a tin roof.

"Here you will sleep," Abuelita said. "Your father's old room."

Inside it was cool and dark. There was no furniture except for a thin mattress on a rusted bed frame, and some broken crates piled against the wall. What creatures lived in that heap of scraps? Mice? Snakes? Definitely spiders; I spotted one crawling casually across the floor, as though this were his territory, not mine.

"Would you like to eat now or rest first, *mi amor*?" Abuelita asked.

"Rest," I said, trying not to let my voice shake. I let my bangs fall into my face to hide the tears welling up.

"You will be happy here," Abuelo said uncertainly. "You can take walks in the woods. You can help us with our work. . . ." His voice trailed off.

Abuelita patted his hand and led him out. "Rest now, *mi amor*," she told me, and closed the door, leaving it cracked.

Once they had left, I lay on the blanket and breathed in the musty air. Everything was a little damp—the planks of the floor, the scratchy wool blanket beneath me. I heard a noise under the bed, the faint rustle of tiny footsteps.

Sixty days stretched before me, empty and endless as sand dunes. No movies, no computer, no entertainment. My portable CD player's batteries would run out soon, and then there wouldn't be music, either. It was a naked feeling. *Who am I without all these things that fill up my life?*

I closed my eyes tight and tried to imagine my bed at home, the fresh flannel sheets, the down comforter, the pile of pillows. But it was impossible to ignore this lumpy pillow stuffed with balled-up fabric scraps. Or the springs inside the mattress that jutted into my back. Or the ancient, moldy odor.

I turned onto my side and pulled my shirt over my nose. I breathed in the last remnants of fabric softener. When I was a little kid, at sleepovers, sometimes everything would suddenly feel wrong, and I'd call Mom at midnight to come get me. Wishing for a phone, I fell asleep.

●

A patch of light on my face woke me up. It was coming through the crack of the heavy wooden door. I got up and walked outside and squinted in the bright sunlight, only half knowing where I was. I stood, dazed, rubbing my sore shoulders. To my left, fields of leafy stalks waved in the breeze. Behind them towered green lumps of mountains. Over the peaks, a few clouds spotted the deep blue sky.

I slipped on Abuelita's sandals and walked to the back of the hut. From here, the plants—corn plants, maybe—stretched over the hills. There were a few shacks way in the distance. I walked farther around the building, skimming my fingers along the rough plank walls.

When I turned the corner, I faced a garden overflowing with petals and leaves of all shapes and sizes. Their scents mingled together on tiny breezes—a honey-sweet smell, a sharp spicy one, a cool mintiness. All of a sudden, the urge to explore this place swept through me. It was the same feeling I had that first night I went into the woods in Walnut Hill. The feeling that something was calling to me, something waiting to be discovered.

I reached the front of the hut again, and there stood Abuelo, in the big patch of dirt and weeds between the four shacks. Chickens swarmed around him, pecking at the corn he scattered from a sack.

"Finally, *m'hija*! You're awake!" he called out. "Do you know you slept all morning?"

I shook my head.

"Why don't you go into the kitchen and meet Loro?" He motioned toward a bamboo shack where smoke rose from the roof. Who was Loro? A neighbor, maybe? Someone my own age might be nice. Maybe he had a TV.

Inside the kitchen it was dark and smoky. Once my eyes adjusted, the first thing I saw was a giant green parrot, perched on a rafter. He opened his beak and screeched, "*¡Hola hola hola!*" Hello hello hello!

Abuelita, holding a big tortilla, stood underneath him. "This is Loro," she said, "and Loro, this is Clara."

Abuelita showed me how to feed Loro bits of tortilla. He plucked the tortilla pieces from my hand, one by one, and I laughed at the way his beak tickled my palm.

"Loro has been on this earth nearly as long as I have," Abuelita said. She turned back to the fire to stir something in a clay pot with a long wooden spoon. Her bare feet seemed to merge with the packed-dirt floor beneath them, like aboveground tree roots.

Suddenly, Loro shrieked. "*¡Ánimo! ¡Ánimo!*" he cried.

I jumped, not only because it was so loud, but because that was what Dad would say to me when I felt upset. It meant something like "Cheer up" or "Have courage" or "Get your spark back." Whenever I acted pouty or grumpy, rolling my eyes and stomping around, he'd grin and say, "*Ánimo*, my daughter!" and I'd roll my eyes even more, trying to hide my smile. Or, the times I felt truly sad, he'd smooth my hair lightly and whisper, "*Ánimo*." It did cheer me up, but I never told him that.

Again, Loro opened his beak and screeched, "*¡Ánimo, Silvia! ¡Ánimo, doña Carmen!*"

"Silvia? Doña Carmen?" I asked Abuelita. "Who are they?"

Abuelo breezed into the kitchen. "Old friends of your grandmother's," he said, looking at her with a devilish grin. "Right, *mi vida*?"

Abuelita raised her eyebrow.

She motioned for us to sit on the wooden chairs, and began serving hot milk with cinnamon and chocolate, rich and foamy. I waited for her to explain, but all she said was "They were threads in the web of our lives." Talking with Abuelita was like diving for pennies. She'd drop some words that flashed like coins. Maybe it was up to me to dive down to find them.

She handed us thick tortillas folded in half, filled with orange squash flowers and melted cheese, cooked over the fire on a clay plate—a *comal.* Then she perched on a wooden chair, smaller than the ones Abuelo and I sat on—kind of a doll's chair. She seemed comfortable with her legs drawn up under her and a tortilla balanced on her knees.

I took a small bite, chewed cautiously. "Good," I said, surprised.

"Your father's favorite food, squash flowers," Abuelo said.

I didn't correct him. It might make him sad that now Dad's favorite food was marshmallow brownies. *But is it possible,* I wondered, *that deep inside, Dad does like squash flowers best?*

Abuelita rested her hand on my shoulder for a moment. Her touch made me remember what had been nagging at the edges of my mind all day, even in dreams during my nap. "Abuelita. Before the bus wreck—why did you squeeze my hand?"

She and Abuelo looked at each other.

"Your father has told you about me, no?" she asked.

"Well, a little." I searched every cranny of my brain, trying to find a story, a quote, any piece of his past with Abuelita in it. When I was small, he used to sing songs from his village and tell me stories about the rabbit and the moon. He'd always make me speak Spanish with him—but we'd just talk about everyday things, like what time he had to pick me up from art class. He'd never given me details about his childhood or his mother or father. All I knew, really, were the bare bones of his life. Finally, I thought of our conversation the evening the letter had arrived. "He did say that you *know* things."

Abuelo set down his mug. "Know things," he repeated proudly. The firelight glinted off his eyes. The green one looked translucent, like some kind of gemstone, and the brown one glistened like melting chocolate. "Your grandmother can see a whole world that the rest of us cannot."

Abuelita playfully poked his shoulder. "More hot chocolate, Clara?" she asked, standing up.

I nodded, watching both of them. Suddenly, more than anything, I wanted to know what she knew.

"Abuelita," I said. I was ready to take a deep breath and dive under to get the shining coins. *"Cuénteme."* Tell me.

She passed me the steaming mug, settled back into her small wooden chair, and began.

Helena

SUMMER 1934

The most beautiful things in life are unexpected, Clara. They tear at the fabric of the everyday world. The world of patting tortillas and fetching water and washing dishes. They show you the deeper world, where you talk with the spirits of trees. Where you see silvery threads connecting a leaf to a star to an earthworm.

I was just a young girl, about eight years old, the night I made my first soul flight. The whole day I'd spent working. Cooking, washing, sweeping, as always. That evening we were drinking hot cinnamon milk around the fire—Uncle José, Aunt Teresa, my cousin María, my grandfather Ta'nu, and me—when we heard something strange. The hoofbeats of a burro, growing louder, closer.

Ta'nu somehow knew. He put down his milk and said, "Ita"—that's what he called me, Flower—"bring me the *mezcal*. And gather *ruda* and white lilies from the garden."

He walked out the door. He was a small man, stooped over. A calm man. A man who never rushed, never panicked.

I leaped up and collected some cups, the *mezcal,* and a jug of water.

Uncle José muttered, "All these strangers coming. I'm tired of it."

Aunt Teresa looked down and said nothing. She hid her eyes whenever Uncle was near. She was a wide, round woman, but she tried to make herself small around Uncle. Small like a mouse hiding in the corner.

"Bring me another cup of hot milk," Uncle José barked at me, just as I was hurrying out the door with my arms full.

Aunt Teresa whispered in a brave mouse voice, "Child, go help your grandfather. I'll give José his milk."

Uncle shot her a dark look.

Before he could say another word, I stepped outside and into the dusk. A man and a woman stood by the burro. They held a child, a little girl, maybe four years old. Her body hung limp, like wet laundry. Ta'nu took the things from my hands. He led the family down the hill, into the curing hut.

I knew what to do. You see, I had been helping Ta'nu heal from the time I could walk. From the time my parents died. I ran around back and picked bunches of *ruda,* breathing in the smell. A sharp, strong smell. Then I gathered an armful of tall, white flowers, still damp from the afternoon

43

rainstorm. I ran back to the hut in the faint light. Mud squished between my toes and splattered my *huipil*, but that didn't matter.

Inside, on the table covered with statues and pictures of saints, candles were lit. The smell of smoking pine filled the room. On the dirt floor, on a woven mat, lay the girl, barely breathing. Poor thing, she looked like a wilted plant, a plant so close to death.

"My daughter was down at the stream," the woman said, "playing, while her sisters gathered water." She spoke slowly, trembling, wrapping her braids around her fingers. Her eyes were swollen from tears. "They said my daughter fell. *Crack*, her head hit a stone. And, still, she hasn't woken up."

Ta'nu took the white lilies and *ruda*, dripping with rain. He swept them over the girl's body. He sang and sang. Waves of words he sang, words that rose and fell. Words that moved up and down with his arms. That wove around us, then up through the cracks in the roof. Over and over, he called to her spirit. He asked it, again and again, to return to her body.

Soon, I knew, he would need the *mezcal*. I opened the bottle. Our *mezcal* was made from cactus juice from a nearby town. How it burned going down your throat, how it made your skin tingle! *Mezcal* has great power to heal, you see, when it's mixed with herbs. But some people—like Uncle José—gulp *mezcal* down. They drink it because they have a thirst for something else, only they don't know what their thirst is for. They gulp *mezcal* down until they collapse, dizzy. And oh, how they make their families suffer.

I passed the bottle to Ta'nu. He used *mezcal* only for cures. He took a mouthful and sprayed it on the girl in great gusts. Gusts like wind in a sudden storm. He called to her spirit, reminding it of the pleasures of life. "Hot cinnamon-chocolate milk," he said. "Warm hearth fires," he said. "Music, laughter, your mother's touch," he said.

But she did not wake up. There she lay with her braids half undone, a few fine hairs damp against her cheeks. Again and again, Ta'nu blew, but the girl remained still. Still as a tree on a day without a breeze.

Ta'nu brushed a piece of copal incense over her. Onto her wrists he rubbed it. Onto her forehead. Onto her temples. Onto her neck. Then he set it in the clay dish of smoldering pinewood. Clouds of smoke spiraled upward. Sweet smoke. Smoke that whispered a kind of language. If you paid close attention, it told you hidden things.

Up and up the smoke moved, and Ta'nu watched it. He watched it to find out what was wrong with the girl. I understood the smoke too, but he didn't know that. No one knew that. You see, every time I helped Ta'nu with his ceremonies, I knew what he would say, because I knew what the smoke had said. This time the smoke told us that the girl's soul was captured. Held prisoner by the spirit of the stream.

A stream spirit! Oh, stream spirits are known for their raw tempers. Up they rise, like whirlwinds. Up they rise, spewing dark water, angry waves, furious white foam. You can never tell when a stream spirit will fly into a rage. When it will lash out for something as simple as a girl stepping onto its favorite rock. So you can see why my heart was pounding fast, why fear was spreading over my skin like cold fingers.

"When your daughter fell," Ta'nu said to the parents, "her soul left her body for a moment. And in that moment, the spirit of the stream snatched her soul."

The mother bit her bottom lip, so hard it drew blood. "How can we find it?"

"It will not be easy," Ta'nu said. "She is very young. Her soul is just weakly attached to her body." He closed his eyes.

We watched him. We waited and waited.

Finally he announced, "I will find her soul and bring it back."

Before he even had to ask, I ran up the hill to the kitchen to prepare the sacred tea. The kitchen was empty of people. By this time, Aunt Teresa, Uncle José, and little María had all gone to bed. I stoked the hearth fire, then unhooked a small metal pot from the rafters. Into it I poured water from our heavy clay jug. I rummaged through the sacks of dried chiles and hardened corncobs piled in the corner. There it was, the crate packed with baskets of dried herbs. I laid the herbs I needed by the hearth and waited for the water to boil. Back and forth over the dirt floor I paced. Back and forth, skimming the bamboo walls with impatient fingertips.

Finally, bubbles began to rise in the pot. I dropped in three leaves of *yuku kuaa*, six of *ita tikuva*, ten of *yuku nuxi*. They steeped and I prayed. I prayed for the spirits of the herbs to help the girl, to give Ta'nu a safe soul journey. Then I poured the tea into a clay cup and brought it to Ta'nu. I was careful, very careful, not to spill a single drop.

Now a cloud of panic filled the room. Tears streamed down the mother's face. The father looked stunned, like a sleepwalker caught in a nightmare. Only his hands were moving, wringing each other out like rags.

"Ita," Ta'nu said to me. "We must do it now. The girl stopped breathing for a moment. She has started again, but the string that connects her soul to her body is fragile."

Ta'nu gulped down the cup of tea without letting it cool. It must have scalded his throat, but that didn't matter to him. His song started again, a song that rode on ripples of a stream. A leaf, floating away. His voice sculpted the night air like hands shaping clay. His voice created another world. A world of giant oceans and shooting stars and mountains. Of tiny hummingbirds, butterfly wings, new buds.

The song faded and his body fell limp against the wall. His journey had begun. Now his soul was traveling through the night, to the stream, to the girl's spirit. We watched his chest rise and fall, rise and fall.

"Is he all right?" the woman asked me.

I nodded. "Soon he'll be back," I assured her.

But Ta'nu wasn't back soon. Time passed. Much more time than it had ever taken him before. The girl's parents barely moved. Their eyes flickered back and forth between their daughter and Ta'nu. Back and forth, back and forth. Watching and waiting. Once in a while they looked at me with faces full of questions. But what could I tell them? I kept watching Ta'nu's body closely, making sure his chest rose and fell. Something wasn't right. This was taking too long.

He'd always told me never to touch him, never to wake him during a soul travel. It was too dangerous, he'd said. A touch could break the thread from his body to his soul. But he'd never told me what to do if he didn't come back.

Time passed. A dog barked in the distance. Silence again. Then another sound. A wilder sound pierced the night. The cry of a jaguar.

Soon the roosters would crow. Loud noises like a rooster's crow could also break the string. Ta'nu had to come back soon. Why was he taking so long?

His chest stopped moving. He lay still, perfectly still.

The woman turned to me. Her mouth hung open in alarm.

I closed my eyes. I willed Ta'nu to take another breath. *Breathe . . . breathe . . . breathe . . .* On a tiny current of air I entered his lungs. I entered his lungs and urged them to rise.

My eyes opened and his chest rose. He was breathing again. Breathing, but faintly. Very faintly.

"Wait here," I told the girl's parents.

I ran to the kitchen. Some tea remained at the bottom of the pot, a half cup's worth. That should be enough for me. I was half the size of Ta'nu. I ran back to the hut. My feet slapped the mud. I kept one hand over the cup to keep it from splashing. Back in the hut, I sat down, took a deep breath, and drank the cold tea. Oh, it was bitter. So bitter, I almost spit it right out.

I sang, the same way Ta'nu did. I asked the spirits and saints and God for help. The rhythm carried me, the rhythm of my voice. A voice that spiraled upward with the copal smoke. My tongue and lips felt numb, yet I heard words coming out of my mouth. Words that I couldn't feel myself forming. Behind my eyelids I saw swirls of light. Pulsing whirlwinds I saw. Whirlwinds pulsing with cricket sounds, with my heartbeat, with the light drumming of rain.

Then I was outside, in the night. But I felt no earth under my feet. I hovered above, at the treetops. Everything glowed. Only a crescent of moon showed that night, but the leaves and branches glimmered, silver. And everything pulsed with life. The trees whispered to me, the corn murmured. Even the stones were breathing. Over the treetops I moved. Below, I saw threads, like spiders' webs, connecting everything.

Walking, it would have taken hours to reach the girl's village, but my flight lasted only minutes. Soon I reached the shiny curving stream that marked the outskirts of the village. I floated above the woods at the water's edge, then made my way downstream. There they were, Ta'nu and the girl! On top of a cluster of stones in the middle of the river. Two wispy figures, glowing faintly. So faintly I'd almost missed them. Their soul strings seemed to be knotted together and pinned down with rocks.

But just behind them was something else. Oh, it was something so cold! Something that chilled my bones. Something that made me want to fly home as fast as I could. The spirit of the stream. He hadn't seen me yet, but I saw his eyes. Eyes that formed dark whirlpools, sucking me in, threatening to drown me.

I hovered, hidden in the leaves, helpless. If I tried to untangle their strings, the spirit of the stream might capture me, too. I looked around for a sign of Ta'nu's spirit animal, a deer with eight white spots. No deer to be seen. Perhaps the spirit of the stream had pulled the deer under its frothing waves. Ta'nu and his deer spirit had been rescuing souls all their lives. So what could I, a little girl, do?

There I lingered, at the edge of the woods, hoping the spirit of the stream wouldn't notice me. Then, below me, a noise. A rustle in the underbrush.

It was the shiny form of a jaguar! His spots shimmered like tiny moons, and he stood so close underneath me I could nearly touch his powerful shoulders. He looked up. Moonlight glinted in his eyes. Then, in one swift motion, he loped over to the stream and lapped at it with his tongue.

The stream spirit froze. The black pools of his eyes filled with fear. He backed away, downstream.

I watched the jaguar. Water dripped from his jaws. He looked straight at the stream spirit, opened his mouth, and let out a cry. A cry that ripped through the night like lightning.

In a flash, the spirit of the stream disappeared underwater.

Now was my chance. I descended from the leaves. Little by little I moved toward Ta'nu. His eyes held terror. Terror was something I'd never seen there before.

I looked at the girl. Her spirit body was thin and trembling. First I loosened the knots at Ta'nu's wrists. All the time I felt the eyes of the jaguar behind me. And I realized something. I realized he was not stalking me. No, he was guarding me, protecting me.

Untangling took a long time. Imagine the worst tangle you've ever gotten in your hair, how much patience you need to smooth it out. Then, after the soul strings were untangled, it took all my strength to heave aside the rocks. One big push on the last rock, and there, Ta'nu was free. He kissed my forehead, then helped me let the girl loose. How fast he was! His fingers were well practiced—quick and nimble like a weaver's. Soon enough, the girl was free too. She shook out her arms, and a trace of a smile came to her face.

I looked back at the jaguar. Still, he was watching me. His gaze was steady and tender, as a mother looks at her baby. How can a jaguar have tenderness, you wonder. A creature that weighs more than a man, that kills its prey with a single bite through the skull. A creature that dwells in secret places, where people never see. But I tell you, this jaguar looked at me with a fierce tenderness. I had no fear.

The jaguar took a last lap at the stream, then, with a flick of his long tail, turned and sauntered off into the forest. Into the thick foliage he went, where sunlight doesn't pass, where even moonlight doesn't pass.

Ta'nu and I held tightly to the girl's hands. Together we flew back over the trees, across the hills, into the yellow glow of the hut.

●

The next morning, the girl and her parents left for their village. They gave us a sack of *pitayas*—cactus fruit—as payment. Outside in the morning sunshine, Ta'nu and I ate them together. We leaned against a tree, worn out as old sandals, tired from the long night. Tired but content, eating the sweet fruit. One after another we ate the *pitayas,* our fingers sticky with red juice.

"Ita, little one," Ta'nu said. "You saved us last night. Thank you."

His words made me flush with pride.

But then he sighed. "Who knows how the stream spirit caught me? He sucked my deer spirit underwater and carried her downstream so she could not help me. Even so, I shouldn't have been caught. Oh, perhaps I am too old . . . perhaps it is nearly time. . . ." His voice dwindled. "Still, Ita, you have much to learn before your next soul flight."

"Why, Ta'nu?" I wanted to fly again, soon.

"Soul flights are dangerous, very dangerous, my child."

"When can I go again?" I pressed.

"You know your spirit animal now. You must thank him. That way he will always protect you."

Ta'nu sliced open another *pitaya* and handed it to me. The red seemed redder than ever. The shiny seeds blacker than ever. My life up to then had been like a forest reflected in water, I thought. A flat forest. Now I was beginning to understand the deep places, the high places, the hidden places. The caves and mountains and tree hollows. Oh, part of me was flying as I sat under the tree.

"I won't have to wait long, will I?"

"I don't know." He hesitated. "I've suspected that you would be a healer, Ita. As your father was. But the life of a healer is difficult. More so for a woman. I feel sad for you, little one." Again, he paused. "Yet I feel happy for you too."

"Why?" I asked, confused.

"Sad for the suffering you will endure. But happy because you will help others live." He took a bite of *pitaya* and chewed thoughtfully. "Through that, Ita, you will know what it means to be alive. Truly alive."

My cousin's shrill voice broke our peace. "*Helena!* Come help us make tortillas! Hurry! Before my father wakes up!"

It wasn't fair! Ta'nu always rested after staying up all night on a soul journey. I wanted to curl up under the tree too. Curl up and sleep, right next to him. Happy and full of red *pitayas.*

He looked at me with tenderness and brushed the hair out of my face. "I wish you could rest here too, Ita. But for women, life is work."

"Helena!" Aunt Teresa appeared outside the kitchen door. "The tortillas!"

I sighed and took a last bite of *pitaya.* Slowly, I chewed it. So slowly, keeping it in my mouth as long as I could. I rolled the seeds around on my tongue while I dragged myself into the kitchen. My tongue rolled the shiny black seeds as I patted out the corn dough, trying to remember the deep places and the high places. Trying to hold on to that flying feeling.

Clara

After Abuelita's story, I couldn't stop thinking about souls. Was my soul what made me different from the plastic doll? My soul, my inside self. When I was younger, my outside self matched my inside self, like a shoe fitting perfectly over a foot. But the shoes I'd been trying on for the past year just didn't fit right. They were too loose or too tight in places. Too stiff or too flat. All year in eighth grade I tried to get into things that Samantha and our other friends were doing. We went to the mall and walked back and forth past the plastic trees and the fountain with the fake waterfall. But it didn't feel right.

For a while I'd wondered if I needed to know more about

my Mexican roots. One day, my social studies teacher asked me to describe how Mexicans celebrate the Day of the Dead. I said I didn't know. Then red-haired, blue-eyed Hannah O'Neil raised her hand and talked about sugar skulls and altars for dead relatives. I sank down in my seat, feeling stupid.

As far as I knew, there weren't any other kids with a Mexican parent in my school. Some of them had Spanish last names but didn't speak any Spanish. Some of them had a parent from another Latin American country, like Venezuela or Argentina. Once, a girl in my math class with an Argentinian father invited me to her house. *Maybe everything will fit together there,* I thought. But they spoke Spanish with strange sounds in a strange rhythm. And when her father, a surgeon, asked how my own father ended up here, I turned red and said I didn't know. I left her house with a heavy feeling in my stomach.

Really, I didn't even know what my inside self *was* anymore. It seemed all jumbled up, like puzzle pieces that got dropped and somehow didn't fit back together.

I thought of the little girl's spirit that Abuelita rescued. I hoped my spirit was still all in one piece inside me, not trapped by an evil spirit in a rack of jeans at a department store.

All this was going through my head as I walked along the edge of the cornfield, toward the mountains that towered over Yucuyoo. My belly felt full from a late breakfast of beans and tortillas and lemongrass tea. Abuelita had said they grew almost all their food themselves. She'd shown me the bean vines, the tall clumps of grass that smelled, strangely enough, like yellow Life Savers, the dried corn still on the cobs that she stripped and boiled and ground to make tortillas. After the meal, I'd stayed alert for signs of Montezuma's revenge, but so far so good. Of course, the outhouse had been gross, and I had to sit over the wooden hole a full ten minutes before I was relaxed enough to go, but everything came out normal. Mom would have been happy that Abuelita boiled the drinking water in a giant pot over the fire to kill all the germs.

When the neat rows of corn ended, the land grew rocky. A steep dirt path led up through grasses and wildflowers. Hummingbirds and butterflies wove in and out of my path.

Abuelita's sandals felt solid under my feet. I'd told her this morning she could have her shoes back. I said I could wear my gypsy shoes with two pairs of socks so that I wouldn't get blisters. "No, *mi amor*," she said. "Wear my sandals. My feet prefer touching the earth as they walk."

Sometimes when you wear another person's clothes, part of that person rubs off on you. Maybe it was Abuelita's sandals that made me start thinking about hidden things. I pictured my life as a big forest. Up until a couple of days ago, I'd only lived in one little clump of trees. I'd thought that was all there was. But Abuelita had pulled me into another clump— another world. And here I was.

Now the path grew shady, with trees and moss-covered boulders along the way. I breathed in the smell of wet earth. This place reminded me of my nights in the woods at the edge of Walnut Hill, when I had the feeling that every cell of my body was tingling, ready for something big to happen.

The trail ended at a small stream, about knee-deep, maybe ten feet across. Water bugs ran across the surface and tiny fish flashed underneath.

I stopped and sat on a rock to map out the route so far. See, anytime I go somewhere new I make a map and think about the place from all perspectives. I imagine I'm a bird, looking down at the scene from above. I opened my sketch-book to a fresh page. With my pencil, I began tracing the path along the cornfield to the stream.

That was when I noticed the sound.

At first I thought it was the wind . . . but there was no wind. The leaves hung still. Maybe there was a highway nearby—it could be the rush of trucks. But no, that couldn't be it—we'd traveled hours on one-lane dirt roads to get here. And the stream was too small to make more noise than a soft gurgling. What it really sounded like was a waterfall—a muf-fled waterfall. If that was it, it had to be farther upstream. I slammed my sketchbook shut, stuck it in my backpack, and started jogging along the stream.

A little while later, I paused to catch my breath. I shrugged off my backpack and leaned against a rock face. It felt cool on my back. The rock outcropping towered above me. Vines draped over the rock's surface like a curtain of ropy hair. I had the urge to move back the vines, the way Mom always tried to push the bangs out of my face. The rushing sounded louder now, like a tub faucet turned on full force behind a bathroom door. But I didn't see a waterfall anywhere.

The sun was high in the sky, already past the middle of its arc, now dropping toward the mountains. My grandparents ate lunch in the late afternoon, and I'd told them I'd eat with them. I took one last look around and then jogged back downhill. My legs kept going faster and faster, until the rest of me was just trying to keep up with them.

Thunder rumbled in the distance, and soon, dark clouds blew in. The wind picked up, whipping branches this way and that. Green shadows flew past me. I leaped over fallen logs and ducked under low tree limbs. And you know the strange thing? All this wildness didn't scare me. It felt good. It felt right. What was *outside* me matched what was *inside*. I could feel my heart racing—*boom-BOOM, boom-BOOM*— and my blood pulsing under my skin—*shh-shhh, shh-shhh*— and my breath moving in and out like wind through a tunnel—*oo-hoo, oo-hoo*. They were the sounds of the water-fall, the sounds of a seashell pressed to your ear. Rushing blood mixed with pounding rain until the two things be-came one and the same.

●

Rain drummed on the kitchen roof. Over lunch, Abuelita had told me that in the rainy season buckets of rain fell every afternoon. I sat by the kitchen fire in jeans and my fuzzy green sweater with holes in it. I liked the holes. They were souvenirs from a hike Dad and I took through a thorny field in Maryland early last fall when the sky was unbelievably blue. No wonder Dad was so crazy about nature, after grow-ing up in a place like this, tucked into mountains and forests.

That hike through thorns in the fall was the last hike Dad and I took together. When I'd told Samantha about the hike at school on Monday, she said, "Clara, you are, like, the most wholesome girl in our entire school." After that, whenever Dad asked me, I made up some excuse about homework or hanging out with friends. He would look down at the ground and say softly, "Okay, then. I'll go alone. *Yo solo y mi alma.*" Just me and my soul.

Once Samantha hinted that my dad was stuck with his landscaping job because he hadn't gone to college like her fa-ther. It felt like a kick in the stomach. I didn't know what to say. Mom always bragged that Dad came over as a penniless fruit picker and was smart enough to work his way up to owning a business. Of course, I didn't tell Samantha that. I didn't want anyone to know that my dad was ever an illegal fruit picker. But if Samantha were here now I'd tell her that maybe he just wanted to be outside, around plants, because that was how he grew up.

I wondered what Dad and Mom and Hector were doing now. Dad, especially. I wondered if he was thinking about me, thinking about his parents, about Yucuyoo. I had a flash of inspiration and decided to fill my sketchbook with drawings for him. On the first page was the little pink house with shutters and flowers in the windows. I labeled that *What I Imagined.* On the second page was a picture of the shacks and outhouse and wild gardens nestled in a valley that I'd drawn my first evening here. *What Is Real.* I looked at the two pictures side by side. If you wanted something familiar and predictable to hang over your sofa, you'd pick the first picture. But if you wanted a picture that held surprises and secrets, a scene to look at closely and explore, you would pick the second.

I flipped to the page with the map I'd drawn of the path up the mountain. *Path to a Waterfall?* I wrote as the caption. I still didn't know where to put the waterfall, but I felt sure it existed.

"Abuelita," I said. I blew on my chamomile tea. "Do you have a map of Yucuyoo?"

She smiled, then laughed. "A map?" She shook her head and her earrings clinked like tiny wind chimes. "Oh, *mi amor,* there has never been a need to make a map of Yucuyoo!"

"Why not?"

"We know this land well. As well as our children's faces."

I took a careful sip of tea. "I just thought maybe for tourists . . ."

"Clara, *mi vida*! No tourist has come here before. You are the first."

I stirred a little more honey into my tea. I'd liked the idea of keeping my explorations secret—it made them more exciting—but it looked like I'd have to say it outright. "I heard a waterfall today."

"Ahhh," she said, nodding. "The spirit waterfall."

At that moment, Abuelo came into the kitchen in a dripping rain poncho, carrying an armful of firewood. "The spirit waterfall," he echoed. "The waterfall that is heard but not seen." He began piling the wood neatly in the corner.

"People of our village are accustomed to the sound," Abuelita said. "For us, it is part of the mountain sounds, the insect songs. Part of the breezes and the birdcalls."

"And no one's ever found it?" I asked. Now, here was a real, genuine secret mission.

Abuelo shook his head. "No one of this earth."

"The young people ask about it from time to time," Abuelita said. "But to my knowledge, no human eye has seen it."

My heart was nearly jumping out of my chest. Now all the pieces seemed to be coming together into a picture. My spirit was starting to feel more like a clear moon again. I remembered the way the waterfall sound seemed to call to me. Maybe even back in Walnut Hill it had been calling to me. I opened my tin of pastels, pulled out a brilliant green, and began shading the trees. "I'll find it," I said. My voice sounded a little more confident than I felt. "And," I added, "I'll mark it on my map. Yucuyoo's first map."

What I love about making maps is that they tell you what to notice. My map showed landmarks like the high rock face, with its scars and wrinkles, crisscrossed with cracks and vines. It showed a fallen tree covered in moss, like a woman sleeping under a fleecy green blanket. It showed two trees bent over the path with their leaves dangling in an emerald arch. You know, when I draw these kinds of things, I notice them more the next time I pass by. I almost feel like waving at them, as though we're friends.

Abuelita began collecting our empty cups in a metal bucket. She looked at my map a moment, and I felt suddenly shy.

"Perhaps it will be you, Clara," she said. "The first one who sees the spirit waterfall."

●

A while later, I looked up from my sketchbook and out the doorway and saw that the rain had stopped and darkness had come. Here it got dark earlier than in Maryland in the summer. I remembered the astronomy chapter of my science book, the diagrams of a blue-swirled earth and a bright yellow sun. It made sense that the days didn't grow as long here, since we were closer to the equator.

The only light came from the fire, warm and orange. A bare lightbulb dangled by a wire from the ceiling, but it was turned off. Even though my grandparents had electricity, they didn't seem to use it much. There were no appliances except for an abandoned-looking blender stuffed in a crate in the corner. Abuelo stood underneath Loro in the kitchen, offering him bits of stale tortilla. I shut my sketchbook, took a tortilla from the basket, and helped Abuelo feed him. Abuelita was taking eggs from another basket and cracking them, one by one, into a blackened pan of hot oil.

As Loro snatched bits of tortilla from my palm, I realized I felt comfortable here. Then I realized how unexpected that was. Most kids in my school would have freaked out in the middle of nowhere with nothing to do.

"What made you ask me to come here?" I asked Abuelita.

She smiled. "Your spirit was restless."

"It was," I said. "How did you know? Did Dad tell you in a letter?"

Abuelo shook his head and winked. "Remember, *m'hija*, your grandmother knows things. Now, me, I was worried you wouldn't like it here. I stayed awake at nights telling your grandmother, 'Oh, but Clara is used to TV and computers and city life! What if our food tastes bad to her? What if our life is too humble for her? What if she turns her nose up at our dirt floors?' But your grandmother said, 'This is what Clara's spirit wants. No distractions.' And it's true! You feel good here, no?"

I nodded. Nearly every minute in Yucuyoo I noticed another difference between it and Walnut Hill. Most of the differences either made me laugh or made me a little nervous. Things that made me laugh were the newspapers and old schoolbooks piled up in the corner of the outhouse to tear up and use for toilet paper, the glittery plastic purple jelly slippers that Abuelita gave me to wear in the bathing hut (which was a tiny shack hidden among the banana trees), the Barbie doll dressed in a poofy knit dress in my grandparents' bedroom—a souvenir from a neighbor's birthday party ten years earlier. Things that made me nervous were having no refrigerator (germs!), the fact that no one in the village seemed to own a car or a phone (emergencies?), and all the bugs and rodents living in my bedroom (just creepy).

Some things seemed plain strange, like the way pets were fed only leftovers. "Pets in the U.S. get their own special food," I said. "Bird food, fish food, cat food, dog food . . ."

Abuelo grinned. "You're joking!"

"Then what do you do with stale tortillas and burned rice?" Abuelita asked.

"Throw them out." I didn't want to get into explaining garbage disposals.

Abuelo's eyes got big. "So, there the dogs are very fat and happy!"

"Well, not too fat because fat dogs get fed *diet* dog food," I said.

Abuelo's mouth dropped open. Abuelita held a cracked eggshell in midair and stared at me. "Diet dog food?" they said at the same time.

I nodded.

They started laughing, first in little titters, and then in deep belly laughs. Abuelo clutched his belly, doubled over, nearly falling to the floor. And Abuelita buried her face in her hands. Her whole body shook. Every time it looked like they were calming down, Abuelo gasped, "Diet dog food!" and they shrieked with laughter all over again. For three minutes straight they laughed. They laughed until smoke began rising from the pan.

"The eggs!" Abuelo cried.

Abuelita grabbed the pan with a towel and spooned the eggs quickly onto our plates. "Ayy, Clara!" she sighed. She wiped her tears with her wrist.

I was trying hard to put myself in their shoes and see

what was so hilarious. Maybe diet dog food was as funny to them as using a math workbook for toilet paper was to me.

I took a bite of the eggs, which were only a little brown in places. I ate the way my grandparents did, tearing off a piece of tortilla and using it to scoop up some eggs. They didn't use forks and knives at all at the table, and only sometimes spoons. Tortillas were their utensils. They used tortillas as napkins, too, to wipe off the sauce around the corners of their mouths.

"How come the eggs don't go bad, sitting out?" I asked.

"Sitting out?" Abuelita asked. She tilted her head, puzzled.

"At home we always keep them in the fridge."

Abuelita squinted at me. "The hen laid them only a few days ago, *mi amor*."

"For what do we need a refrigerator?" Abuelo said with a proud shrug. "Even if we could afford one, we would never use it."

"Here our food is fresh." Abuelita smiled. Her gold tooth caught the firelight and made her look like a queen. "Good for you."

Abuelo added, "Nearly everything you eat here came from our land and our animals. Only a few things, like honey, we buy at the market. We pay with the money our coffee beans bring us. Which isn't much." He glanced at Abuelita and laughed.

I had to admit, the eggs were delicious. Much better than old eggs from a cardboard carton from the store. Like fresh-squeezed orange juice compared to the frozen stuff in a can. They were the tastiest eggs I'd ever eaten.

The next morning when I came into the kitchen, Abuelo exploded in another fit of laughter. "I couldn't sleep last night, *m'hija*! The diet food for dogs! Every time I drifted off, I thought of it!"

"It's true," Abuelita said. "Oh, how he laughed! For hours, Clara! I almost sent him out to sleep with the chickens."

As we ate, I noticed quiet sounds—the wood fire crackling, Loro rustling in the rafters, a pot of beans simmering. Sounds you might not be able to hear over the hum of a refrigerator. Maybe when you took the extra noises away, you could notice hidden messages. You could hear what your spirit was telling you.

After breakfast, Abuelita packed me squash flower quesadillas for lunch. She wrapped them in banana leaves, which she used like plastic bags. I stuck them into my backpack, along with a water bottle, two red bananas, a pencil, my sketchbook, a flashlight, a pocketknife, and a yellow rain poncho. The poncho looked silly on me—something I would never in a million years wear in Walnut Hill. But Abuelita made me put it in my backpack. "For later, Clara, when the waters come with such force you won't think of how you look. The trees will not care. The animals will not care."

That was another thing we had in common: We both liked to be prepared. Mom always called me a pack rat and complained about how I dragged my backpack around everywhere. For even a ten-minute car ride, I had to have books and snacks and CDs and my CD player and sketchbook. But it pays to be prepared. If I'd been allowed to bring a third suitcase, I would have had a pair of hiking boots with me. Abuelita's sandals were starting to grow on me, though, so maybe it was a blessing in disguise, as Mom would say.

All morning I wandered along a maze of trails on the mountain. I even explored places without the waterfall sound. I figured there might be echoes that tricked you. By the time the sun shone from directly overhead, I'd circled back to where the sound was the strongest. I sat down on a rock by the stream and watched the wispy-thin water bugs, and right then it occurred to me I might be lonely. Not completely lonely, since I had Abuelita and Abuelo and Loro, but lonely for someone to explore with me. Sometimes I just had the urge to point out neat things to someone else. I used to do this with Dad, and Samantha, too, until she changed.

"Hey, look at the shadow of that water bug!" I would say if a friend were with me. "Look at the perfect little ribbons the water makes in the sand!"

I leaned back on the rock, with my face to the sky, and then I squirmed around a little because a sharp point was jabbing me in the back. I sat up and thought. Maybe I could turn the rock over to lie on its smooth side. I wedged my fingers underneath the rock and pushed it over. I was so absorbed in my work, I didn't notice him coming up behind me.

"Don't move!" a voice yelled.

I froze.

"Let go of the rock and move back slowly!" the voice said. The voice was sharp. It was a guy's voice, I realized.

I felt the rock under my palms. I thought of murderers and gang members and genuine lunatics. The rock was too heavy to pick up and hurl at him, so I took a deep breath and turned to face him.

The boy was my height, and staring me straight in the eyes with a crazy look. Sweat was beaded up on his forehead and dripping down the sides of his face. We stood facing each other—him breathing hard and me just trying to breathe at all.

Our bodies were tensed, like two deer with their ears perked up, ready and waiting.

He took a step toward me. Then I noticed that his eyes weren't focused on me, but on the rock I had turned over. I looked at the rock. The bottom of it seemed to be moving with swarms of creatures that looked like small brown lobsters. They waved their claws above them and grasped angrily at the air. I stepped closer and bent down to inspect them.

The boy grabbed my arm. He pulled me back so hard I fell against him.

"Do you . . ." He paused to catch his breath. "Do you know what these are?"

I shook my head.

"Scorpions."

The word made my stomach freeze.

"Do you know what would happen if one stung you?"

Again, I shook my head.

"One sting on your toe would make your whole leg ache all day. Then it would feel prickly—like ants were crawling around under your skin. Three or four stings in the right places could kill you. The worst is if you're allergic to scorpions. Then, with one sting, your lungs would close up and you'd be dead in fifteen minutes."

At least a dozen scorpions covered the rock. I took a few more steps back and glanced nervously down at my legs to make sure none was crawling up.

"I didn't mean to scare you," he said.

I shrugged. My mouth was dry. I couldn't form words.

"Just—don't move the rocks," he said. Now his voice sounded gentle, like I was a scared dog he was trying to calm down. "Be careful."

He walked to the edge of a rock outcropping and yelled, *"Chchchchchchivo!"* Ggggggggoat! I walked toward him and peered over the edge. There were nine or ten white and brown and black goats scattered across the hillside, chewing leaves. Slowly, they wandered toward us.

Now that I was standing close to him, I noticed a strange smell—wet wool and sweat mixed with something sweet. He wore a T-shirt that looked like it had been handed down twenty times. It was so thin that light came through. He had on faded red pants, too big for him, held up by a frayed rope around the waist. And the weirdest thing: Sticking out below the cuffs were pointy black shoes—old-man loafers. They were strangely shiny, with decorative fringe on top.

He had on a woven-palm hat that was worn and comfortable-looking and fit his head perfectly, like it had been molded on there. And under the shadow of the brim were pink cheeks, brown skin, and sharp eyes watching the goats. It was the kind of face you wanted to keep looking at, soaking in every detail.

"See you later," he said with a sideways glance, and disappeared down the hillside.

●

During the afternoon storm I sat cross-legged under a rock ledge and watched drops slide off the points of leaves. The smell of rain and the sound of drumming water wrapped around me. Nature was becoming a wild force, bending the trees and turning the ground into a mud slide. A thrill swept through me. There was nowhere I'd rather be than this place on this mountain at this moment.

What was the boy doing now? Watching the rain? What was he thinking about? Was he used to these rainstorms, or did they make his heart race too? Was he someone I could tell about the water bug shadows and the ribbons of sand? Through the sheets of water, things lost their outlines and became blurred shapes and watery colors. I could be anyone, anywhere in the rain, and it would be the same. I could be Abuelita, my father, the boy, at any point in time, just sitting in the rain.

I asked myself a question. *Why were you restless in Walnut Hill?* A feeling washed over me: being underwater at night in the woods. *Remember this feeling, Clara.* Abuelita had said that the world before her spirit journey had seemed like reflections on water, and that afterward, she saw what was underneath. Maybe that was what I wanted, deep inside—to see the world that Abuelita saw, the world of spirits and webs of light.

●

When I bounced into the kitchen that afternoon, the green bird greeted me, "Clara, Clara, Clara!"

"Loro, Loro, Loro," I sang back.

"How fast he's learned your name, *mi amor!*" Abuelita said. She was dropping squares of chocolate into the green pitcher of milk on the fire. Abuelo sat at the table, bent over a sandal he was sewing. He glanced up at me and smiled. "Another pair of sandals for your grandmother." Then he bent his head down again and threaded the thick needle through the goat hide.

I grabbed an old tortilla out of the basket and tore off a few pieces. Loro carefully plucked them out of my hand. His beak looked ancient, covered with cracks and scars. "Clara!" he called again and again, between his tiny mouthfuls. I felt proud that he had learned my name; I was part of this odd little family already.

Now Abuelita was rolling a wooden stirrer between her palms to make the hot chocolate foamy. It seemed to whip things up just like an electric blender. I liked her strange kitchen utensils—a stone bowl to grind chiles and tomatoes, a clay *comal* to cook the tortillas, and wooden spoons, some as small as my pinkie and others as long as my arm.

"You seem happy about something, *mi amor*," she said.

"Yes," I said. I was surprised at the flush I felt coming over my face. "Well, nothing special." I tried to make my voice sound casual. "I met a boy." It ended up sounding too melodramatic. So I shrugged and mumbled, "He saved me from scorpions."

Abuelo looked up from his sewing. "What?"

I blushed. Now I'd made him sound like a heroic prince who'd rescued me.

"Scorpions," Abuelita said, raising an eyebrow. Not much surprised her besides diet dog food. "Who was the boy?"

"I don't know. He was about my age. He had a lot of goats with him. He was wearing red pants that were too big for him." I didn't say anything about his smell.

"It must be Pedro." Abuelo glanced at Abuelita. "You think so, *mi vida*?"

She nodded. "Yes, it was Pedro." She poured hot chocolate into our brown clay cups.

I took a sip, breathed in the cinnamon-chocolate steam. "So, who is he?"

"Past the cornfield, a few hills over is where he lives. With his mother. Only the two of them." Abuelo knotted the thread and bit off the end with his teeth. "All alone, she raised him."

"His great-grandmother was a dear friend of mine," Abuelita said. "Since he was born I have known him. Since he was this tall"—she held her finger at knee level—"he has had the gift of music."

Music? I wanted to know more but was too embarrassed to ask: How old was he? Why did he wear those shiny old-man loafers? Did he go out every day with the goats? Would I run into him again on the mountain?

As though she'd heard my thoughts, Abuelita said, "Oh, you will see him again, Clara. Of this I am certain."

●

The following day on the mountain, after hours of wandering, I thought I saw Pedro and his goats on the next mountain over. A tiny patch of red and a bunch of white and black dots moved through the brush. For some reason, my pulse quickened. He was too far away for me to call out to. I just squinted at him until he disappeared over the top of the mountain.

I didn't come across the waterfall, either, but I did find some bluish green mushrooms and tiny snails, which I sketched in my book. The caption read *Remember These, Dad?* He loved small, unexpected things in nature. He always marveled over the undersides of mushroom caps and squinted for minutes at the smooth spiral of snail shells.

I was wary of scorpions now. I inspected every rock carefully before I sat down. But I did feel prepared, since Abuelita had made me bring along a bunch of garlic to keep snakes and spiders and scorpions away. She said they couldn't stand the smell of garlic. "In all my years on this earth," she said, "no creature has poisoned me, and this is why. Garlic! Garlic, *mi amor*. I go nowhere without garlic." She wanted me to keep it in my pocket, but I was afraid my jeans would get stinky, so as a compromise we decided I'd keep it in my back-pack.

That night, halfway through our hot chocolate, Loro screeched so suddenly we all jumped. "¡*Ánimo, Silvia! ¡Ánimo, doña Carmen!*"

"Loro is making a demand," Abuelo said. "A demand to hear more of your grandmother's story." He gave a sideways glance at Abuelita.

"Yes! Who are these people?" I asked. "I still don't know. Silvia, and doña Carmen?"

Abuelita squinted, gazing into the fire, as though it were an old photograph. "Well, first you must know the path that led me to the city . . . ," she began.

I got comfortable, wrapped my fuzzy green sweater around my shoulders, and tucked my knees under my chin. I watched Abuelita's eyes turn younger and younger as she talked, until her face became as fresh as a girl's, her whole life before her.

Helena
SUMMER 1935–FALL 1937

For years, Clara, my life was drenched with aromas of herbs and spices. Day after day I hovered by the fire, tending to pots and stirring with my long wooden spoon. Stirring cinnamon into hot chocolate. Stirring oregano into soup. Stirring lemongrass into tea. Only a few precious hours in the afternoons were mine. I would slip away from my kitchen chores and find Ta'nu. Far into the mountains we walked, to places where the powerful herbs grew. We left gifts to thank the spirits for the plants. Gifts of eggs and green feathers and cocoa beans. Back home, we hung some of the herbs to dry in the rafters. Others we mixed fresh, with *mezcal.*

The second time I drank the sacred tea was not long

after my first soul flight. Ta'nu was out chopping firewood. A neighbor stumbled to our house, crying and carrying his young boy. The child's skin burned with fever. His eyes could see nothing. His mouth could form no words. His spirit had left his body.

As the tea brewed, I fetched a bucket of cold water at the spring. Back in the kitchen, I poured it into a tin. With his father's help, I heaved the boy into the water. Then I lit the candles and copal. Sweet smoke spiraled upward as I swallowed the tea. Softly, I chanted. I called on the saints, the spirits, God.

After a time, a table appeared before me. A table with two cups, beautiful cups, shiny silver. And a deep voice, a woman's voice, said, "Choose which you will drink from, the cup of good or the cup of evil." I chose the cup of good, and drank down every last drop. It was golden and sweet, like honey, and filled me with light. When I drank that light, I made a promise. A promise that always, I would use my powers for good, whenever I was called upon.

The boy lived. Word spread about my healing powers. As young as I was, people trusted me to heal them. And always, I used my powers for good.

When I was eleven, Ta'nu began to grow breathless at every hill we climbed. Oh, his mind still flowed clear as a stream, and people still came to him for cures, but he had little strength. Only enough to do a few cures a week. More and more often, Ta'nu entrusted me to drink the sacred tea, to make the soul journeys. When I'd return to the hut after rescuing a patient's spirit, Ta'nu would ask me, "What did you see, Ita? Whom did you meet?" and as I told him, he listened closely, nodding. "Ah, that must have been the swamp spirit," he would say. "Slimy, isn't he?" Or "Oh, that was the spirit of the clay cliffs—a tricky one, that spirit." When I told him how my spirit animal protected me on my journey, his eyes lit up. "Granddaughter, what a mighty spirit, this jaguar." His own spirit, the deer, was swift and strong and helpful, he said. Yet the jaguar! Oh, the jaguar! Raw power wrapped in silky fur. Only once in a while now did Ta'nu make a soul flight himself. When he did, it left him tired for days. How it pained me to see the deep circles beneath his eyes, to hear him struggle for breath.

Uncle José seemed almost happy about Ta'nu's weakness. No, I don't think he wished for Ta'nu to die. But he couldn't wait to replace him as head of the family.

One evening by the fire, while I was heating the milk, Uncle said something that would change my life forever. He took a long swig of *mezcal* and turned to Ta'nu. "I've decided that Helena will go to the city to be a maid."

My stomach jumped. I stopped stirring and turned to face them.

Ta'nu sipped his milk. Nothing shocked him, you see.

"She's useless here," Uncle insisted. "María and Teresa can do the chores without her."

I doubted María and Aunt Teresa would agree with that.

"You promised we would take care of her," Uncle said with a sneer. He pointed his bottle toward me. "But now she's old enough to leave."

"True, I made that promise to her mother," Ta'nu said. "At the time it seemed that your wife might never have a child of her own. I knew she wanted one. I knew she'd make a loving mother." Ta'nu's voice lowered to nearly a whisper. I could barely hear his words. "And, son, I thought it would give you a chance to forgive yourself. To let go of your bad feelings about your brother's death."

"What bad feelings?" Uncle cried. He threw his arms up, and some of his *mezcal* splashed out of the bottle.

"I am too old to argue with you, son." Ta'nu sighed. Orange light flickered over his face. Already he was turning into shadows. Already fading. "I only hope that someday you will be at peace with Ramón's death—and with his daughter," he added, glancing at me.

I lowered my gaze to the foaming milk. Rarely did people dare to mention my father's death. They feared fanning the flames of Uncle's anger.

"You spoil her, just as you spoiled her father!" Smoke from the kitchen fire moved over Uncle's face. He tried to blow it away. He swatted the air with his arms, furious. "You take her away from doing women's work. And why? For nothing, so she can waste time walking around in the hills."

"Helena is learning to cure, son, to continue my work," Ta'nu replied calmly. "And she will continue it. She will continue it far better than I ever did. Far better than even my own grandfather. This I feel."

My face grew warm.

"I don't see her bringing in any money." Uncle let out a forceful cough and fought his battle with the smoke. He tried to flick it away with his bottle. Still, the smoke moved toward him in a steady stream.

"Oh, in time she will," Ta'nu said in a voice full of confidence. But his eyes looked tired, strained.

"She's a woman," Uncle pushed. "She'll stop curing when she gets married anyway. She's more useful as a maid."

Ta'nu took a deep breath. Slowly, he let it out. He closed his eyes and leaned back, as though he were preparing to say something important. And then he snored.

My heart sank.

Uncle sneered and shook his head, coughing and laughing. I could tell he felt full of strength. Full of strength now that Ta'nu was losing his. For the first time he glanced over at me. I tried not to let my rage show. I tried to hold it in, but it shot out of my eyes. Like sparks, it burned into him.

He looked away and mumbled, "Leave."

I took the pot of milk off the hot coals. As I turned to go, Uncle added, "And don't look at me again with those eyes. Just like your mother's. Witch's eyes."

●

No one ever told me the whole story of what happened the day of my father's death. But I have been able to fit some things together, like pieces of a broken plate. Bits of conversation and stories here and there. People said that from the time he was three years old, my father had a calling to heal. Barely walking, imagine! Ta'nu began teaching him, and soon he was curing neighbors and relatives. Word spread, and soon people knew his name in far-off villages. Soon they spoke of him like a saint, a worker of miracles.

Uncle José was a year older than Ramón. You see, the elder brother should be the more important, yet José lived in the shadow of his younger brother. The kernel of envy grew bigger and bigger inside José, until that was all he was: the jealous brother. People said that he picked on my father every waking moment. Teased him, tripped him, played cruel jokes on him. But no other boys laughed; no other boys joined in. Instead, they leaped to my father's defense. And this fed José's black ball of envy even more.

The day after Uncle announced I would go to Oaxaca City, Aunt Teresa and María and I went to gather mushrooms in the forest. Every moment with them felt precious now that I knew I might be leaving. Every moment golden. Since María had heard the news, early that morning, her hand had stayed firmly attached to mine. Hardly a minute passed without her throwing her arms around me, begging, pleading, "Don't leave, Helena!"

Through the woods we walked, swinging our baskets. Aunt began speaking. "When your mother and I were young girls, Helena, we used to gather mushrooms together. Once we left the village, we'd make up stories. We'd wade in streams and climb trees. . . ."

"Let's climb trees now!" María shouted.

Aunt laughed and shook her head. "No, love. Your father will be angry if we don't have our baskets full."

I waited for Aunt to tell more. Memories of my mother were gems I collected. Precious little gems that I saved for sad times.

"I always wished I could be strong like your mother," Aunt said. She dropped a blue-green mushroom into the basket.

"Strong?" But I'd thought my mother was weak. So weak that after my father died, she grew sick from grief. So weak that she let herself die. Why hadn't she found strength to stay alive for me? How could she leave her two-year-old daughter? This was what I had always wondered.

"And brave, and honest . . . ," Aunt continued. She picked another mushroom from the base of a tree. "One morning, just after breakfast, before the men went out to collect firewood, your uncle José was in a dark mood. Oh, who knows why—you know his moods. José told your father he was more of a burden than a help with the heavy work. You see, your father was smaller than the other men, but he worked just as hard. As always, Ramón let the cruel words slide off him, like water over rocks. He left the table to join the other men, but José stayed behind, drinking the last of the tea. That's when your mother said to him, in a voice sharper than a machete, 'You, José, are a weak man. A shameful, weak man.' "

"She said that to Father?" María asked, her eyes wide.

Aunt nodded, smiling softly.

"And what did Uncle do?" I stared at Aunt. The mushroom basket dangled at my side, forgotten.

"He hung his head. He never could look into her eyes again. And he never taunted Ramón again. At least not whenever your mother was around."

Tingles swept over me, tingles of pride. My mother had stood up to Uncle!

I'd already heard the rest of the story. One afternoon, when I was two years old, a terrible storm struck. They say it was the most violent storm in years. Thunder cracked so hard, the ground trembled. Blinding bolts of lightning crisscrossed the sky. The men ran in from the cornfields, into the nearest house, for shelter. They began drinking *mezcal* to calm their nerves. Soon a boy burst into the house. Through tears, he sobbed that his goats were running, frightened, toward the river. And the river was rising. My father told the boy not to worry. "I will bring your goats in, child," he said. "Your goats will not drown."

They say the other men tried to stop my father. "You'll be killed!" they cried. But Uncle, drunk by then, said, "If my brother wants to play the hero, let him."

My father rounded up every one of the goats and led them to shelter. As he ran back across the cornfield toward the house, a bolt of lightning struck him. The goats lived. My father died.

That evening, after Ta'nu finished his chamomile tea, he stood next to me by the kitchen fire. On my shoulder he rested his hand gently, then asked me to do as Uncle said. "In the city, Ita, you will learn Spanish. To speak Spanish is a powerful thing."

"Why?" I asked.

"When we speak Mixteco the government treats us like squawking birds. In Spanish, they will listen." He grew silent. Then he added, "And, Ita, I fear your uncle's tempers. Of how he would treat you if I weren't here. Maybe it is better that you go. There in the city you will depend on no one. No one but yourself."

"But what about curing?"

"I have taught you much already, nearly as much as I know. The rest you will learn from other teachers who cross your path. Spirit teachers and human teachers."

"I don't want to go to the city, Ta'nu!" I threw down the spoon into the pot of tea. My tears spilled over. Yes, I still had a bit of a whiny little girl in me. But soon that would be gone. "Who would I work for?"

"At the bar, your uncle met a man from Oaxaca City. Don Manuel García López is his name. His family wants a maid, a quiet girl from the country." Ta'nu stroked my hair, trying to calm me.

"What will happen to you, Ta'nu?" He was fading, you see. His voice, his breath, fading. Lately his body seemed almost transparent, like fine lace. Like a mist blowing apart in a breeze. And at the bottom, this was my fear: that if I left, I might never see him alive again.

"María will help me with the chores. And soon I will need to stop curing." He paused. "Will you go to the city, then, Ita?"

I felt a sharp tugging inside, as though a rope held me to the smoky bamboo kitchen. To the mountains whose forms I knew as well as the lines on my own palms. To the stream whose water flowed through my veins. To the cornfields that nourished my body. This land was a part of me, as much as my legs and arms and fingers were part of me.

But if Ta'nu wanted me to go, there must be some reason, some dream he had, some vision, some words from the spirits that told him this was right.

"Yes," I agreed finally. "I'll go."

Three days later, I found myself walking along the path to town with Uncle José. I carried a big basket packed with my other *huipil* and skirt, a shawl, a blanket, mangoes, tortillas, salt, and limes. In a small sack tucked at the waist of the skirt I wore, I carried my herbs. They were wrapped carefully in dried corn husks, along with a flask of *mezcal* for making medicine. I hadn't eaten that morning. My stomach was too full of worries, too full of questions. Where would I make offerings to the gods and my spirit animal, so far away from the caves of my village? How would I find the spirits? How would they find me?

I worried about María and Aunt Teresa. María had cried all morning long. She'd buried her head in my shoulder, and her stream of tears had soaked my *huipil*. Already I missed how she touched me on the arm as if we were sisters. Already I missed her funny stories, how she imitated the silly things Uncle did when he was drunk. And already I missed Aunt

80

Teresa's soft, timid face. How she brought bowls of chicken broth to me when I was sick, how she placed her hand on my forehead when I had bad dreams.

Uncle had me wait at the doorway of the darkened bar full of men. Rowdy men, laughing and shouting. I watched him walk over to a man standing in the corner. The man was a head taller than the others and wore an expensive-looking leather hat. He had fine cheekbones and full lips. And a smug smile. The kind of smile that said he knew how charming he was. He strutted toward me and threw back his shoulders. His torso formed a perfect V.

When Uncle introduced us, don Manuel lifted one corner of his mouth. I offered my hand, but instead of touching it lightly, he gripped it. The way a hand clamps onto a chicken just before snapping its neck. His eyes moved over me. I wanted to run out the door and hide behind a tree.

"We'll be on our way, then," don Manuel said, touching the back of my neck. I cringed.

For a moment Uncle looked uncertain. He glanced at don Manuel, then at me, then back at don Manuel. Maybe he wouldn't make me go after all.

"Don't worry, José," don Manuel laughed. "She's a little too young for me."

Uncle hesitated. I held my breath. Then his face relaxed into a grin. He reached out his hand to shake don Manuel's. Uncle turned to me, and for a few seconds, he looked as though he might hug me, or at least touch my hand. But he only nodded at me, then disappeared into the bar.

For a moment, I thought about running back home. Instead, I took a deep breath and looked up at don Manuel. He motioned for me to climb into the back of his wagon with the baskets.

I sat on the wood planks. On one side of me was a tall basket of guavas that kept rolling onto my head during the journey. On the other side, a giant sack of corncobs, which I tried to use as a lumpy pillow. Don Manuel's business, Ta'nu had told me, was buying fruits and vegetables from the villages and selling them in Oaxaca City to market vendors.

I'd never been to the city before, but Ta'nu had said it took a couple of days of travel. At dusk we stopped at a small wooden shelter by a trickle of a stream. Don Manuel said we would sleep there. He gave the horses water, then ate some dried meat and tortillas and drank *mezcal*. He didn't offer me anything. This surprised me. You see, in my village there was a saying: We all eat from the same tortilla. This means that everyone should share. Everyone should respect each other, because at the bottom, we are all people.

I squeezed some lime onto my tortilla, sprinkled it with salt, and chewed slowly to make it last longer. Then I walked behind the trees and relieved myself. By the base of a tree I squatted, looking around at the needle-sharp leaves, the thorny shrubs. The plants were different here. We were no longer high in mountains that touched the clouds. Tall cacti covered the land, and the air felt dry. What a thirsty, lonely feeling it gave me. *I could run now,* I thought, *run and live on food from the land and sleep in caves.*

I didn't run. I tell you, if I had known what was going to happen over the next year, maybe I would have. But that is not how life works. Life is a tree, branching out here and there, and there is no sense in asking, What if I had followed this branch, not that one? Later in my life I would run away, not once, but twice, from different places, different dangers, but now was not the time for that.

I ducked inside the shelter, spread out my *petate*, and lay down. I covered myself with the wool blanket. Don Manuel laid his *petate* down beside mine, so close I could feel his breath moving my hair. I stood up suddenly and snatched up my blanket and *petate*.

"I'm sleeping in the wagon," I said, looking down at him.

He stretched his arms behind his head. "Suit yourself." He let out a smug laugh. "But as I said, you're too young for me anyway."

In the wagon, I curled up by the baskets of food. My muscles stayed as tense as violin strings until I heard his loud snoring. Only then did I let myself sink into sleep.

●

We hardly spoke for the whole trip. The next evening, in the low mountains, we turned a curve and Oaxaca City came into view. It was a forest of houses, more houses than I'd ever seen in one place. On the outskirts were huts of wood and clay and bamboo, like the ones in my village. But in the center, the stone buildings towered high like churches. I had never seen houses of two floors before. And some of these had three! And glass windows and carved wooden doors, and fountains in the courtyards. When we passed the market there were so many people I couldn't find my breath. Like ants in an anthill they scurried around. I imagine everyone had some task to do, but I could find no order.

I felt small suddenly, like an ant myself. I could be crushed, killed, and things would go on. Who would notice? In my village, life had felt solid, like a mountain. But here it was a fog that could disappear by late morning.

Don Manuel seemed excited to be back in town. Finally,

he started talking to me. He spoke Mixteco with an accent, so I had to listen closely to understand. He had left the village as a boy to live in the city, where people speak Spanish. His tongue had forgotten the rhythms of my language, just as his mind had forgotten our customs.

"This is the market," he pointed out. "Here you will come to buy our food every day."

How would I find my way through this place? It terrified me! How strange that my spirit had traveled to distant lands and fought evil spirits, yet in this city I felt like a frightened baby bird plucked from its nest.

Some people looked like me—two long braids and a red *huipil* and black skirt that just covered my knees. Other women wore *huipiles* in patterns and colors I had never seen. *Huipiles* with white ruffles embroidered with pink roses. *Huipiles* with flouncy yellow and purple skirts and short tops covered with finely stitched flowers. And some women wore long dresses of thin, flimsy fabric, tight at the top. How could they bend over to gather firewood without tearing those seams? Or roll up those narrow sleeves to wash clothes? Or catch stray goats on cliffs with those tiny pointed shoes?

And the men wore black! In my village they wore white, except for gray wool ponchos when it was cold. Some of these city men were dressed all in black, right up to their hats. But their faces were bone-colored.

"The rich-folk section of town," don Manuel said.

We turned down a street with fewer people now. The building on the corner had no glass in its windows, only iron bars.

"The jail."

A pair of hands stretched through the bars. They

clutched half a *tamal* that a passerby placed in them. The hands pulled the *tamal* through the bars and then reached out, empty now, grasping for more.

"My neighbor was in there. After his wife died, no one brought him food." Don Manuel shrugged. "He's dead now."

What kind of place was this? Neighbors letting neighbors starve? How could they do this, when we all eat from the same tortilla? Already I did not like it. I would bring the prisoners food, I decided—old tortillas and fruit and any leftover meals.

Our wagon pulled up to my new home. Don Manuel clanked open a tall black gate. He led the horses and me into a courtyard. Oh, it was a pretty place, filled with trees and flowering bushes. From one of the trees, a call rang out. A shrill, piercing voice. "*¡Buenas tardes buenas tardes!*"

I looked closer. Feathers rippled, feathers the brilliant green of newly formed leaves. It was a *loro*—a talking parrot—and his greetings were the first Spanish words I learned. He would become my teacher, and my best friend.

Don Manuel's wife came out of a doorway, stuffing a pastry into her mouth. She looked like a big ball of tortilla dough squeezed into a dress, bursting out at the openings. She said something to don Manuel in Spanish. I didn't understand the words, but the meaning was clear from the greedy look in her eyes. She poked through the bags in the back of the wagon. Her husband handed her three guavas from the sack. She crammed the rest of the pastry in her mouth, then started on the guavas.

"My wife, Carmen," he said. "She and my daughter speak only Spanish. You will learn quickly how to follow their commands. That is all the Spanish you will need."

A daughter! Someone to be sisters with! Like María, to laugh with as we cooked together. Maybe I wouldn't be so lonely after all.

Doña Carmen pushed me inside the kitchen. She motioned to the corner of the room, gesturing that I would sleep there. In that corner I would spread my *petate* out at night and roll it up in the mornings. She showed me the bucket and rags, the basin where I would do the washing. She showed me every corner of the house I was to clean.

Meanwhile, I watched her munching on the guavas. My mouth watered, and oh, how I wished she would offer me some. I had eaten my last tortilla that morning. In my village, you see, people always offered food the moment someone walked in the door. First offered them food, then offered them a wooden chair to rest their legs.

Doña Carmen led me into a room where a girl a little older than me sat in a chair. She sat slouched, staring at herself in a mirror. First she pouted her lips out like a grumpy baby, then puckered them in like a bitter old woman. Then she raised and lowered her eyebrows, then turned her head this way and that.

Doña Carmen spoke to her in a guarded voice. A voice you might use to talk to a wild, snarling dog. "Silvia."

They rattled away in Spanish until the girl pulled something out of a drawer. She walked over to me and dropped it in my lap without meeting my eyes. It was a white skirt, trimmed with pink ribbon, torn at the hem. Silvia yelled at her mother. Oh, how that girl could yell! She spit out a string of words I didn't understand. With a frown, doña Carmen handed me a needle and thread, and gestured to me to mend the skirt.

Later I would realize that this fighting was nothing unusual in the García López household. And Silvia, it turned out, would be far from a friend. She would treat me like a cockroach. A slightly useful cockroach who could cook and mend clothes, but still an insect.

●

My days were the same: wake up in darkness, fetch water from the pump, heat the water, make tortillas and beans, serve breakfast to the family, eat their leftovers, wash the dishes, heat more water, wash the clothes, hang them to dry, sweep the courtyard, mop the floors, dust the furniture, shine the wood, polish the glass, go to the market for food, make lunch, clean up, mend their clothes, and on and on until they finished their hot chocolate at night and went to sleep. I would sip the leftover hot chocolate, wash the dishes, and then, past midnight, unroll my *petate* and sleep. For a few precious hours I slept, until the church bells woke me up before dawn again. My body felt worn out, like an old grandmother's. And I was only eleven!

During that time I learned to love dawn, the moments before the chores of the day had begun to weigh heavy. At dawn the world was all fresh pathways, waiting to be followed. There was only a whisper between the living and the dead. Sometimes at dawn I felt that I could reach out my hand and touch my parents. That just outside the firelight, there they were, sitting in the shadows, watching me.

At dawn the *loro* fluttered with excitement. He greeted me with whistles, with *"¡Buenos dias buenos dias!"* Good morning good morning! How good it felt to have some creature happy to see me! When I'd first seen him, he'd looked sickly and sad. Droopy eyes, droopy head, droopy wings. He had been a gift from don Manuel to Silvia. Yet she barely looked at him, barely fed him. She never spoke to him with kind words, only shouts and curses.

Oh! But I loved that bird! I whispered to him as I washed dishes in the courtyard. I sang him songs in Mixteco. I told him stories about the rabbit and the moon, about the coyote and the snake, about the devil in the cave. And would you believe it? He started speaking Mixteco! In the mornings he greeted me with *"Naja iyo nuu?"* How are you? And I'd answer, *"Iyo va'a nii."* I'm fine.

Sometimes I practiced Spanish with him. *"¡Ánimo!"* I taught him to say. Have courage! One morning, I had a dream about the mountains where I used to gather herbs. A dream that made me ache for my village, that left the taste of cool springwater on my tongue. My body felt heavy as I stood up, rolled up my *petate,* and walked into the courtyard to start working. My eyes filled with tears, so I couldn't see the pot or the firewood. All I wanted to do was go back to sleep and never wake up. I let myself collapse to the ground. I pulled my knees up to my chin and buried my face in my *huipil* and tried to enter my dream again, with the mountains and springwater. At that moment, a shrill whistle broke the silence.

"¡Ánimo!" Loro cried. *"¡Ánimo, Helena!"*

I wiped my eyes, stood up, and started working. You see how important it is to have one true friend in the world? Later I learned that *ánimo* also means soul. Spirit. And really, Loro had seen my spirit empty of hope, slipping away into the shadows. He called to it, called to me, and yes, my spirit stayed. For that, I always thank him.

●

Within a few weeks, the market changed from a place that frightened me with its noise and commotion to a place I enjoyed. A place of colors and songs and smells and so many people! Old and young, pale and dark, so many people with their own worries and hopes. There at the market, our paths all crossed. I began to greet the vendors and the other maids who came to the market, toting their baskets like me. I learned the names of the children dressed in rags who picked through the garbage for food. Always, I set aside a bit of my wages to buy them pastries.

Every day, on the way to the market, I passed by the stone jail. Every day I stood outside the barred windows and unwrapped a small bundle of food. Leftover tortillas, scraps of meat, cheese, soft fruit. I never stayed long, for fear that Silvia or don Manuel or doña Carmen might walk by and forbid me to give away their food. Because of the dark shadows inside the prison, I never knew the prisoners' faces, only their hands, their voices. Voices pleading and thanking. Hands grasping and clutching whatever I offered. Then stretching out again, empty, asking for more.

But one pair of hands stood out from the rest. One pair of hands moved with grace and dignity. The hands were held out tenderly, cupped together, as though they were waiting for a dove to land in them. They were a woman's hands, with thick brown fingers. They were hands of a woman who had worked hard in her life, a woman like Aunt, a woman like my mother. The hands held wisdom, like the hands of Ta'nu, who loved tending to his herbs and patting soil gently over seeds. I had the feeling that those hands belonged to someone I would like to know. I remembered what Ta'nu had told me about learning from teachers who crossed my path. Yes, those hands could teach me something.

Ta'nu was also right about learning Spanish. At first I thought I'd no sooner understand Spanish than the language of birds. I couldn't imagine my tongue making that strange trilling sound. I couldn't grasp the rhythm, a cricket song rising and falling. But little by little I found myself understanding a word here, a word there. And little by little I heard myself stringing the words together. And yes! People began to understand me. Instead of pointing to fruits and vegetables at the market, we used words.

And as I understood more and more Spanish, I understood the García López family better and better. I understood why don Manuel often returned home at dawn smelling of perfume and liquor. The maids at the market always joked about how he juggled mistresses the way a street performer juggles oranges. Whenever he stayed out all night, doña Carmen would order me around more than ever the next day. In a voice like a knife in my ear she'd call from her bed, "Bring me a dozen cherry pastries!" And when I returned from the market, "No, these are cherry. I asked for lemon, you fool. Go back and bring me lemon. And this is coming out of your wages, girl." I said nothing and did as she said, trying to bury my anger like hot coals under ash.

One morning, I was in Silvia's room, making her bed. Doña Carmen stood in front of the mirror, behind her daughter. She was arranging Silvia's hair into a fancy bun that looked like a woven basket.

"I wish my face were whiter," Silvia grumbled. "It's Papá's fault. His skin is so dark. Why did you marry a man from the country?"

"A handsome man from the country."

"Ayyy! You're pulling my hair."

"I was hardly older than you when we married," doña Carmen said. "Your father talked so smoothly. Like rich custard."

"He still does," Silvia said. "Yesterday I saw him talking that way." She narrowed her eyes. "With the beef lady at the market."

Her mother stiffened.

"You're weak, Mamá. You let him make a fool of you."

Doña Carmen gave Silvia's hair a tug.

"Ayyy! Go away, Mamá! I'll have the maid do my hair!"

Doña Carmen heaved her body up. She dragged herself toward the door. I pretended to be busy smoothing out the bedspread. On her way past me, she commanded, "Bring me a cake. Chocolate cake."

For the rest of the afternoon she devoured the cake, piece by piece. Like a wild dog she attacked the food. She ate and ate, barking orders and spewing bits of chocolate and saliva everywhere. She devoured it, trying to fill the emptiness inside her. By nightfall her belly was full, but her heart was still empty.

6

Clara

Even the birds flying close overhead didn't notice me hidden in the shadows between two boulders. I could be just another wrinkle in the stone, or a patch of moss. Without watches and mirrors, I could be someone else, someone from another time. I could be Abuelita, before she went to the city—just a girl in the timeless mountains, resting on a rock for a moment.

With my eyes closed, the sound of the waterfall became clearer. And other sounds stood out. It was like listening to a song on the radio and picking out the guitar, then the piano, and the violin, and all the other instruments, one by one. In this song there were insects' wings drumming in waves, and about seven different bird tunes, calling back and forth.

Little by little I noticed something else blending into the song. A person's voice. It was faint, but it grew louder as the person grew closer, until he must have been right above me, on top of the rocks. He sang in Spanish, to a tune I liked but had never heard before. The singing stopped and I heard "Chchchchivo," and then the scuttle of goat hooves.

The footsteps grew closer until there was a goat next to me on the rock. It was caramel-colored with a skinny neck and a long nose and ears that stuck straight out. I'd never been this close to a goat before, so close I could see the sleep in the corners of its eyes. It watched me for a while, as if to say, What are you doing here? Then it seemed to shrug and started chewing at a shrub by my foot. I breathed in that same sour sweetness that clung to Pedro. The singing started again—a sad song about nighttime flowers. I stood up slowly, very careful not to startle the goat, and tilted my head back.

"Pedro!" I called. "Your goat's down here!"

The singing stopped. His head peeked over the cliff and then disappeared. I heard him skid down the trail along the side of the boulders. He was a burst of color, like a tropical bird. He wore an orange T-shirt and the same red pants and carried a guitar with a green and yellow woven strap slung across his shoulder.

Would he act embarrassed? If someone caught me singing when I thought I was alone, I'd turn bright red and stumble over my words and run away the first chance I got. But no, he looked happy to see me. His teeth glowed white next to his rosy cheeks. He swung his guitar around and sat down on the rock. He motioned for me to sit, like a waiter at a fancy restaurant pointing out a seat. Without a single word, he pulled out a few notes.

And here's another amazing thing: He looked at me as he sang. Really looked. At first my eyes flickered away, the way they sometimes do during a movie that makes my skin tingle because it feels like *too much*. But he kept on singing and I let myself look back at him. An ocean was filling me, and I felt like something flimsy, a Tupperware container maybe, something that couldn't possibly hold an ocean. The salt water rose up inside me, higher and higher, until it nearly overflowed. Once, early in the morning on Mom's birthday, Dad and I filled the bedroom with daisies, and when she woke up she smiled and cried and tried to talk but couldn't find words. She must have felt the ocean too.

The words to the song, in Spanish, formed a vivid picture in my mind: galaxies, the Milky Way, planets, jewels, brilliant colors, love, beauty, a soul, a kiss. Everything swirling around. I couldn't tell you what the song was *about* or how the words all fit together. I just felt each word's power, the way the words flew from his mouth, like pieces of a mosaic that my mind caught in midair and rearranged into its own creation. My fingers itched to draw it all in my sketchbook. After three songs, Pedro stood up. He moved his eyes away to the wandering goats. I realized I had been holding completely still, barely breathing. I wondered if he knew how he'd made these waves swell up inside me like the moon tugging at the tide.

"The goats are ready to move on," he said.

"What do you do with the goats?" I was stalling. I didn't want him to leave.

"I make sure they don't get eaten by coyotes or mountain cats. I take them to places with shrubs to eat and keep them out of the cornfields and make sure none wander off. Very exciting." He laughed.

"Oh." The waves were still moving inside me. There was a silence while I searched for something else to say.

"Well, thank you for listening, Clara." He slung the guitar across his back.

"Pedro." I stood up. My legs felt shaky. Why was my body acting this way? "Can I walk with you?"

He nodded and smiled. His teeth were as straight as if he'd just gotten braces off, although I doubted his family could have afforded braces for him. "You know my name?"

"My grandparents guessed it was you," I said. "You know my name too."

"Your grandmother told me she was inviting you here. And every time I saw your grandfather, he told me exactly how many days left until you came. Then last Saturday at the market, everyone was talking about the American girl. I knew it must be Clara Luna."

I felt my face grow warm. "That's weird you think of me as American. Back home when I meet new kids, they ask if I'm Mexican. Or they just say, 'What *are* you?' "

We were quiet for a moment as we climbed up a steep part.

"What do *you* think you are?" he asked.

I thought for a moment. "I don't know. I can only see myself from the inside."

"What do you see?"

"A person who likes to draw maps." I laughed. "And who likes chocolate and birds." I paused. Something about the way he listened made me want to tell him things I wouldn't think about telling anyone else, things I used to tell Samantha before she changed, things I used to tell Dad before *I* changed. "I'm more than that," I added. "I'm someone who swims in the forest when everyone else is asleep." I wondered if he'd think I was a lunatic.

He nodded like that was the most natural thing in the world. "And maybe there's more that you haven't figured out yet."

I gave him a sideways glance. "What about you? Who are you?"

"A smelly goat-boy from Yucuyoo. Almost fifteen years old, with no father and no money and nothing. Nothing except for my mother and my guitar." He was smiling a little, so it was hard to tell if he was serious.

"Is that what you see from the inside?" I asked.

He paused. "Here in Yucuyoo we have a saying: The land is our body and its streams are our blood. And its waterfalls, our pulse." He stretched up and brushed his hands through the leaves over our heads. "That's what I see from the inside."

It seemed like a good opportunity to ask him about the waterfall sound, but then I reminded myself that finding the waterfall was my own secret mission, so instead I said, "You're a singer, too."

"A listener," he said, after a moment. "I listen to things and try to turn them into music."

I lay in bed that night trying to untangle Pedro's smells. There was the sour goat smell and the clean fruit smell of his soap. There was the smell of damp wood soaked up from nights sleeping in his cabin and morning trips to gather firewood for his mother. Maybe that was why bits of bark clung to his hair. And there was a brown sugar smell that his skin just seemed to give off.

Pedro's pointy shoes with that decorative fringe looked like something my American grandfather might wear Friday nights out at the Budget Buffet. Pedro wore them with white sports socks that bunched out over the sides, exactly the kind of thing that kids would tease him about if he spent even one recess at Walnut Hill Middle School. Since he was almost fifteen years old, he'd be going into tenth grade. This fall would start my first year of high school, so I couldn't imagine what high schoolers would say about those socks, but I suspected they wouldn't be any kinder than middle schoolers. Pedro must have shined the shoes that morning, because they still gave off the faint smell of polish. That smell made me want to hug him.

Of course, I wouldn't hug him. He didn't seem like the kind of boy I'd have a crush on. At school, there was a circle of popular boys who nearly every girl drooled over. Those boys only went out with the popular *girls* who nearly every *boy* drooled over. In my case, I'd chosen Mark G. to like, and Samantha had chosen Mike M., and we both knew that since we weren't popular, they'd never like us back. All the same, Samantha and I passed notes all day long, in code, with the guys' names backward. *Kram looked soooo good today!* or *I'm soooo in love with Ekim.* It's true, I admired how they strutted around in their name-brand clothes, how they slouched, impossibly cool, in their chairs and flirted with teachers. But crushes on them were like crushes on movie stars: fun, but hopeless.

Once I said to Samantha, "What if the unpopular girls and unpopular guys went out with each other? Then we could all have real live boyfriends." She rolled her eyes at me. "Clara, the unpopular guys are all dorks!" She would definitely write Pedro off as a dork. *Friend material, maybe,* she would say. *But a boyfriend? Ugh! With that stinky shoe gunk?*

It was the pungent smell of Pedro's shoe polish that made me think of Dad. He polished his shoes every morning too, only he wore big clomping boots. Every morning he smeared them with brown goop and then rubbed them hard with scraps of old sheets. I loved watching the way his wrists gave the rags expert flicks. Then he would carefully scrub his hands with soap in the bathroom sink and leave for work in his red truck. He spent his days planting and digging in other people's yards. By the time he came home, the boots would be dull again and he'd stick them in the garage. He'd come in wearing socks and slippers, hug me, and give me a smooth stone or a single flower or a dried cicada shell or a broken blue eggshell, whatever small thing he'd found that day. When I was little, these presents thrilled me as much as a trip to the toy store, but as I grew older, I saw that my other friends' parents got them highlighter pens or dry-erase boards or little sticky notepads, all with fancy company logos on them. Dad's wilted flowers and bug carcasses started to seem pitiful.

All last year I'd wished for a father like Samantha's, who left for an office every weekday at 8:20 in a silvery four-door car with plush seats. Not a father who came home from work in a red truck with LUNA LANDSCAPING stenciled on the door, a father with soil under his fingernails, grass stains on his jeans, burs and thorns stuck to his socks.

Mom loved this about him, how he always brought bits of nature into the house with him. That was what made her fall in love with him. I loved hearing the story of how they fell in love. When I was little, I would ask to hear it as a bedtime story. It sounded like a fairy tale to me. Dad did lawn maintenance at Mom's apartment complex while she was in graduate school. When he found out she was studying to be a teacher, he asked her if she could tutor him in English. He worked as a dishwasher at night, he said, so he only had Saturday mornings off, and could she teach him then? She looked at the burs stuck to his pants and breathed in the fresh grass and earth smell that clung to him, and saw how sincere he was and said yes.

Every Saturday he showed up at her door, freshly showered, smelling of shoe polish and soap. She smiled at the neat comb lines in his hair and the ironed creases in his button-down shirt. Every Saturday he brought her a small present— a bouquet of wildflowers, a woven wreath of daisies, an abandoned bird's nest. Sometimes they went for a walk after their lesson or had brunch with Mom's parents. When Dad asked Mom how her parents felt about him being an immigrant, she looked him straight in the eyes and said, without a pause, "They admire you. My ancestors came from other countries too. France and Norway and Wales. Most Americans have immigrant roots, you know."

All week long she counted the days to their next lesson, and during the lesson, she wished she could stretch out time. One day, Dad offered her a pinecone and said, "Look at how perfect the spiral is." She watched his face watching the pinecone. And she realized she wanted always to feel the way she felt when she looked at his face. That was my cue to end the bedtime story: "And then you were in love!" I shouted triumphantly. "And then we were in love," she whispered, and kissed me goodnight.

Days passed. I saw Pedro every afternoon on the mountain. He showed me how to weave *petates* out of palm. At first he'd tried to teach me how to make a hat like his, but after a few tries that turned out like sloppy birds' nests, we realized I'd have to start small. So we worked on miniature *petates*. My fingers were clumsy, and none of the edges turned out straight. I ended up with tiny amoeba-shaped coasters— presents for Mom, I decided. Pedro laughed a lot too, like my grandparents, only he wasn't as hyper as Abuelo. When Pedro laughed his eyes crinkled up, the way they did when he sang or listened to me talk. Watching his eyes crinkle gave me a warm, liquidy feeling. I wondered if he felt that way when he watched me laugh.

I showed him how to do origami, which I'd learned from a book Dad got me for Christmas last year. After fifteen minutes Pedro had mastered the swan and dragon and was already inventing new ones—scorpions and guitars. His fingers moved as quickly as they did plucking guitar strings or weaving hats.

Every day we followed the goats around. I called *"Chchchchivo"* when they wandered, and they even began listening to me. Sometimes Pedro would ask me what my life was like in Maryland, and I'd try to explain how everyone had a cell phone with call-waiting and redial and caller ID, and computers and e-mail and Internet and DVDs, and how you have to remember numbers and codes and passwords for everything.

He would ask a few questions and then suddenly stop. His eyes would lose their crinkle, and the rosiness would leave his cheeks. He'd begin walking a few steps ahead of me in the middle of the trail, leaving no room for me to walk next to him. I'd straggle behind, watching his hair poke out below his hat, watching him take long strides in his old red pants and black shoes. I'd promise myself not to talk about the U.S. again. But it always came up. It was part of who I was, like it or not.

"Is Mexico how you thought it would be?" Pedro asked me one day.

I shook my head. I didn't even have to think about that one. I was sketching a picture of him with that high rock face in the background. I'd already done the nooks and crags, the plants growing out of the cracks, the vines hanging down like a woman's hair—that part had taken me a while. The rock face was almost a real face, with lines and wrinkles, and holes like eyes and ears. Now I was sketching in the strong arch of Pedro's eyebrows, leading down into the shadow under his cheekbones. I could fill up my whole sketchbook with pictures of Pedro and not get tired of it.

"Don't move your mouth so much, Pedro!" I laughed.

"Well, what did you expect Yucuyoo to be like?" he asked through his teeth, trying to keep from smiling.

"Like the Mexico in Disney World. You walk around a lake and stop in all these pretend countries. What I remember from Mexico was a bunch of ladies in ruffly white skirts and two braids and lots of lipstick. They danced around with giant white smiles. And there were burros dressed up in red and green and white blankets."

He let out a smirk.

"Ped-*ro*! *Hold still* if you want this to turn out good!"

"Okay, okay!" he said, trying not to move his mouth. "And then you came here and saw these shacks made of metal scraps and cardboard."

I smiled. "And no dressed-up burros!"

He did not smile back. "And you see me with this old orange shirt that says—how did you say it in English—'Rrrrockveel Soccerrr League.' Probably a rich boy in your country decided he didn't like it anymore."

I stopped drawing. My pencil hovered over the paper. His voice had turned bitter.

"And his mother gave it to a secondhand store, and somehow it made its way down here, and a mother bought it, and her first son wore it, then her second son, then her third son, then her sister's son, and then her neighbor's son, and that's me, and here it is."

His eyes were changing somehow as he talked. I erased the eyes, blew off the dust, and tried to get them right. I studied him closely. Where had those new shadows come from?

"You're moving again, Pedro," I said softly.

"You're wondering how a goat-boy like me knows that, aren't you? Well, my friends' fathers have been to Chicago and Los Angeles and they bring back new T-shirts with the tags on that still smell like the store."

"I wasn't wondering that, Pedro," I said.

"I know all about your country. My friends' fathers send back videos of their big apartments and giant TVs. I know all about it, even though you think I'm just a goat-boy."

"I don't think that." I wanted to ask him, *What about your own father? Where is he? Why doesn't he send videos?* But I had the feeling that if I asked him this, he would snap and growl at me like a cornered dog. So I held my tongue.

I wanted that lightness to come back into his eyes. For a few minutes I sketched a line here, erased it, sketched another one there, erased it. It was strange how someone's face could be warm one minute, and the next, cold as stone.

Finally, I decided to change the subject to something that would make him happy. He loved his guitar, so I said, in a strained voice, "Where'd you get your guitar from?"

"Marcos. My sixth-grade teacher. When he was eighteen, he taught for a year here in Yucuyoo. Everyone here loved him."

Pedro was moving his face too much now for me to finish the drawing. But at least his eyes had more life. I set my pencil down.

"Marcos taught me to play guitar." Pedro picked out a few notes on his guitar, and I wished he would start playing and singing and looking into my eyes. But he kept his eyes on his fingers. "When Marcos left at the end of the school year, everyone threw him a big fiesta. The women made *tamales*, and the men roasted two goats in his honor. The band played songs and he danced with even the oldest ladies and the littlest girls. When he left, people cried for days. Marcos gave me his guitar the day before he went away. Instead of crying, I played it all the time."

"Do you think he'll come back?"

Pedro shrugged. "Who knows," he said flatly. "I'm used to it now. Everyone I care about leaves." He gave me a cold look. "They go away and forget about Yucuyoo."

His face had changed again. The shadows were back. He sighed like an old, tired man. "Did you finish the drawing?"

"No. It's about to rain. I'll do it later."

But I never did. I could never draw him in a way that satisfied me. Whenever I thought I'd captured something on paper, his expression changed, and I'd think, *No, that's not him, that's not him at all.*

●

"What do you know about Marcos?" I asked Abuelita. We were washing clothes by the banana tree. Well, she was washing and I was watching.

She thought about my question. She sprinkled white powder into the concrete sink, and with a gourd, added water from the giant metal barrel that collected rain.

"Marcos was a poet," she said finally. "A poet with plans to change the world. And maybe he did, the year he was here. In his own way."

"How?"

"He taught Pedro many things. He taught Pedro that while his roots grow deep into the darkness, his face turns to the light." She scrubbed my jeans, which were coated with mud and turned the water brown. "Pedro's father left when Pedro was a small child, you see. When you feel that life has treated you badly, it is easy, so easy, to let your heart fill with anger. Marcos showed Pedro how to fill his heart with music instead."

"But then Marcos left him."

Abuelita wrung out the jeans and set them aside, then moved on to my orange sweatshirt. "Yes, Marcos was a boy from the city, you see. How could he stay in our village his whole life? But, oh, what goodness he left behind. He told Pedro, 'Stay in school and help me change the world.' Three boys in Pedro's class studied past their eighth year of school. Pedro was one of them. All the other boys stopped to help their families in the fields. During the school year, Pedro wakes up before dawn and gathers firewood for his mother. Then he takes the goats out with his books. Then he goes to school with his books. Then he takes the goats out again with his books until darkness falls."

I thought of how much I complained to Dad about my

only two chores—taking out the trash and the recycling. A little wave of shame swept over me. Abuelita wrung out my green sweater and put it on top of the pile of clothes. She took a gourdful of water and rinsed the rest of the suds down the hole in the sink. The water poured out below into a mud puddle, and little rivers trickled past the banana tree down the slope. Then she plugged up the hole with a wad of cloth and poured clear water into the sink. She added the clothes to rinse them. She did this all so fast, you could tell she'd been doing it all her life. It occurred to me that maybe I should pay attention so that I could do a load of laundry now and then.

"Your grandfather and I, we are glad for your friendship with Pedro." She swished the clothes around in the water and squeezed out the last of the suds. "We were worried he would be hard on you."

"Hard on me? How?"

"Oh, his life has not been easy." She said this slowly, and I could tell she was thinking hard about what words to use. "When people here think of your country, they think of money, of streets paved with gold, and diamonds on the trees." She twisted out the clothes one last time and piled them in a bucket. She carried it over to the clothesline, and together, we began pinning up the clothes.

"Is that why Pedro's father left?"

"In a way." She unpinned the shirt I'd pinned up and turned it inside out. "Like this, *mi amor*. So the sun does not fade your lovely clothes."

"Oh." I felt like a two-year-old around her sometimes when she was doing chores. All I knew how to do was throw clothes into a washing machine, the hot setting for towels and sheets and T-shirts and pajamas, and the cold setting for nice clothes.

"Years ago we people of Yucuyoo sold our coffee to a company. And this company sold it around the world. Imagine. People in far-off lands drinking coffee I picked with these hands!" She stretched out her fingers, red from the cold water and harsh soap. "And then, the trade rules changed. The companies began buying coffee from other places. Our coffee prices started to fall. They fell and fell like a dying bird. Oh, it was a terrible shock. You see, it began to cost more to grow the coffee than to sell it. That is when Pedro's father left. That is when many men started leaving. Because there is no way to feed a family with nothing." Abuelita pinned up the last shirt, my art shirt, splattered with red and yellow paint.

"Who changed the rules? Why?"

"I will tell you a story that happened years ago. Here, in our land, by the marketplace. There was a high stone wall, and on the other side, a tree. A huge old tree, as wide as I am tall. A tree whose branches gave shade for the grandmothers to gather and talk, for the children to play. Then one day a man came to town and bought the piece of earth on the other side of the wall. Oh, he was not a bad man, but he was a man who stayed inside his walls. He did not understand that this tree gave us shade and joy. He did not understand that the roots of the tree spread out beneath us all. That the branches spread high over us all. No, all the man knew was that the tree would make a fine table and fine chairs in his house. So he had his sons chop it down. Since that day, the grandmothers and children no longer gather in the cool shade."

Abuelita sighed. For a moment it didn't seem like she had a powerful jaguar inside her. She looked like a small, old, tired lady. A sad feeling stayed inside me all afternoon until late that night, in my bed under the wooden rafters. Falling asleep, I saw a tall stone wall. From the other side of the wall came music, notes from Pedro's guitar. I tried to climb over the wall. I tried to dig under it. I tried to knock it down. Finally, I gave up and sat against the wall and listened, and that's all I remember.

●

"You should have flown over it," Pedro said when I told him about the dream.

"I forgot you could do that in dreams," I said.

"You can do anything."

A picture flashed in my head, me stepping forward and kissing Pedro on the mouth. It shocked me. *Where did that come from? Do I want to do that?* But Pedro was . . . Pedro. I imagined him standing next to Mark G., code name Kram, the third-coolest guy in my grade. I imagined Mark looking at a place beyond my head, too cool to actually look at me. He wore his attitude like another layer of name-brand clothes, his real self buried somewhere far beneath. And I saw Pedro, looking into my eyes, into the inside of me, making me feel like an oyster with a perfect pearl in its center. Then I pictured Samantha looking at Pedro's outfit with her nose wrinkled up. *Clara, he is so not your type. Not anyone's type.*

I pushed the pictures out of my head. I wasn't in Walnut Hill. I was here. Walnut Hill had its own set of rules. But those rules were flimsy and didn't make sense and I didn't have to follow them, did I?

I looked at Pedro's face, rosy and damp with sweat. "You're right," I said. "I can do anything."

We spent the morning looking for hummingbirds, just to

watch them dart and swoop around from flower to flower, sticking their long tongues into the spirals of petals. We'd counted sixteen so far. Pedro started talking about Marcos, and I felt like he was talking about an old friend.

"Marcos collected stories from our village and put them together in a book." Pedro said this with a proud smile. "And he taught us other stories, stories from before the Spaniards came. When there was a great civilization here."

He talked for a while. The thing that caught my attention most was that hundreds of years ago, his ancestors worshiped a hummingbird god, and a feathered serpent god, and another called Smoking Mirror, and a goddess called Obsidian Butterfly.

"What's obsidian?" I asked.

He scanned the ground for a few seconds, then picked up a tiny shard of glassy black rock and held it up. I imagined a butterfly made of this, something so airy and delicate and sharp and strong.

"Tomorrow let's find pieces of obsidian," I said. "We can lay them down in the shape of a butterfly and leave them on a rock as an offering."

"An offering to who?"

"To the Obsidian Butterfly goddess!"

Pedro smiled. "Marcos always had ideas like that too. He said we should be proud of our ancestors."

Our ancestors. Was Pedro including me with him and Marcos? *His ancestors are Dad's ancestors,* I thought, *which means they're my ancestors too.* This gave me a shiver of pride and made me feel close to Pedro and close to Dad, even though he was thousands of miles away.

That afternoon, Pedro and I sat on a rock side by side,

cooling off our bare feet in the stream. Pedro was playing his guitar and humming softly. Underneath our legs, a line of ants trailed along the bank, carrying pieces of leaves twenty times their size. Each one looked like a sailboat, struggling to stay steady in the breeze. "Look at them!" I said. "Isn't that neat?" As I said this, I remembered how I'd been wishing for someone to point out neat things to. I smiled and tucked my chin into the crook of my elbow and breathed in the smell of the sunshine and sweat on my skin, and felt the ocean filling me. *You can do anything, Clara.* Again, the picture of me kissing Pedro crept into my head. Did he ever think about kissing me? The way he sang to me made me think he might.

Pedro looked like he was thinking about something else. He played some more, and sang the song about the galaxies and jewels, the first one he'd ever played me. I had drawn pictures of this song in my sketchbook—diamonds and emeralds and sapphires spiraling with stars. That was how I thought of our time together, something glittering, as big and important as the Milky Way.

Pedro kept playing, but stopped humming, and said, "Clara. Do you understand what the words to my songs mean?"

My brain started sifting through bits of his other songs. It was hard; I'd always listened more to *how* he sang the words, with so much feeling. I heard the words, but I'd never thought about the layers of meanings beneath them. At the core, they had to be about how he felt toward me. I felt like chocolate in the sun, a sweet, melting feeling. *This is it. This is the precise, magical moment he's going to tell me he likes me.*

I took a deep breath. "I guess—mostly they're about . . ."

I was going to say love, but my mouth wouldn't form the word, and I felt my face flush. Luckily he was looking down at the ants. "Well, I don't know."

"Listen carefully, Clara."

He kept playing the song, but now sang the words extra clearly.

> *"Jewels had no souls*
> *They were only mirrors, brilliant colors . . .*

"See, Clara, the words show how wealth isn't important, how it distracts us from important things. The way the money in your country distracted my father. These are songs of protest. Songs to unite the poor people to stand up against the rich."

My heart was starting to sink right down to my feet. "What are you talking about?" I whispered.

"Marcos says the rich treat us like those ants"—he pointed to the endless line of leaf pieces moving in the shadow of our knees—"doing backbreaking work for the people lucky enough to be born with money."

This was what Abuelita had tried to prepare me for, I realized. But I hadn't expected it to feel like this. I'd been flying with the stars, and suddenly, *bam*, I was knocked down.

"You mean they're not about . . . love?" I asked in a small, humiliated voice.

"They're about love . . . ," he said, and paused.

I held my breath and waited.

"Love for justice and dignity," he said.

But they weren't about love for me. I wanted to tear up the galaxy picture in my sketchbook and throw the pieces at him. "Pedro, those are just Marcos's words coming out of your mouth. They're not how you really feel."

He looked confused. "Who cares whose words they are? They're true." He stood up, picked up his shoes, and slung his guitar over his back. He looked at me for a second as if I were a math problem he was trying to figure out. Then he said, "Forget it. Let's go. It's going to rain."

I didn't move. I didn't think my legs would work. All this time, I'd thought every song he'd sung had been a gift especially for me. How stupid I was, to listen to every song as though I were hypnotized. I'd trusted him with my most secret things, things I would never tell Samantha. And all along he'd really been lecturing me about politics. What I wanted now was for him to hurt the way I was hurting. I raised my chin and said in a voice that didn't sound like my own, "You wish Marcos were your dad because you don't have one anymore."

He looked like I'd slapped him. His mouth fell half-open in disbelief. Then he shook his head and said slowly, "Your father's no better, Clara. He ran away too."

"He didn't *run away*."

"Yes, he did. And found an American wife and had a kid and forgot about Yucuyoo."

"He didn't *forget*."

"Then, Clara, why didn't he ever come back to visit? Not once in how many years? Twenty years?"

"You don't know anything about my father!"

"It's a small village. Everyone knows everything."

I picked up my sandals and slipped them on even though my feet were dripping wet. I fastened them, fumbling. Pedro had a point, although I wasn't going to admit it. Why hadn't

Dad ever returned? I searched for a way to defend him. "Maybe he felt guilty," I said finally, "because for all those years while he was illegal he couldn't go back. He had to work and save money and learn English. And it would have been dangerous to cross the border again. People die crossing. And then when he married my mom, and he finally became legal—maybe he was afraid people here would be mad if he showed up."

"None of the men care once they leave," Pedro said.

"But he did try to remember Yucuyoo," I said, hearing my voice grow louder. "In his own way." Every nature walk Dad and I had taken was an echo from his past that he'd shared with me. And I'd stopped going. There was the tea he made for me when I was sick—chamomile and oregano and lime and honey and garlic. When I got older I refused to drink it and demanded normal cold medicine, bright red syrup in a bottle. All the bits of his past that he offered, I rejected. "I'm the one who didn't care."

My body tingled with some kind of furious electricity. I stood up and faced Pedro.

He stood there, hands awkward at his sides.

I picked up my backpack and turned away. I ran down the trail, half tripping over rocks as I went. My backpack bounced clumsily against me, and I hoped he wasn't watching me stumble along with my arms out, trying to balance. I was a wounded bird, crashing through tree branches and vines. The rain began, and I slipped and slid downhill as the ground spit up mud at me. My skin felt raw and cold, but I didn't bother stopping to put on the plastic poncho. I let the rain pelt me like hard little bullets.

By the time I made my way across the stretch of corn-field, I was hungry, thirsty, tired, and angry. Angry at myself for being so stupid. *I want to go home,* I thought. *I want to go back to where I understand things.*

It was still drizzling a little when I reached Abuelita, out in the yard. She was holding a bloody machete and standing over a freshly killed chicken on a tree stump. It was headless and some of its feathers were stained red. She dipped it into a pot of steaming water for a minute, then pulled it out and tore out feathers by the handful. Then she slit open its skin, pulled the guts out, and plopped them into a bucket. Chicken blood and goop dripped from her hands. My appetite disap-peared.

She looked up and noticed me gaping. "Chicken soup for dinner tonight, *mi amor*. And chicken in chocolate-chile sauce for lunch tomorrow," she announced.

I felt my lip curl up. "At home we buy chicken already plucked and cleaned and wrapped in plastic. You can buy a package of all legs or all thighs or whatever you like best." My voice sounded like the popular girls' voices, talking about whose clothes were cooler or whose parents' car was more expensive or whose DVD collection was bigger.

"What about the feet and guts?" she asked, curious.

"I don't know—maybe they just throw them out—make dog food with them or something."

"Or diet dog food!"

I didn't laugh.

"Well, Clara, here we use most of it. Except for the beak, of course, and the feathers, and some of the innards. And al-ways, we boil the goodness out of the bones in a soup."

That night, when Abuelita handed me a big bowl with a chicken foot sticking right out and bits of fat floating around, my stomach turned. At first I thought the foot was a decoration like parsley, but then I saw Abuelo sucking and chewing on his. I ate a lot of tortillas and some of the broth, but I stuck the foot in my pocket to throw down the hole in the outhouse later. Abuelita probably knew, but I didn't care.

They talked about the coffee harvest, switching to Mixteco at times. I stayed silent. My hand touched the slimy, bumpy chicken foot in my pocket. I ran my fingers over the soft claws with their rubbery ridges and felt very, very far from home.

●

That night in bed I let Pedro's words come back to me, hard and powerful, like punches. I let his eyes come back too, frustrated and honest. His face, its shadows and light, its curves and dips. I wanted to sketch his face again and again. How had this feeling snuck up on me?

I wondered if I would ever smell his shoe polish again, its sharp, sad scent. That smell brought back another memory of Dad. We were living in an apartment in Baltimore at the time. Even though Dad was doing plumbing and pool cleaning for the apartment complex, he still polished his work boots in the mornings, out on our little balcony. In nursery school one day, bratty Allison S. had been bragging about how many birthday presents her grandparents had given her—all four grandparents. I remember lying and saying I had five grandparents, just to beat Allison. That afternoon I sat on my usual place on the balcony, cross-legged on the Astroturf, watching the rain, wondering how I'd gotten ripped off with only two grandparents. Mom was inside unloading the dishwasher.

"Mommy!" I called inside. "How come I only have Grand-mom and Pop-pop, and Allison has four?"

"You have four also, hon," she called back. "The other two live far away." She started loading the dirty dishes from the sink. Her hair was long then, and she wore it in a high ponytail that bounced around as she moved.

"I want to see them!" What I really meant was *I want presents from them!*

Her ponytail stopped bouncing and she walked to the sliding glass door, wiping her hands on her jeans. "Tell that to Daddy, Clara," she said softly. "They're his own mommy and daddy. He hasn't seen them for almost fifteen years." She looked at me through thick glasses that made her sad eyes look twice their normal size.

Imagine not seeing your parents for so long! I sat outside on the balcony, watching water drip from the rail, sipping my orangeade. The smell of rain blended with the shoe pol-ish odor from the box of stained rags that Dad kept under the lawn chair. *Poor Daddy.*

Every once in a while another wave of sadness would hit me, usually at times when Dad was hurt. Once he slipped on the ice in the driveway and couldn't get up until I came over and helped him. Another time he got twenty-three hornet stings from a nest he disturbed out back. He ran into the house with panicked eyes, and his whole body grew redder and more swollen by the second. Or, the most recent time, in May, when I walked in the sliding glass door at four a.m. and saw him standing in the shadows, his face wet. For the past couple of years, whenever a feeling of tenderness would float up to the surface, I'd try to push it back down again, like an inner tube that you jump on, and for a moment it goes under-water, but it always rises up again.

Here's the last thing he said to me, at the airport, while we stood by my pile of bags, waiting to board: "Clara, from the moment I crossed that border, I put all my memories of home in a box and sealed it shut. For almost twenty-five years the memories moved around inside, pressing on the walls, leaking out here and there. When you left the house that night, the box exploded, and all the memories shot out and lodged themselves all over—in our house, our yard, our furniture, on me, on you. And since then I can't look anywhere without seeing a memory, and I know I will never be able to collect them all together and shut them in again."

Over the loudspeaker, they announced rows fifteen through twenty-four. I was row nineteen. Mom hurried over from the gate where she'd been giving the flight attendant special instructions about me and began picking up my bags. "Get your ticket ready, sweetie. You've got your wallet? Your travelers' checks? The credit card?" and on and on, while Dad hugged me and whispered, "Clara—you're my pathway home."

●

Abuelita yanked a giant weed out of the soil, then paused to wipe the sweat from her forehead. Her hand left a small streak of mud just under her hairline. I didn't say anything about it—I thought it looked nice. I pulled out a few small weeds, careful not to disturb the roots of the chamomile flowers. I tossed them onto our pile of wilting leaves, which was growing into a small mountain.

Yesterday I'd felt like one of these uprooted weeds, but this morning I'd helped fix a tasty breakfast and washed the dishes and fed Loro and done a pile of laundry, and all this made me feel useful. I didn't even care that the harsh laundry and dish soap made my hands red and swollen and sore. Today, I decided, instead of wandering around the mountains, I would help Abuelita. And of course there was another reason: I was afraid of seeing Pedro, afraid he would say hi in a cold voice with a cold face, or worse, that he might not say hi at all.

I glanced up at Abuelita again. With the soil on her forehead, she seemed part of the garden. I imagined her when she was a girl, ripped away from her land, an uprooted plant in the city without a single person who cared about her.

"Abuelita." I paused and sat on my heels. "How did you get out of the city?"

She wiped her forehead with the other hand now. It made a matching streak. She sat back on her heels, facing me. "I left alone, in the moonlight." She laughed, tilted back her head, and looked at the sky for a moment.

Moonlight. I smiled and picked some dirt out of my fingernails and waited.

"First, Clara, you must know more about Silvia. More about doña Carmen. And most of all, you must know about a particular three-toothed woman. And then, *mi amor*, the moonlight . . ."

Helena

WINTER TO SPRING 1938

"I wish that bird would hush up!" Silvia was in a dark mood.

Loro ignored her and kept whistling his good-morning song.

"It's not even lunchtime yet and I'm already bored." She pushed her lips out in a pout.

"*¡Ánimo, Silvia!*" Loro shrieked. Lighten up!

I tried to hide my laughter. I was feeling happy, humming and washing the breakfast dishes in the yard. Breathing in the freshness of the morning. Watching light bounce off bubbles. It reminded me of the forest by my village, the way the sunlight shone through the leaves at this time of day.

Silvia stomped over to Loro and held her fist up as Uncle did when he was angry. *"Hush! Up!"*

Loro opened his beak wide and let out a cackle of laughter. A cackle like the shriek of a trumpet. Silvia jumped and backed away.

"Silvia, why don't you like Loro?" I asked. "I'd be happy to have a bird like him." I scraped my spoon at some hardened rice stuck to the bottom of the pot.

"He's a devil bird. He makes my nerves twitch, the way he screams." After a pause she added, "Papá gave him to me as a gift. At first I liked him. Then I found out that Papá had a new mistress—the woman who sells birds at the market. Why should I be nice to a bird that came from her?" She made a face at Loro. Curled up her lip, bugged out her eyes. How ugly she could make herself look.

"But Loro's not to blame," I said.

She shrugged. "I can't wait to leave this family. Like my older brothers and sisters did. I'll leave and never come back." Everything about her was sharp. Her nose, her eyes, her pointy chin, her narrow lips. The words shot out of her mouth like hard bits of hail.

"You're lucky to have a mother and father at all," I said, putting the last of the dishes into the rack. "My parents died."

She ignored me. "Thanks to Papá I have skin like a coat of dirt. People think I'm from the country. That I speak an Indian language. Someone thought I was a maid once. That's why I always wear fancy dresses at the market now. And powder my face white."

She smoothed the ruffles of her skirt. The satin sash had come undone. She turned her back to me and snapped her fingers. "Tie it, *muchacha.*"

I wiped my hands on my *huipil* and tried to even out the bow. She'd been making me tie her sashes more often lately. And braiding her hair. Why, I wondered. To be close to me? Uncle used to do something like that. He would stand by the kitchen door and criticize Aunt Teresa's cooking. The tortillas were always too small, the meat too salty, the sauce too spicy. Really, I think he was lonely. Lonely because people kept a distance from him. But he wanted someone to listen.

Silvia kept talking. "Every time I pass a beggar child I think, *That could be a half brother or sister of mine.* You, *muchacha,* you could be one."

"I am not," I said quietly. My parents' love for each other was famous in my village. Two lovebirds. One could not survive without the other.

Silvia craned her neck around to check the bow. It must have looked good enough because she didn't make me redo it.

I turned from her and tore up a leftover tortilla for Loro. In Mixteco I whispered to him, "Don't mind that girl's harsh words, Loro. I could listen to you sing for all my life."

"Don't talk about me!" Silvia snapped. "And stop speaking that Indian language!" Into the house she stormed.

"*¡Ánimo!*" Loro called after her.

●

Oh, there was so much evil air inside that house. I had to give myself *limpias* to clean my spirit. I used leaves from hidden *ruda* bushes I'd planted next to the avocado tree. Really, I should have given a *limpia* to the house, but Silvia protested. "Mamá! Don't let her do those devil Indian things!"

Little by little, Silvia and doña Carmen were pushing me into a corner. Something was going to happen. Just before a storm begins, the air smells of thunder. This is what I felt. The first drop of the storm was when doña Carmen started paying my wages late. The tenth month she did not pay me at all.

One afternoon in the eleventh month, I decided it was time. Time to demand my money and stand up for myself. I brought her a bowl of rice pudding she'd ordered and set it down in front of her. Politely, I said to her, "Doña Carmen, excuse me, but you haven't paid me this month."

"Ay, girl, leave me alone now. Can't you see I'm eating?"

There I waited, outside the door of her bedroom. I waited and waited, until she finished every last bit of pudding. My heart beat fast as I took her empty bowl. "Now, could you please pay me?"

Her jaw dropped at my boldness. Then her lips twisted into a smirk. "Later. I'm taking a nap." She stretched her mouth into a fake yawn.

A week passed. Every day, doña Carmen fanned the coals of my anger more and more. She fanned the anger I had tried to bury under ashes, hoping to smother it. And now the anger threatened to burst into flames. When I talked to another maid about it at the market, she said, "Be glad the *señora* doesn't beat you." I couldn't help smiling at that. Imagine the effort doña Carmen would have to make just to haul her body out of the armchair! Then imagine the effort it would take for her to raise up her great arms and hit me. No, she would collapse in a pool of sweat, gasping for breath.

"I won't let her treat me this way," I said. "She's no better than me. We all eat from the same tortilla."

"What are you going to do?" the maid asked.

"I'll think about it." And I thought. The next morning, I washed the piles of clothes that never stopped coming.

And as I washed, I whispered to Loro, "I could just take the money she owes me. But then I'd be fired. Or worse."

Then, even though it made me shudder, I thought of the curses I'd heard of in my village. "I could put a sharp rock into her belly. Make her roll with pain. Or I could steal her soul so she's left with no will. Or make a snake bite her." All the herbs I needed were with me. If I saved chicken bones from the next meal and collected blood from the fresh-killed goats at the market, then I could do the curse.

Loro gave a shrill cry, a cry that pulled me out of the dark hole I was sinking into.

"You're right, Loro," I said, feeling ashamed. "I'm a healer. I harm no one."

At that moment doña Carmen came out of the house. She was huffing like an old burro under her load of dresses and shirts. She dumped them on top of the pile. "Do these. And make them white this time."

I took a deep breath. "Not until you give me the money you owe me."

She looked at me as though I'd slapped her. "Never . . . *never* tell me what to do, girl. You are nothing. You are"— and she looked around the ground—"you are this ant under my shoe." She raised her fat foot over a long line of ants. Each ant carried a piece of yellow petal ten times its size. She smashed down her foot. "That is how little you mean to me. How little you mean to this world. Now wash the clothes, girl."

I obeyed her. But the blood rushed to my face, blood full of heat and fury. Again, I began planning the terrible curses I would put on her.

The next day, I came back from the market carrying a basket of meat. I opened the gate, swatting the flies away. Inside the courtyard were doña Carmen, don Manuel, and two policemen, one short and round like a hog, and the other lanky as a hungry horse.

Before I could say a word, doña Carmen snatched the basket from my hands. The policemen grabbed me by the elbows.

"You're under arrest," the stout one said. He forced my wrists behind my back. With a rope he tied them together.

"For what?" I had trouble finding the words in Spanish.

"You know what."

But I'd decided not to curse her! Had my powers spun out of my control?

"For stealing," the taller one said finally.

"Stealing what?" I thought of the leftover tortillas and meat scraps I'd brought to the prison. My pulse quickened.

"Don't play stupid, *señorita*," he said. "Stealing the *señora*'s ring. She found it hidden in your bag of herbs."

"But I didn't." I looked around for help. My eyes rested on don Manuel.

He shrugged. "My wife says you did." His gaze moved to his boots.

I looked at doña Carmen, but she, too, refused to meet my eyes. Flies buzzed around the meat basket she held. What a vulture she was, what a fat vulture.

I tried to keep my voice steady. "I don't know how her ring appeared in my bag. But I did not hide it there." Desperate, I searched for a kind face. Loro stayed quiet and solemn, as though he were praying at Mass.

"Doña Carmen says your actions have been suspicious for a long time," the thin policeman said. "She says you've

123

stolen pastries from her too." With dull eyes, he watched my reaction.

I bit my lip to hold back tears. No one believed me. I was as helpless as an ant after all.

"First the pastries. Now the ring," the short one grunted. He nodded, and the rolls of skin beneath his chin jiggled.

With that, they led me to the gate. I looked back at Loro. Beyond him, Silvia stood in the shadows of the doorway. Half hidden, she watched us, with narrowed, bitter eyes.

●

"You will stay here until your trial," the guard said. He guided me down the hallway toward the cell. His face looked pale and sickly. Crescents hung, deep and purple, below his eyes. The building smelled cold, like death.

Stay calm, I told myself. *Stay calm. Remember the spirits of your mother, your father, the jaguar. Remember that all the time, they are here, protecting you.* "When is the trial?" I asked.

"Who knows." He hacked up a glob of phlegm and spit it onto the floor. "Depends how fast the judge hears all the other cases. Could be a week. Could be a month. Six months."

Six months? "And what if they find me guilty?" I asked quietly.

"For stealing a ring? Who knows. Depends if the judge is having a bad day. One year. Ten years." He coughed and spit again. The packed-dirt floor was spotted with mucus.

Maybe this was a nightmare. I closed my eyes. *Helena,* I told myself, *when you open your eyes you will wake up in your village. You will wake up on your* petate, *next to María laughing in her sleep.* But when I opened my eyes we were standing in front of a door. A thick wooden door with bars set in a small window.

"You'll have a cell mate," the guard said. Out of a pouch at his side he pulled a large ring of keys. "We call her doña Three Teeth. She doesn't talk." He placed a key in the lock and turned it. The door creaked open. He nudged me inside. My legs shook like a scared goat's.

The cell door shut behind me. Slowly my eyes grew accustomed to the dim light. There, in the corner, was the skeletal form of a woman. A woman with skin like dried leaves draped over bones. She sat with her feet tucked under her and her *huipil* untucked, spread around her, faded and filthy. Who knew where her *huipil* ended and the dirt floor began? Her hair hung in two long, thin braids. Like little brooms, they brushed the packed dirt. The only color in the room came from the orange ribbons woven into her braids.

How long until I'd turn into her? A stale old skeleton, barely alive?

"I'm Helena," I whispered in Spanish.

Silent, she watched me from the shadows.

"What's your name?" I ventured. I hid my hands behind my back so that she wouldn't see them shaking.

No answer.

I took a step closer. And another. And another. Now I was close enough to see the design on her *huipil*. Small rows of zigzags. It was familiar.

It was almost the same pattern as mine! She must be from a nearby village.

Now I tried in Mixteco. *"Na ka'an no'o ñuu savi?"* Do you speak Mixteco?

A slow smile spread across her face, a smile that unveiled three crooked teeth. Speaking Mixteco, she replied, in a rusted voice, "You're the girl who passes me tortillas through the bars."

Yes. Her hands. I recognized them. Her hands had always stood out from the other hands stretched between the bars. The others were clutching, grasping, desperate. But her hands were graceful. Always, they had taken the tortillas with dignity.

I took a step closer. I reached out and placed my right hand against hers. Lightly, our hands touched, as is our custom.

You know, you can learn much from touching a person's hand, if only you pay attention. As our hands touched, I heard a faint echo of music. I saw trails of sparks from nights of dancing. I felt a pulse of passion buried deep. And in her eyes I sensed a trace of playfulness. "I am pleased to finally meet you," I said.

"Are you a healer?" she asked.

"Yes!" I said, surprised. "How did you know?"

"From the way you look into me. Not *at* me, but *into* me. You see who I used to be, not just who I am now. Don't you?"

I sat down next to her and leaned against the cold wall. "I hope so." I paused and looked at her closely. Old laugh lines ran like riverbeds over the hills and valleys of her face. "You don't belong here," I said. "No more than I do. Why are you here?"

Doña Three Teeth's story lasted from noon until night-fall. The words that she had kept inside her for so long flowed out. They drifted around the room like spirals of incense smoke. As she spoke, the square of light from the window grew orange with the sunset. Then the cool purple of dusk. And finally, darkness. I closed my eyes and let her words wrap around me.

As a child, she said, she had been like a firework, always on the brink of exploding with joy. She threw herself into everything she did: embroidering otherworldly animals on *huipiles,* climbing up guava trees like a squirrel, searching for healing herbs with her grandmother. One night at a village fiesta, she fell in love with a man named Pedro Victor, a violinist who played music from his soul, music so rich it brought tears to your eyes. No one was surprised that she let his music carry her away on bird wings. No one was surprised at how sudden and deep her love for him ran. But no one was surprised, either, that her parents refused to let her marry him. In her parents' eyes he was just a poor wandering musician from a far-off village, a stranger who was not to be trusted.

So she ran off with him. She ran off with him even though her parents warned she would never again be welcome in their house. She and Pedro Victor moved to the Mixteco neighborhood of Oaxaca City, and there they thrived. "Oh, Helena!" she said. "We loved everyone! We loved everything! And everyone loved us! Everything loved us!" How good that they loved so much, so deeply, because it did not last long. Seven years. They lived seven years of a poor but enchanted life, with three healthy children and one in the belly. And then, one day, a runaway horse galloped down the street and crashed into Pedro Victor. His head hit a rock and he died at once.

"At that moment, Helena, at that very moment, all the joy inside me left. All the music. All the sparks." She miscarried her baby from grief. Still, she had to feed her other children—a one-year-old, a three-year-old, and a six-year-old. A friend found her a job as a maid for an elderly woman. She washed clothes and mopped floors with her baby playing at her side. Her two older children wandered around the market, scrounging for food like dogs. There by the fruit stands they ate black bananas and half-rotten mangoes that had fallen on the ground. Imagine how much it hurt her heart to know that her children were eating like dogs. She could count every rib on their tiny bodies.

That winter her youngest child fell ill. He could keep no milk or food down. "Oh, Helena! If only I'd been in my village! So many herbs growing wild in the hills. So many herbs that could have cured my son!" Her child grew weaker and weaker. She could not ask her friends for money; no, they barely scraped together enough for their own children. Finally, she asked her employer for a loan of five pesos to bring the child to a doctor. But even after she showed the *señora* how pale and thin the boy had become, the *señora* said no. "If I give you five pesos," the old woman snapped, "soon every beggar in this neighborhood will be at my door."

The next morning the child never woke up. That was when doña Three Teeth decided to lower her head and take her other two children back to her village. She would have to ask her parents for help. But first, she needed money for the passage back. As she was dusting the old lady's bedroom one afternoon, she opened a shiny silver jewelry box and took a pair of earrings.

"Listen, Helena," she told me, her face dark with shame. "You must understand this. I had no other hope! I imagined all the people I loved dying. One by one. And nothing, I tell you, nothing is worse than seeing your child die."

But the old lady was sharper than she had thought. Eyes

sharp as a hawk's. She noticed the missing jewelry the next morning. Soon, the police were pounding on the door of doña Three Teeth's shack. They found the earrings hidden underneath her straw pillow and carted her off to jail. The big green stones in the earrings were emeralds, worth far more than she'd thought. The crime was much graver. And so was the punishment.

The worst of it was, her children were sent to an orphanage. "One tiny moment they gave me to kiss my children goodbye. How could I know that might be the last time I'd hold them? The last time ever?" She thought of her children with every breath she took. All she could do was pray that people were treating them well. She prayed that the oldest remembered the name of their village. Then maybe they could leave the orphanage and live with their relatives.

"Ahhh, Helena, they say they will free me next month. Can you believe it? After ten years! But you know something? My stomach is full of fear. I fear going back to my village. I fear that my children will be there . . . and feel shame for me. And at the same time, I fear that they won't be there . . . that never again will I see them."

In silence we sat until the guard's footsteps sounded in the hall. He opened the door, coughing, and handed a heavy jar of water to us. We drank in gulps, doña Three Teeth and I, passing the pitcher back and forth. Then he set down a clay plate with a few tortillas and a bowl of black beans. The tortillas were stale and the beans cold, but that didn't matter. We shared the food, nibbling like rabbits, trying to make it last longer. Of course, my cell mate had only three teeth, so she had no choice but to chew slowly.

I left the last tortilla for her, and the last bit of beans. But she refused. "No, love, you take it."

"No, please, you."

"No, you!"

So we tore it in half, and in half again, and again, until the tortilla pieces were the size of my little fingernail. And when we tried to part it further, we fell into a fit of laughter. Oh, such a fit that the guard's face appeared at the door's window to see about our uproar. Who knows what he thought when he saw us rolling on the floor? Rolling and laughing so hard that tears rolled down our cheeks.

Once he left we caught our breaths and our laughter faded into sighs. Night fell, and we lay on the dirt floor with our braids overlapping. Above us, a fly buzzed through the air. This close to doña Three Teeth, I caught a whiff of her real smell. It pierced through the stench of old sweat and mouse droppings. Her smell made me think of a fresh lime. A lime just sliced open, tart and sweet in a fine spray.

I told her about Ta'nu and Loro and Aunt and María, the beings I loved in this world. When I imitated Loro shrieking "¡Ánimo!" she giggled like a young girl. After a moment, I said, "Tell me more about your village. About when you were a child. When everything was good."

She talked and talked. As her words poured out, she seemed lighter. Her voice turned warm and soothing as lemongrass tea.

I closed my eyes and let her paint pictures of the green fields around her village. Of the mossy springs where they collected water. Of the secrets in the mountain forests. I listened to the *shhhhhhh shhhhhhh* sound her voice made when she talked of the spirit waterfall. A waterfall that you could hear but not see. The sound of moving water had sung her to sleep as a child. And it sang me to sleep there in our cell. It made me forget about the floor beneath me, cold and hard. It made me forget about the rats scuttling in the corner and the cockroaches crawling over my ankles.

In peace, I slept.

8

Clara

Night after night I lay under my scratchy blanket, staring at the wooden beams in the ceiling. It took hours to fall asleep, and even when I slept it was only halfway. During the days since the fight with Pedro, I hadn't been walking in the mountains. Instead, I stayed in the yard by the shacks, watching the chickens fight over bits of old tortillas. Sometimes I helped my grandparents work, but mostly I sat alone on a wooden chair, feeling bored and sorry for myself, wishing for a TV. Some part of my mind was always thinking about Pedro, replaying every conversation we'd had, regretting some things I'd said, wishing I'd said others.

Jewels had no soul. They were only mirrors, brilliant colors.
I thought about the song's words from all angles, like a puzzle. What they made me think of was the fake miniature neighborhood at the spring fair and the feeling that my life in Walnut Hill was reflections on the surface of water. Flat, like Abuelita's life before her first soul flight.

One night, about a week after the fight with Pedro, no matter how many times I changed positions, sleep would not come. Had I forgotten how to sleep? Was it a skill that you could just forget? I sat up, threw my pillow against the wall, and stepped out of bed onto the cold wooden floor.

Outside, the night held tiny water droplets. They hung in the air and pressed on my skin. There was a fuzzy halo around the half-moon, and only a few stars flickered. Most of them were hidden behind clouds. The air smelled musty, like a forgotten corner of an attic. Clothes on the line moved in slow waves, and beyond that, mist drifted over the mountains. The air was so thick that flying seemed almost possible—swimming through the night.

A voice called out, "Clara."

It was Abuelita, walking toward me.

"What are you doing up, Abuelita?" I asked, surprised.

"I'm going to give you a *limpia, mi amor.*"

"A *limpia*?"

"*Limpia* means clean. Clean inside, in your spirit. We will blow away the clouds, lift up the fog."

In the moonlight, we collected *ruda* and basil and white flowers from the garden, in a basket. In her curing room, Abuelita lit candles on the altar and began chanting in Mixteco in a low, soft voice. I stood still while she brushed the wet herbs over my head and neck. Little droplets of water trickled down my forehead, tickled my face, ran over my shoulders, down my arms. I giggled, then shivered, and then my breathing fell into the rhythm of her chanting.

Through half-closed eyes, I saw her take a mouthful of *mezcal*. Then, in a burst like Coke exploding from a just-opened bottle, she sprayed it all over me.

The shock of cold wetness.

Tingling skin.

Every inch of my body woke up, as though I'd just leaped into a swimming pool.

Then the tears came, warm, out of my eyes, down my face, and I heard myself sobbing, for so many things—for rolling my eyes at Dad's stories, for yelling at Pedro, for all the people who'd crossed the desert, their abandoned villages, the families they'd left behind. Wave after wave of cold *mezcal* soaked me until I was drenched.

Finally Abuelita stopped, wrapped a blanket around my shoulders, and chanted again softly. She made crosses in the air with her hands over my head, chest, and stomach. Then she gathered up the wet herbs in the basket and led me along the edge of the cornfield, up through the wild grasses, and into the woods at the base of the mountain. When we reached the stream, we stopped.

The water ran fast, with little flecks of white foam spotting the blackness. She handed the limp herbs to me and whispered, "These have passed over your body, over your spirit. They have taken out all the *mal aire*—all the bad things. Now the *mal aire* is in these plants. Throw them in the running water, *mi amor,* and watch the current carry them away."

I tossed the herbs into the water. The stream swallowed them up. Above us, in the branches, something moved. There,

134

on a twisted tree limb, stood a large white bird, watching us. A heron, it looked like. It had a long neck and long legs and a peaceful air. It gazed at me with fondness, like an old friend who could guess my thoughts. I was about to point it out to Abuelita, but before I could open my mouth, the bird spread its great wings, rose up, and disappeared into the trees.

That was when I knew it, as though the heron had somehow flown inside me and spoken to me. *You are like your grandmother. You are a person who looks deeply, into the insides of things.*

I whispered "Thank you" to the heron. *My spirit animal,* I thought with a shiver of pride. An animal who could fly across borders and over walls, who could see forests and deserts and fields spread out below.

Abuelita and I walked back, and with every step, I grew lighter and lighter. It wouldn't have surprised me if with the next step I'd floated right up into the air. By the time we reached the field, the clouds had broken up. The half-moon was as clear as a paper cutout. *Luna clara.* Clear moon. More and more stars came out from the mist until pinpoints of light spotted the entire sky.

●

The next morning, I sketched another picture for Dad. The background dissolved into shadows, purple-blue night air with wisps of trees, a glimmer of light off the stream. At the center, under a glowing moon, the heron rising. Underneath I wrote, with confident strokes, *Your Daughter, Clara.*

After the *limpia,* other things became clearer—unexpected things. Things I'd never thought much about before. I started to appreciate washing dishes outside, how the sunlight shone through droplets of water and made starry reflections on the sink and turned the bubbles into heaps of rainbows. I began helping Abuelita more with other chores too—making tortillas, carrying big containers of water from the spring, walking to neighbors' houses with a sack strapped to my forehead, full of dried beans, bananas, and tomatoes to trade. She showed me how to string the herbs up to dry, and we tied them to the kitchen rafters, where they dangled just below Loro.

In my notebook, I sketched the herbs, their leaves laced with networks of veins. Some leaves' edges were smooth arcs, others jagged like the teeth of a saw. Leaves of all sizes, fuzzy and silver, or slick and green, nearly black. I labeled them with their names and healing benefits. I felt thirsty for everything Abuelita knew. Her knowledge was a cool stream that I could dip a cup into and drink up.

During the day I focused on working and learning, but at night Pedro started taking over my thoughts. I saw my feelings for him more clearly now. They were like an obsidian butterfly, fragile and solid and glittering, impossible to ignore. I sketched a picture of an obsidian butterfly for Dad and labeled it *Pedro and Me.*

In the mornings I started helping Abuelo gather firewood and pile it onto the burro's back, and chop down weeds along the path to the cornfield using a long machete. Who knows what Mom would have said if she'd seen me strutting down the path swinging a knife as long as my arm? She always worried that I'd cut off a finger from something as simple as chopping carrots or slicing a bagel. A few mornings after the *limpia,* I came outside and found Abuelo standing behind a thick log set on its end, as high as his waist. He held a big wooden club with both hands and moved it up and down in the hollowed-out tree trunk. I came closer and saw that it was smooth inside, and half full of coffee beans.

"Try it, Clara," he said. He held the club out to me and sat down on a little wooden chair, sweat dripping down the sides of his face even though it was still morning. Lifting up his hat, he smoothed back his hair and wiped the moisture off his face with a faded red bandanna.

"What does this do to the beans?" I asked. The club was heavier than I'd thought. It threw me off balance at first, like when you pick up a bowling ball.

"It takes the skins off," Abuelo said. "Next we'll separate the skins and beans, then roast them, then grind them. Part of it we'll sell at the market, and the rest we'll use in our own coffee."

How could someone so old do this work for hours? At first I felt as clumsy as a dog trying to use a pencil. But eventually I fell into a rhythm, pounding slowly and listening to Abuelo's rough, comfortable voice.

"This work is nicer when you have someone to talk with," he said. "Your father used to help me. We had two of these logs. Side by side, we used to work."

"What happened to the other one?"

"Oh, when I realized he wasn't coming back, I sold it in town."

I wiped the sweat from my face, pulled off my sweater, and tossed it onto a cardboard box. How could Dad have left his father alone? How could he stand to never hear Abuelo's hyper little laugh? It didn't make sense. "Abuelo," I said. "Why do you think my dad left here and never came back?"

Abuelo looked at me for a minute from under the brim of his hat. "Ay, *m'hija*! I was hoping you would tell me."

"He doesn't talk about it," I said. I gripped the club to begin pounding again.

Abuelo stood up now, took a handful of coffee beans, and sifted the skins through his fingers. His palms and fingers were solid calluses from years of hard work. I'd always figured that Dad's calluses had come from the landscaping business. But those calluses must have started here, in Yucuyoo. The bottom layer of tough skin on his palms had grown thick right here, while he pounded coffee beans next to his father.

"Now comes the part that your father always loved best," Abuelo said. "Separating the beans from the skin. And see? What luck! There is just the right amount of wind for this today."

We spread *petates* out over the area between the kitchen and the outhouse, a flat stretch of dirt where the chickens usually scurried around. Then, using a gourd, Abuelo scooped out the beans from the tree trunk and threw them up into the air. The wind caught the lighter bits—the dried wispy skins—and carried them off toward the banana trees. The beans were heavier, and they fell onto the mat. They were the part we needed.

Abuelo handed me another gourd. "You can use this one, *m'hija.*" I took it and noticed words carved on the bottom. *Enrique Hector Luna Estrada, Yucuyoo, 1980.* It had been Dad's.

Abuelo saw me running my fingers over the letters. "Enrique was your age when he carved that."

I tossed a gourdful up into the air, imagining I was Dad, before he had any idea he'd be moving to the U.S. and marrying an American and having a daughter. The wind caught the beans and held them in the air, hanging there by sunlight, as if the beans and skins were deciding: *Stay or go?* And the heavy beans fell, while the skins flew off in waves, rising and falling and making small circles in their flight toward the trees.

Abuelo threw another gourdful into the air and squinted into the sun, watching the skins disappear. "The day after Enrique left was a little windy like today. I got up early to pound the beans before breakfast. I waited for him to come out and help. I waited and waited. He never came."

"He didn't tell you he was leaving?" I couldn't believe it—Dad would get mad at me if I rode my bike down the block without telling him first!

"No. Perhaps he wouldn't have been able to bear seeing our faces when he said goodbye. He knew he would be leaving us all alone. He was the only child we were able to have. He slipped away in the middle of the night."

"How old was he?" I asked.

"Sixteen, nearly seventeen. He was restless, you see. I think he saw his life here stretching out forever, harvesting coffee and barely making enough money for food. A few months before he left, he told us something in a serious voice. 'A friend of mine is going to Arizona to work,' he said. 'And I'm thinking about going too.' "

Abuelo was sitting down now on the mat, surrounded by shiny beans. I threw the last gourdful into the air and watched the skins fly away. I sat down next to him, cross-legged, and felt the sun warm on my face.

He rolled a few beans around in his hand. "Clara, I have only seen your grandmother cry one time. And that was the day Enrique told us he might leave. The only time, *m'hija.* She sat there by the fire and a single tear slipped out. Months later, on the morning after he did leave, I had breakfast alone with your grandmother. And do you know what she told me? 'He will be gone for a long time, years and years.' 'But no,' I told her, 'he'll be back as soon as he saves up money.' She put her hand over mine and shook her head. And then I cried enough tears for the both of us."

Abuelo began collecting the beans and dropping them by handfuls into a tin bucket. I started to plunk them in too.

I thought about how Pedro's face grew red and angry when he talked about men in the village leaving. "Were you angry at Dad?"

"Mostly sad. That is where the wind has taken him. Like the coffee skins. Why struggle against it?"

"But he could've visited you, at least!" *I* would've been mad.

"He hasn't forgotten us. From time to time a postcard comes. Always blank. Empty of writing but full of shame. And every once in a while an envelope comes with some money and photos in it. Never a message, just the return address."

"Why?"

"Perhaps he hoped that one day we would ask him to come home. Or perhaps that one day we would ask his daughter."

The bucket of beans was full to the brim now. Abuelo heaved it up and carried it to the shed. He walked into the shadows at the back corner and dug out a small wooden box from a pile of tools and crates.

I opened it and pulled out a thick pile of postcards. One from Arizona—sunset over cacti. Then one from California— the beach and palm trees—postmarked a few months later. Then one from Washington State—giant pines.

"This must have been when Dad was traveling around," I said. "Picking fruit and vegetables for money."

Abuelo took out a thin stack of photos from the bottom of the box. "Look at this, *m'hija*. When you were born he sent us this." He pointed to a baby picture of me, swaddled up, a fat little ball, in the middle of Mom and Dad's green bedspread.

The photo was familiar—it hung on the family room wall at home. On the back were my name and birthday, written in Dad's precise handwriting. The next picture was me, two years old, picking a purple crocus. And four years old, digging in a sandbox in a red sweater. And then baby Hector, plopped down in the surf at Ocean City. And on and on until the most recent, fourteen-year-old me, drawing in my sketchbook on the couch, so intent on what I was doing that I was caught off guard by Dad taking the picture. My mouth was slightly open in surprise and my eyes looked wide and confused—I was hovering between my inside world and the outside one.

"I didn't know he sent you these, Abuelo!"

I flipped through the rest of the postcards now, all the places Dad had worked.

"And how lucky that he sent them. That is how we knew your address. This spring, your grandmother told me that she felt your restless spirit. Searching, she said. She would get out of bed at night and wander outside. Night after night, like a jaguar. She said she could feel you better then. One morning she said, 'Come to town with me to mail a letter.' You see, she had asked Pedro to write it the night before."

"Pedro wrote that letter?" I felt myself smile, even though I was trying not to. I liked the idea that there was a connection between Pedro and me before we ever saw each other. It sent a shivery thrill through me to think of my hands holding the same piece of paper that his had held.

Abuelo nodded. "Your grandmother said you would come in June on the full moon. And Clara, when I heard that, my heart soared like a bird. I went into Enrique's old room and aired out his mattress and blankets and scrubbed the walls and floor. And on the way to the airport, I kept pestering your grandmother, 'What if she's not there? What if she decided not to come?' Oh, I was just like a child!"

I laughed. He *had* reminded me of an excited little kid when we first met at the airport.

"And as you were coming off that plane, Clara, my heart was so flooded with joy, I thought I would burst!"

●

After each day of hard work, I'd lie on my mattress and listen to rain beat overhead on the tin roof. I'd feel my tired legs and exhausted shoulders. And all the while, bits of Pedro's music ran through my head, flitting around like butterflies—they entered my dreams and stayed with me until morning, when I found myself humming his songs as I got dressed. I started taking short afternoon walks in the mountains and scanned the trees for a glimpse of his red pants. I listened hopefully for the scuttle of goat hooves. I sat by the stream at the spot where we used to meet, wishing he'd show up. He was avoiding me, that was obvious.

At the market on Saturday, Abuelita and I were picking out avocados when I spotted Pedro in his orange T-shirt. He was over by the clock tower, where a bunch of women in long braids and checked aprons sat behind low tables. The tables were spread with half-gourds full of wet cheese. The women were swatting away flies with palm fans and stirring the cheese with wooden spoons. Next to them, Pedro was cutting chunks of solid cheese into squares and wrapping them in banana leaves.

Something inside me jumped. Tingles spread over my skin. He must have felt my gaze because he looked up at me, straight into my eyes, right through the crowd of people and the piles of chiles and the bundles of flowers. He handed his knife to the woman next to him. She was small and fragile-looking, with thin wrists and pointy shoulders. He said something to her and pointed in my direction. Then he wiped his hands on his pants and began to weave his way toward me. I tried to look interested in the avocados, but my heart was beating fast.

When he reached us, he greeted Abuelita in Mixteco and touched her hand. Then he said to me in Spanish, "Hello, Clara."

"Hello," I said coolly.

"My mother wants to meet you." It was hard to tell if he was still angry at me or not. His face was empty of expression. Even so, the way he said my name sounded nice. It rolled off his tongue like tiny crystals.

"Here I will wait for you, by the tomatoes," Abuelita said.

I followed Pedro as he wound back through smells of frying meat, simmering corn soup, hot cinnamon coffee. A warmth moved through me like bathwater, and it amazed me that just being near a certain person could make me feel this way. We reached the cheese section.

"Have a spoonful of cheese," Pedro offered. "It's from our goats' milk."

The cheese looked disgusting—snotty and goopy, with a damp, moldy smell. And even with the women fanning, a few flies were managing to land in it here and there.

"No, thanks," I said.

"Please, go ahead," urged the fragile woman, who I guessed must be his mother. She would have had a nice smile if two of her teeth hadn't been rotted.

After a deep breath I took a nibble off the spoonful she handed me. It was rich and creamy. "Not bad," I said, licking the spoon clean.

His mother touched my hand lightly, the way people here shake hands, like they're afraid you might break. "My son thinks very highly of you," she said.

So he must have said good things about me. He must have been thinking about me.

Pedro pretended not to be listening. He acted completely absorbed in fanning the flies. But I noticed his cheeks growing pinker. His mother gave me a square of cheese wrapped in a banana leaf to share with my grandparents. "Come visit us soon," she said. "Our house is your house." After I thanked her, Pedro and I made our way back to the vegetables. But Abuelita wasn't by the avocados and tomatoes anymore. We walked all the way to the end of the row, scanning the crowds. The nasal sounds of Mixteco surrounded us—people bargaining, chatting, calling to wandering children, soothing babies, joking and laughing. Salsa music blared from a giant speaker at a CD stand nearby, where a group of boys had gathered.

"Eh, Pedro!" a boy in a baseball cap called out. "Introduce us to your woman!"

"I'll just go back to Abuelita," I mumbled. I tried to spot her in the crowd of dozens of other women, who all had long braids woven with ribbons.

By this time three of the guys had walked over to us.

"*Hola, guapa,*" the biggest one said. The one in the baseball cap whistled and looked me up and down.

This was only the second time in my life when any boy had looked at me that way—the first time had been the year before at the Ocean City boardwalk. And the boys might have been whistling at Samantha rather than me. We'd felt giggly and flattered then, but now I just crossed my arms awkwardly, then uncrossed them, then held them stiffly by my sides.

"How does she like it here?" asked the big guy. He wore baggy jeans and a black T-shirt and two gold chains. Even though he was right in front of us, he had to yell to be heard over the music.

"Ask her yourself, Felipe. She speaks Spanish," Pedro said. He kept looking over his shoulder, like he wanted to get away as soon as he could.

Felipe said to me, "Marry me and take me back to your country."

I wanted to shrink or hide or become invisible.

"Let's go," Pedro said. He walked away and I turned to follow him.

"Ah, Pedro's the one she'll take with her," said the boy in the baseball cap.

"Pedro's going to disappear from here, just like his dad," the youngest one added, smirking.

As soon as the words were out, Felipe gave him a shove. "Shut up, Diego!"

Pedro stopped in his tracks. He turned around and slowly walked up to the younger kid.

"Pedro, calm down," Felipe said. He backed up, pulling the younger one with him. "Diego didn't know any better."

"If he *ever* says anything like that again . . ." Pedro's fists

145

clenched and unclenched. Was he going to hit someone? But no, he turned and ran away, disappearing into the crowd, leaving me alone with the group of boys.

I straightened up and lifted my head high like a heron's. I hoped I looked graceful. That was how I felt, at least, and it surprised me. I looked each one of them straight in the eyes. My stare wasn't as strong as Abuelita's, but it seemed to work. They glanced at each other sheepishly and hung their heads.

On the way to the sink that night with my toothbrush and toothpaste, I noticed the moon, perfectly full. I could see the shape of the entire rabbit inside the circle. A song that Dad used to sing came back to me, the song that told the story of how the rabbit got stuck in the moon. A farmer was angry that a rabbit kept nibbling at his crops, so he rolled a big ball of candle wax toward it. The rabbit got caught in the wax ball, which rolled faster and faster until it left the earth and flew into the sky.

A full moon. It must be July then, exactly one month after I'd gotten here. Now I understood why Abuelita hadn't given a calendar date in her letter, but moon time instead. Here, times and dates didn't matter. There were rhythms— of the moon, the sun, the afternoon rains, hot chocolate at night, patting tortillas in the mornings.

One month left. Suddenly I missed the strumming of Pedro's guitar so much, I felt a sharp pain in my stomach. I stood in the cool air with toothpaste foam dripping down my chin, halfheartedly brushing. I looked past the cornfield to where Pedro's house was just a little point of light.

Should I walk over there, barefoot, like Abuelita did more than two full moons ago? The only thing stopping me was some kind of pride mixed with shame. Maybe it was the same thing that kept Dad from visiting his parents, or at least writing them a real letter. Maybe what people really wanted was to touch souls with other people, but the problem was that other things kept getting in the way. I thought of doña Carmen and her husband, and Silvia, and Uncle José—who would be my great-great-uncle. What each of them really wanted were threads of love like a spiderweb connecting them with other people, but they couldn't quite get it right.

But I was going to get it right, I decided. I could go to Pedro's house with an offering of roasted coffee beans. Yes, I would do it. I would go tomorrow night, when he'd be at home with his mother, having hot cinnamon-chocolate milk. After all, she had invited me.

I spit out the toothpaste, rinsed my mouth, and wiped my face on the sleeve of my sweatshirt. Through the banana leaves, the wind made a soft rushing sound, light as someone's breath. The *shhhhhhhh* made me think of the hidden waterfall. One month left to find it. I walked to my room slowly, following my long moon shadow, looking back every few steps, back toward Pedro's house.

In bed more words of his songs came to me. *Nighttime flowers.* Flowers that you can smell only at night. The scent of flowers like souls, something you can't touch, something hidden in the night, something you find if you are brave enough to go into the darkness, into strange territory. I had found Pedro's soul and he had found mine, but then, somehow, we'd lost track of them. All these thoughts and words and songs darted around my head like hummingbirds until I fell asleep.

147

The next morning while we were sipping chamomile tea after breakfast, Loro *sang*! I'd heard birds sing with whistles and chirps before, but never with words. And best of all, I recognized the words—it was the rabbit-in-the-moon song.

"Dad sang that song to me when I was little," I announced, once Loro had finished.

"He probably learned it from Loro," Abuelo said, grinning.

"Or from me," Abuelita said. Her voice wavered a little. Her gaze sank down to her cup. "I used to sing it to him. Before I'd put him to bed."

"Where did you learn it?" I asked her.

"Doña Three Teeth." Abuelita took a deep breath, raised her head, and offered us the next piece of the puzzle of her life.

Helena

SPRING 1938

After my first night in jail, I awoke to a square of light shining through the window, right onto my cheek. Doña Three Teeth slept soundly beside me. I stood up and stretched my back, stiff and sore. I pressed my face against the bars and breathed in the fresh morning smell. People breezed by on their way to market. A mother pulled her curious children away from the bars. "No!" she warned. "Dirty!" A few people I recognized passed—three maids I knew from the market and two vendors.

And then, Silvia walked by. She wore a white ruffled dress with small yellow flowers. Her braid was perfectly curled around her head, every hair in place. Under her hat, her skin was powdered white, as though a sack of flour had burst in her face.

"Silvia!" I called.

She stopped in her tracks and stared ahead. I could almost hear her thoughts: Should she ignore me and keep walking, or come to the window? With every bit of strength, I willed her toward me. Oh, I willed her so hard my body shook. *Silvia, turn your head. Come over.*

And she did. With her feet dragging, she came to the window. She most likely couldn't see my face in the shadows, but she knew my voice.

"Silvia," I said. I wished I could reach out and hold her there.

"I know you didn't steal the ring," she said flatly.

"Your mother planted it there, didn't she?"

"Yes, and I hate her. What a coward."

"Silvia. Tell this to the police. Please."

"It's not my problem. She doesn't matter to me. Neither do you." She turned to leave.

"Silvia, wait!"

She paused. The thinnest thread held her there. Oh, I had to be careful, very, very careful not to break it.

"Silvia, if you don't tell the police," and here I tried to keep my voice from breaking, "if you don't tell them, I could rot in here for years."

It seemed that a veil lifted from her face. Her eyes, for a moment, saw outward, not just inward. From her basket she plucked out a cherry pastry and handed it to me. "I'll *think* about it."

●

150

I gave the pastry to doña Three Teeth. She pretended to drink hot chocolate with it. There she sat like a rich lady, sipping at her imaginary cup with her little finger raised. She helped herself to imaginary seconds and thirds. You know, watching her eat the pastry was better than eating it myself. Oh, how she savored it! She licked her fingers, and laughed and laughed at such a small, rare pleasure.

That night, I decided to enter the dreams of another for the first time. When I was a child, Ta'nu had told me stories of drifting in and out of others' dreams. After two years of training, and many soul flights, I asked Ta'nu to teach me how to enter dreams. He laughed, his eyes twinkling. "Oh, Ita. So eager, you are. But entering the dreams of another, now, that is not easy. I learned to do it much later in life, as an old man. Even now, I need two cups of sacred tea to do it. If, one day, you have a great need, you will find a way." I had no sacred tea in the cell with me. But I did have a great need. More than a need. A desperation.

I took a long breath and looked inside myself, into my calm center. How to do this? First, I decided, I would slip out of my body. My spirit animal would know what to do after that. I had slipped out of my body many times since my first soul flight to the stream, sometimes with the sacred tea, sometimes without. Every time, I remembered the warnings Ta'nu gave me while we were eating *pitayas* under the tree. "Soul flights are dangerous, very dangerous, my child. When your spirit leaves your body, there is always the chance it will never find its way back."

Once doña Three Teeth was snoring softly, I closed my eyes and began chanting. Very softly, I chanted. The words circled around me like a gentle whirlwind. In time, they lifted my spirit up. I hovered over my body and looked at it. There it lay, in its cotton *huipil* and skirt on the dirt floor. As always, I was surprised by the tenderness of the eyelids. The strength of the cheekbones. The full, pretty lips.

With ease I slipped through the bars, out to the deserted street. In midair I floated, calling to my jaguar spirit. A moment later, he bounded down the center of the road and stopped just beneath me. He panted, his tongue hanging out between glistening white teeth. I lowered myself and stroked his ears, smooth as fine velvet. I wrapped my arms around his thick neck and buried my face in his fur. Soon, I felt myself sinking into him.

I let myself *become* the jaguar.

On four legs, I ran down the street, around the corner, down a few more blocks, to the García López house. I sprang over the gate and landed in the dark courtyard. Loro slept soundly; he didn't even stir as I breezed by his cage. I leaped onto the windowsill of Silvia's bedroom and crept softly across the tile floor, my claws *tap-tap-tap*ping. Then I lay down, panting, on Silvia's white sheets.

All night I let her soak up my presence. All night I oozed into her pores, slipped through her fluttering eyelids, came in and out of her breath, until just before dawn, when I bounded out the window, through the courtyard, up the streets, back to the prison.

Hours after the sun had risen, my eyes opened to a small patch of light through the window. Footsteps had awakened me, footsteps coming down the hall. Iron keys rattled. The door unlocked and creaked open.

"Señorita Helena," the guard announced. "The charges

are dropped. You're free." He cleared his throat and added in a low voice, "My apologies for the inconvenience, *señorita*."

Doña Three Teeth was just waking up. She gave me a sleepy, sad smile.

Before I could say goodbye to her properly, the guard took me by the elbow and led me to a main room. There, doña Carmen, don Manuel, and Silvia sat in a row of wooden chairs. In a voice loud enough for everyone to hear, Silvia whispered, "Well, Mamá, aren't you going to offer your apologies?"

Doña Carmen glared at her husband. Like a venomous snake, she spit out, "Keep your daughter under control . . . maybe if you were at home more . . ."

Don Manuel squirmed in his seat as though he'd just stepped on a red-ant hill. "Let's go," he mumbled, and stood up.

"Wait," said Silvia. "My mother owes the girl some money."

The guard rubbed his eyes. "Is this true?"

"Yes," I said, watching doña Carmen's face grow red as a chile pepper. "Sixty pesos, she owes me."

"Pay her now, *señora*." The poor guard looked tired, in no mood to argue.

"But I have no money with me. At home I'll give her . . ." Doña Carmen's voice trailed off.

"*Now*," he said. His voice was raw and hoarse.

Doña Carmen pulled forty pesos out of a pouch around her neck and looked at her husband. He sighed and pulled a few coins out of his pocket.

"Less money for you to spend around town," she hissed at him. She snatched the money and shoved it toward me. Out the door she stormed, cursing under her breath. Don Manuel and Silvia followed her at a distance, don Manuel with his head hanging but Silvia with her head high and proud.

On the way out, I paused and whispered to the guard. "*Señor,* boil some oregano, chamomile, and garlic, then add juice of a whole lime and three spoonfuls of honey. Drink a cup of it three times a day. Your cough will be gone in days."

He gave me a strange look.

I reached out my hand. There I held it, waiting. After a moment he touched it with his own. "Thank you, señorita Helena." The corners of his mouth turned up in a puzzled smile. "I'll try that."

Outside I tilted my face to the sky and soaked up the sunshine like a lizard. Then I walked down the street to the market and bought three mangoes. One after another I ate them. How delicious, to have mango juice dripping down your chin. Yellow sunshine, blue sky, food in my stomach, and freedom.

Back at the García López house, doña Carmen went straight to her bedroom. "Pack your things and be out of this house by tomorrow morning," she snapped at me on her way upstairs.

I smiled calmly. I unbraided my hair and brushed it out with my fingers. In a tin of cold water, I bathed myself and washed my hair, scrubbing away the stale prison odor. I slipped on my *huipil* and skirt and thought about what to do next. I could go door to door, searching for another family who might hire me as a maid. But a wave of weariness hit me, and even though it was daytime, I spread my *petate* on the kitchen floor. There I lay with my eyes closed.

"Helena," a voice whispered just as I was floating off to

sleep. I opened my eyes. Silvia was kneeling beside me, a shadow against the rectangle of bright sunlight in the doorway. "You're not going to leave us, are you?"

"Of course I am," I said without a pause. Did she expect me to stay?

She sighed. Her eyes looked tired, too tired for someone who had never lifted a finger to work. "Take that bird with you."

"Silvia!" I cried, surprised. "Thank you!" I threw my arms around her. My arms wrapped around her skinny shoulders and thin neck. Her body felt stiff as an old tortilla, but she didn't pull away. For a few moments, her face rested in my loose hair.

"Anyway, the bird would just grow ill and die without you here," she said, standing up.

I noticed that her face looked softer somehow. She walked out of the kitchen, then stopped and turned back to me. "Your hair, Helena. It feels like fur. The fur of a cat." She looked into my eyes for the first time. And for the first time, I saw her truly seeing me. How startling life is, sometimes. That souls can touch for a moment, like a flash of light. I wondered: Could a soul pass on a piece of its flame to another, and on and on, forever? Was my soul made of light from the souls that had touched mine? I hoped that some of my light had gone to Silvia. I was certain that doña Three Teeth's soul had passed light to me, and that I would pass it on.

All afternoon I drifted in and out of sleep and dreamed of my grandfather. Not dreamed, exactly, but had visions. I saw him in the room with me. There he stood by the hearth, sitting in the corner, watching me. *Something is wrong with him.* He was entering my dreams the same way I'd entered Silvia's the night before.

When I awoke, it was dark. Everyone else had gone to sleep. I gathered my sack of herbs and my extra clothes. Then I packed some leftover tortillas in a basket along with limes and salt. Fruit I could pick along the way.

I walked through the dark courtyard, past the flowers and trees. "Helena Helena Helena!" Loro called, shifting his feet on his perch, his feathers bristling with joy. I unlatched the door of his cage and kissed the top of his head. Piece by piece I fed him a tortilla. Then he climbed onto my arm with thick, firm claws. He shuffled up to my shoulder, and there he sat, on the long journey back to my village. And, as you know, he's been with me ever since.

●

On the way out of town, I walked down the deserted street toward the jail. The full moon was rising in front of me. A long moon shadow stretched behind me. Music drifted toward me, someone singing. The voice grew louder as I grew closer. It was doña Three Teeth. At the corner of the prison I stood and listened. The song told the story of how the rabbit ended up in the moon. I watched the form of the rabbit in the moon as she sang. Oh, how sweetly she sang. How sadly. You see, when people think no one is listening, their song reveals their soul. And her soul took my breath away. It glowed as strong as a thousand hearth fires.

When the song ended I walked up to the window, where doña Three Teeth peered out. In Mixteco, I whispered, "*Ton kuaa!*" Good evening!

"Helena!" she cried. The moonlight made her face shimmer. She reached her hand out and smoothed Loro's feathers. "And you are Loro, no?"

"*¡Ánimo!*" he creaked.

She widened her eyes and smiled.

I pressed thirty pesos into her palm. "For when you leave here," I said. Gently, I squeezed her hand.

Before she could refuse the money, I left. From behind me she called out, "*Nku ta'a vini,* Helena." Thank you.

Much later that night I realized something. Much later, when the moon was high and small in the sky, when I was outside the city, walking along the road through the mountains. With a stab of regret, I realized that I had never asked her true name.

●

Ten days it took me to return to my village. Ten days, walking. Most likely there was a faster way, a shortcut through the forests, but I only knew the road we'd come on. During the days I slept. During the nights I walked. Oh, I loved this. The moon gave me enough light. And it was cooler at night, no blazing sun to sap my strength. Night-blooming flowers like *huele de noche* filled the air with their scent. I saw no man, no woman. All was peaceful and quiet except for Loro's whistling and talking. Of course I had heard the stories of evil creatures of the night. Creatures of this world and other worlds, creatures that attacked innocent wanderers. Yet there was nothing for me to fear among the trees. This I knew. Remember, the most powerful animal of the night forest, the jaguar, would leap to my defense if anything threatened me. With this knowledge I walked with courage.

At sunrise on the tenth day, after a full night of walking, I arrived. From the mountain that towered over our village, I could see thin streams of smoke rising from the roofs in the valley. Up they rose and disappeared into the clouds. Inside the huts, the women would be starting tortillas and chamomile tea for breakfast.

I ran the rest of the way, smiling, then laughing and hollering. The basket bounced on my back and the sack bumped my thigh, but I barely noticed. My heart felt so full of joy, I thought it might explode.

I burst into the kitchen. Sunshine came through the bamboo walls and lit up María with stripes. She held a half-formed tortilla in her hand. When she saw me standing there, breathless and filthy, in the doorway, she screamed, tossed the tortilla over our heads, threw her arms around me. Both of us were laughing and crying.

Her hair pressed into my face, and I breathed in her clean, sweet smell. Over my shoulder, she screamed, *"Mother! Hurry!"*

Aunt Teresa came around the corner with an armful of firewood, and when she saw me, dropped it all to the ground. She ran to me, wrapped her tortilla-dough arms around my shoulders, pressed me against her big, soft stomach. Imagine how I felt to be suddenly surrounded with so much love. It was like coming inside from a bitter rain, inside to a bright fire.

They fed me a huge breakfast, enough for three men—piles of eggs, beans, tortillas, chile sauce. "How thin you are!" they kept saying. "A sack of bones!" They heaped seconds and thirds in front of me until I could eat no more. I told them everything: about the García López family, my time in jail, doña Three Teeth. They had a thousand questions. Oh, even the tiniest details, they wanted to know. "How do the women in Oaxaca wear their hair? Where do they collect water? Where do they urinate?" And you can imagine how much they adored Loro. In minutes they'd taught him their names. They screeched with delight as he said, "Maríííía! Tereeeeeeesa!"

Finally, I grew serious. "And Ta'nu . . . how is he?"

"He's very ill, Helena," Aunt Teresa said.

"He says he's going to die soon," María added, somber now.

"Well, I won't let him," I whispered.

We sipped the hot milk in silence. Above us, in the rafters, Loro moved back and forth. Outside we heard Uncle's footsteps, his loud yawning.

Aunt Teresa's eyes grew big. "*Ayyyy!* We forgot to make breakfast for your father!" she said to María. "Quick, help me make more tortillas."

Uncle José appeared in the kitchen doorway. For a moment I thought he might welcome me home. Maybe even embrace me. I should have known he wouldn't. Still, my heart sank at his cold eyes. "What are you doing here?" he growled.

"I came to cure Ta'nu."

"Too late. The old man says he's going to die. Nothing you can do."

"We'll see," I said. No longer did I fear Uncle. I had been in jail. I had been alone in a city where no one cared about me except for a bird. I had walked for ten days with little food. For the first time I saw Uncle clearly. Now that I no longer lived in his shadow, I saw who he truly was. A coward who bullied his daughter and wife.

"You shouldn't have come back. You think we're going to feed you now? That you'll live here for free?"

"José! The girl's tired from her journey!" Aunt Teresa said in her brave mouse voice.

159

He shot her a threatening look that silenced her quickly. It silenced her the way the sight of a broom makes a dog crawl away on its belly to escape a beating. My fury was rising. I pressed my lips together.

"Where's my breakfast?" he demanded.

"Almost ready, Father," María said.

"Why isn't it ready?"

"Well, Helena just arrived," Aunt explained, "and we fed her. She was hungry . . . and we haven't seen her for so long. . . ."

"Already eating our food, I see, and distracting us from work."

I pulled out my money pouch and took out two coins. I dropped them onto the table. "This is for your food, Uncle. And don't worry, I'll take no more of it."

"Don't leave again, Helena!" cried María.

"I won't."

"What will you eat then? Dirt?" Uncle challenged me.

"I will cure," I said, hearing my voice strong and certain. "I will help Ta'nu cure."

●

In his room, Ta'nu lay on the *petate,* covered in blankets. Only his face showed. A pale face, nearly a ghost's face already, the light shining through. I could almost see right through him, to his bones and blood and veins. He looked strangely peaceful. Some people, you see, struggle with death, but not Ta'nu. He lay there, tranquil, breathing slowly. His eyes followed me as I walked into the room. He smiled.

I knelt at his side and stroked my hand across his forehead. "I'll cure you, Ta'nu," I whispered. "I'll brew you teas, do a *limpia,* fly to whatever is making you sick, fight for your spirit. No matter if it kills me . . ." I felt his skin warm under my hand. I wanted it never to turn cold.

"It's my time to die, Helena," he said.

"Ta'nu. I don't want to live in this world without you." If only I could sink into him, become part of him, die if he died.

"My body will not be here. But my spirit will. My spirit will visit you always," he said.

What could I say to make him change his mind about dying? "Ta'nu," I pleaded. "No one else in the world cares about me the way you do."

"Ita, one day you will marry. You will have children, grandchildren. They will love you very much."

"I will never marry. I'm a healer. No man wants a wife more powerful than himself."

"You have not met him yet, love, but you will. Ita, I give you my room, my curing hut and the altar inside, and the herbs, and my garden. I wish I could offer you more—"

"*Ta'nu.* I only want you to stay alive. *Please.*"

"Helena. They say that deep in the middle of the earth is a chamber lit by candles. Thousands of candles. White candles. Some tall, some short, all different heights, standing in pools of wax. Each of these candles is a person's life. The tall ones are the newborn babies. They have a whole lifetime yet to live. The short ones are mostly very old people. People whose flame of life is just about to go out. And watching over these candles is the spirit woman in charge of life and death and healing. When a short stub is about to go out, she places a new candle over it. A tall candle. She presses it into the pool of wax. And a new life begins. There must be death for life to happen."

Ta'nu's breathing was strained now. He closed his eyes and drifted off to sleep.

"I understand," I said, not bothering to wipe the stream of tears from my face. "I'll let your candle go out, Ta'nu." And I watched him all day and all night. Beside him I sat, holding his hand as he slowly faded. Just before dawn, his flame went out, and somewhere, a new candle was lit.

10

Clara

The sun hung low in the sky like a squashed mango. I circled the spot where the waterfall sounded loudest. Sunshine was pouring between the leaves and making moving spots of light on the forest floor. Next to me loomed a high rock face draped with vines, and nearby sat a pile of rocks. But no waterfall.

Maybe Pedro knew where it was. I wished I'd asked him. At first I'd wanted to find it alone—my secret mission—but now I wanted to find it with him. Tonight I would ask him, tonight when I went to his house, if I got up the nerve.

I missed watching his fingers weave palm and fold origami and smooth the fur of the goats. If he'd been here, I'd have asked him about the waterfall. *This mountain is our body,* he'd told me. *The streams are our blood, the waterfalls our pulse.*

I walked up the trail along the side of the rock face to a small peak, from which I had a view of the valley below. Suddenly, I heard my name. It echoed through the whole valley, bouncing back and forth and up and down and everywhere.

"*CLARAAAA-Claraaaa-Claraaa-Claraaaa . . .*" Until it faded.

Where was he? I scanned the valley. My heart pounded.

"*DIIIIIIS-CÚÚÚÚL-PAAAA-MEEEEE . . . ,*" he called out. Forgive me.

There he was! On the next mountain over—a little below the peak! He was just a speck of red surrounded by white and black dots, which must have been goats. I stood on a rock, waving my arms over my head.

"*DIIIIIIS-CÚÚÚÚL-PAAAA-MEEEEE . . . ,*" I shouted back. *Discúlpame . . .* My voice came back in waves from the farthest mountains.

●

The next day, I was wading in the stream, watching tiny fish flicker around my ankles, when without a word, Pedro sat down on a rock and played. It was a song I hadn't heard before. The words painted a picture in my mind: Pedro opening a door and watching me come toward him, out of the shadows and into the light. And then came the lines that made me quiver inside.

>*I give you a song when you appear,*
>*The mystery of love . . .*

He watched me closely while he sang. He had to stop for a second in the middle to call out *"Chchchchchivo"* when he noticed that one of the goats had wandered, and another time, to brush away the dragonfly that kept landing on the neck of the guitar. Toward the end of the song his voice grew louder and stronger and the strumming grew harder. The veins in his neck stood out, and beads of sweat formed on his forehead. When he finished, we looked at each other as though a tornado had just whirled by.

After a minute I asked, "What did the words mean, Pedro?"

"What do you think?"

"Were the words for me?"

He smiled. "You and only you. Because I miss you."

That heat went through me again. "It sounded nice."

I waded out of the stream, trying not to slip on any stones. I pulled out a little package from my backpack. "Here are some coffee beans for you and your mother."

"Thanks."

"I roasted them with Abuelita. I was going to bring them to you."

"Do you want to walk with me and the goats?"

I nodded. "I miss the goats." I miss *you*, I wanted to say, but I wasn't quite brave enough. I put on the sandals—now they fit my feet perfectly—and slung the backpack over my shoulder.

"Sorry about Diego and Felipe and Chucho," he said. "Those guys at the market, they're just jealous."

"Of what?" I thought of what Abuelita had told me about the streets paved with gold and the diamonds on the trees.

"That you chose me. As your friend, I mean."

"Oh."

"They should have known better than to talk about my dad." He took a deep breath and let it out slowly. "My dad left when I was a little kid, to go work in Chicago. He was supposed to send money back to my mother and me. He told us he'd come back to visit every couple of years."

"And what happened to him?" I asked.

"He stopped sending money after a few years. Then nothing."

"Do you think he's dead?"

"Sometimes I wish he was." He paused. "A few years ago Diego and Felipe's father came back from Chicago to visit. He said he saw my father there. He was married and had children. He has a whole new family now. He forgot about us here."

We rounded the bend, out of the sunshine, down into the shadows. Here moss hung from tree branches.

"See, Clara, whenever the men who have lived in your country come back here, they show off their video cameras and CD players and cell phones." Pedro grabbed a handful of moss from the tree and began tearing it into pieces. "My father chose all those things over our village. Over my mother and me."

He threw the rest of the moss onto the ground.

"He got distracted," I said. "By the jewels and the reflections and bright colors."

"You were listening," he said, smiling. He climbed onto a high rock covered with light green and white lichen and reached down to give me a hand. From above we had a view of the small, shady valley, of the goats wandering on beds of soft grass.

"But, Clara, you don't get distracted by those things. You're different."

"Different?" I asked doubtfully, thinking of the CD cases and clothes strewn over my bedroom carpet, of my shiny stereo system and waist-high speakers, my closet full of shoes and gadgets that had seemed so important when I bought them at the mall. Not exactly jewels, but definitely distracting things, things without souls.

"You pay attention to what's important," Pedro said. "You let yourself hear my music, really hear it. And you're looking for the waterfall, like me."

"How did you know?" He was so much like Abuelita; he knew things that most people would never have guessed.

"The way you listen, the way you look." Then, almost shyly, he added, "And because I'm looking for it too."

Pedro and I spent the next few days following the goats, on the lookout for any nook or cranny that might lead to the waterfall. He suspected that it was underground, and I thought he was probably right.

During those days we talked excitedly, to make up for our time apart. We talked about God, the universe, souls, life after death, ghosts, spirits, aliens. He told me tales about the rain serpents that live in lakes in the mountains, the lightning and thunder gods who send storms out of the caves, the little frog goddesses that announce the rain, the moon goddess, the sun god, and their children, the stars. He made me tell the plots of all the extraterrestrial movies I'd seen. He had some ideas about spirits and aliens actually being one and the same. He sang songs, and I sat close to him, strumming the guitar at the wide part as he moved his fingers along its neck. Then I breathed in deeply the strange sweet smell that clung to him.

One afternoon, we were huddled under a rock shelter, watching the sheets of rain come down. The goats were gathered near us, sopping wet, pressed against the rock.

"That day at the market, you spoke in Mixteco to my grandmother," I said. "I didn't know you spoke it. Before that, I only heard older people speak it."

He was sitting next to me, wearing a black plastic garbage bag to keep the rain off. I was wearing the yellow plastic poncho Abuelita had given me.

"My mother always speaks Mixteco to me," he said.

I thought for a second. "My dad doesn't speak it. At least I don't think he does."

"That's because he went to school. When he was young, the teacher smacked children's hands with a stick if they spoke Mixteco."

"That's horrible!" I shivered under my poncho and rubbed my hands over my goose-bumped legs. "How come your mother speaks it?"

"She never went to school. She worked at home with her mother and grandmother."

I imagined five-year-old Dad on his first day of school, his skinny legs in goatskin sandals and a little palm hat. I saw him speaking his own language and then *smack*, being hit on the hand. The shock, the sting, the red mark, his eyes welling up with tears.

And Dad years later, with his mustache and a few silvery hairs, wet eyes, watching me come in shamefaced through the glass doors at four a.m. Dad speaking Spanish to me in front of my friends: *"¿A qué hora regresas, Clara?"* When will you be back, Clara? He would not let me out the door until I answered in Spanish. *"A las nueve, Dad."* At nine, Dad. And

I'd sigh and roll my eyes and slam the door behind me and wait for my embarrassment to slowly fade.

●

I began asking Abuelita to tell me the names of the herbs in Mixteco whenever we made medicines. Every time we prepared an herb, she had me rub it between my fingers and smell it and feel it. *Pericón* with its tiny yellow flowers—*yuku taxini* in Mixteco—for women giving birth. Sweet *sauco*—*ita tindoo*—for colds and flus. Bitter *hierba amarga*—*yuku tuchi*—for stomachaches and anger. Some herbs we hung upside down from the rafters to dry for teas. Others we dropped into glass bottles of *mezcal,* where they'd stay until next year, when she'd strain out the leaves.

Maybe I would be here next summer to strain the leaves out myself. But as soon as the thought surfaced in my mind, I pushed it down again. I didn't want to think about this summer ending. I didn't want to think that all this could go on without me. The dishes would get washed, the tortillas made, the coffee beans ground. And I was afraid that when I went back to Walnut Hill, the old Clara would come back, the foggy moon, clouded and confused.

Early one morning, while I was outside at the sink splashing cold water on my face, Abuelita called my name. Her voice sounded urgent. I dried my face on my shirt and ran to the kitchen. She was picking out dried oregano leaves and *carrizo* roots from the rafters and dropping them into a basket with other herbs.

"What's wrong?" I asked.

"I need your help, *mi vida.* Listen."

I heard the *clip-clop* of a burro. Usually they just plodded along, weighed down with sacks of corn or firewood, but this one seemed to be galloping. Its footsteps were growing louder, closer.

"Someone's coming with a child to be cured," she said. "She might have been stung by a scorpion."

"How do you know?" I asked. We had no phone, and neither did the neighbors.

"I feel it," she said. "Put some water on to boil, *mi amor.* Then start brewing this basket of herbs."

I'd never seen her move this fast before. She began grinding garlic and chocolate on the *metate*. I ran outside with the clay pot for the water.

The burros drew closer. There were two of them. One carried a woman and a baby, and the other carried the two boys who had been teasing Pedro at the market—Felipe and Diego. They looked pale, their eyes wide open. The baby girl was about a year old, and she shook with sobs in her mother's lap.

Abuelita came outside and moved her hands over the baby, who was wrapped in a black shawl. "Where was she stung, Verónica?"

The mother wiped her own tears away and pointed to a small red mark on the back of the baby's tiny star-shaped hand.

Abuelita led us into the kitchen. I started to boil water. Meanwhile, Abuelita rubbed garlic on the sting. From our pot of warm milk on the fire, she dipped a cupful and mixed it with chocolate and ground garlic. The mother took it, her hand trembling, and poured it into the baby's mouth. About half dribbled down her chin. She coughed and sputtered hot chocolate everywhere.

"How long ago was she stung?" Abuelita asked.

"Just fifteen minutes ago. She was crawling on the floor while I was making tortillas. She turned over a basket in the corner and then screamed and I saw the scorpion run into a crack in the wall."

Abuelita rested her hand on the baby's damp, red forehead while the mother continued trying to pour the milk into her child's mouth. When water began bubbling, I dropped the herbs from our basket into the pot and stirred it with the wooden spoon.

The boys stood stiffly in the corner, watching everything quietly. The little one, Diego, said in a small voice, "Is our sister going to live?"

Abuelita touched his cheek. "Scorpion venom acts in different ways on different people, *mi amor*. And some scorpions have powerful venom, and some have weak venom. One never knows what will happen. What you can do now, child, is pray for your sister."

Diego moved his hands to his leather Virgin Mary necklace and his lips started moving. I couldn't help noticing the difference between the bratty Diego at the market and the one in front of me now.

Abuelita rubbed more garlic on the baby's hand until the tea had steeped. I poured some into a cup and blew on it.

"Add some honey, then see if it's cool enough," Abuelita told me.

I did as she said and took a sip. Even with two spoons of honey, it tasted strong and bitter. Potent.

"It's okay," I said.

"Give it to the baby." Abuelita kept on rubbing the garlic and massaging the baby. The little girl was calming down. Abuelita seemed to be soaking up the pain and squeezing it out, giving the baby waves of relief.

I held the cup to the little girl's mouth. Without words I begged her to drink. And she did! She drank the entire cup without spitting it out, even though it was as bitter as lemon juice.

The strange thing was that I could feel the baby's pain. It was heavy, like a stone pulling her down. I kept stroking her head, trying to take out the blackness and send her calm blue waves, to give her the lightness of a leaf in the wind. I was the heron, rising up with my wings, lifting both of us up, light as air, above the pain. Every flap of my wings pushed the pain farther away, and we soared over treetops in the cool sky.

After a while her whimpering stopped. I couldn't say how long exactly. I couldn't even tell you if it was seven minutes or seventy minutes. At some point the baby took a deep breath, yawned wide with her whole red face, and looked around the room. Suddenly she was curious as a puppy and kept trying to slide off her mother's lap.

The mother's eyes were wide, amazed. "Should I let her down?" she asked me.

I looked at Abuelita.

Abuelita nodded and sat down in her little chair, watching the child carefully. The girl staggered in a one-year-old way around the kitchen, grabbing at tomatoes in a basket, hitting a wooden spoon against clay pots. When she heard Loro whistle from above, her face lit up, and she glanced around to see where the sound was coming from. Finally she looked up and discovered the giant green bird walking along the rafters. She squealed and laughed, her head thrown back. She looked off balance, and I jumped up and caught her just as she toppled backward. She tilted her face up at me and giggled and played with my hair, trying to stick my ponytail into her mouth. It's strange how life can switch from scary to funny in seconds, how one minute it seems as fragile as a butterfly and the next, as solid as obsidian.

Diego and Felipe sat on the floor by their sister, playing with her. I noticed that while Felipe, the older one, was laughing, a few tears escaped his eyes. Every few minutes he gave his sister a hug, until she squirmed out of his grasp.

They ate breakfast with us, quesadillas filled with cheese and orange squash flowers. Abuelo came back with the firewood and a sackful of wild mushrooms. Some were sea green and some fiery orange. "Fresh-picked mushrooms," he said. "Your father's second-favorite food." I'd thought it was bacon cheeseburgers, but instead of saying anything I just smiled. I'd have a lot to ask Dad about when I got home. Abuelita tucked the mushrooms inside the quesadillas along with the flowers and cheese. Usually mushrooms taste like dirt to me, but these tasted like forest secrets. Like sunsets hiding in tree hollows.

Felipe kept stealing looks at me as we ate, and I wondered what he was thinking. I wasn't annoyed anymore over what he'd said at the market. How could you stay annoyed with someone you'd just seen crying and praying over his baby sister?

After breakfast, I poured the rest of the tea into a bottle and wrapped up a bundle of the herbs for the family to take home.

"One cupful three times a day, before meals, for the next three days," said Abuelita.

I handed the package and the bottle of herb tea to Felipe.

He looked at me for a moment like he wanted to say something but couldn't find the words. "You saved my sister's life, Clara," he said finally.

"It wasn't me, it was Abuelita," I said.

Abuelita laid her hand on my shoulder. "It was both of

us, but mostly God and the spirits and the herbs and chocolate and garlic, and you boys praying, too."

The mother touched our hands lightly. "Felipe and Diego will bring over a sack of corn and vegetables for you tomorrow," she said. "Thank you both."

After they left, Abuelita and I went to her garden to cut lemongrass for tea. "Now do you understand, Clara? Why your spirit was restless?"

I thought for a moment. "Because I was looking for something, but I didn't know what it was. Something hidden. The thing that makes me feel alive." My words came out soft, but certain. "I'm a healer, like you."

Abuelita nodded. "You know, if you accept, it will take dedication. Some people prefer to float on the surface of life. They do not look deeply. They do not listen deeply. As a healer, you will see things that make you freeze in terror. You will see cold things, heavy things, death. Knowing this, do you accept?"

The heron was inside me, rising up bravely. "Yes."

"That is good." She picked a leaf of *hierba buena* and rubbed it between her fingers, releasing the smell of mint. "Those who do not accept cut off something that wants to grow inside them. Like this *hierba buena.* Cut off the stems, yet the roots will continue to grow underneath the soil, spreading wide and deep. Little sprouts will spring up everywhere. A person could spend her whole life trying to cut them off. What you have chosen is good, Clara. To let your talent grow, tend to it, give it room to spread, value it."

"What if other people don't understand?" I thought of Samantha, of what she and other kids would say.

"Perhaps they will see that your talent is good for them, too. Perhaps they will help it grow."

That night I drew a picture of a *hierba buena* plant for Dad, its roots deep in the earth, its leaves in the sunshine. *I am a healer.*

●

The next day, when the boys came to deliver the sacks of food, Felipe walked up to where I was washing dishes outside at the sink. It had just stopped raining, and now the sunlight came through the banana leaves. Droplets were still clinging like glass beads to the leaves.

"This is for you, Clara," he said, holding out a carved gourd. I wiped my hands on my shorts and turned it over in my hands. Patterns of deer and rabbits and birds were etched on the outside. "I made it myself," he said. "My dad taught me before the last time he left for Chicago, two years ago."

"Thanks, Felipe. It's beautiful." I ran my fingers over the ridges. "What does your dad do in Chicago?"

"Works." He shrugged and looked at the ground.

"Doing what?"

He skimmed his fingers over the top of his hair. His haircut looked like the Astroturf on a miniature golf course, short and spiky, only about a half inch long. It was shiny and stiff with hair gel that smelled perfumy and made my nose itch. Finally, he said, "Well, the truth is my dad was doing construction last summer, then they laid him off for the winter, then he was cleaning bathrooms, then he lost that job, and now he's out of work. That's why he hasn't called us for a while. Because he's out of work." He pressed his lips together. "But don't tell anyone."

"Okay."

"Me and Diego ask him to come home every time he

175

calls, but he says he can't because then what would we live on? But I tell him I'd live on tortillas and salt and water if he would come home."

I didn't know what to say. I just looked at his eyes and tried to understand how he felt, the way I'd felt his little sister's pain.

"Clara. You know what dream I have sometimes? Usually I dream it right before I wake up in the mornings. I find a secret passage to Chicago that gets me there in a couple of seconds, and then I see my dad and walk toward him. But before I get to hug him I realize, *Wait a minute, this is impossible.* And he disappears and I find myself back here in Yucuyoo with roosters crowing."

He kicked at the dirt with his big clomping Nikes and fiddled with the hem of his Chicago Bulls T-shirt. His legs were chunky under a pair of baggy basketball shorts. "I'm sorry about that day at the market, Clara."

"It's okay," I said.

"It's just—I thought—I didn't know you were a healer."

"Actually, I just found out myself," I said.

"My mom says you have the same gift as your grandmother."

"Well, I hope I can use it like she has."

"And you know what me and Diego noticed? That you look just like her. Especially how your cheeks push up your eyes when you smile."

"I guess we look a little alike." I didn't mind so much that he'd mentioned my chubby cheeks.

"You remind us of Marcos, too. He's the last stranger who came to Yucuyoo. When you leave us, we'll miss you just like we miss him. People will be talking about you for years, Clara."

"But I'm coming back soon," I said.

He looked at me doubtfully.

"I am," I said.

"Eh! Felipe!" Diego yelled from the burro. "Let's go!"

Felipe touched my hand lightly. "I hope so." Then he left.

I traced my fingers over the carvings. My hand looked like someone else's hand, rough and red from the harsh dish and laundry soap. My fingers and palms were callused from holding hot clay pots and flipping steaming tortillas and carrying heavy baskets from the market and climbing over rocks and strumming guitar strings.

I liked the way my hands looked. I liked the way they felt. These weren't nail-polished hands that could belong to any other girl in Walnut Hill. They were my grandmother's hands, healing hands, working hands. Maybe they had fewer lines and wrinkles than Abuelita's hands, but in the bones, they were the same.

●

"I think Felipe likes you," Pedro announced, pausing in the middle of a song.

"What do you mean?" I set the pencil down on my sketchbook and looked up.

"When you saved his sister's life . . ."

"*I* didn't, *Abuelita* did," I said. "I just helped." I shifted positions on the rock, pulled my legs out of the water, and folded them, my knees under my chin.

"All he talks about is you. Clara this. Clara that. Like you're his new best friend." Pedro's face held a sour expression. Even though he was sitting just across the stream from me, he seemed far away.

"Well, at least he's not teasing you about me anymore, right?"

Pedro shrugged. "He has a giant TV. Did he invite you over to watch it yet?"

I shook my head. "I don't feel like watching TV anyway."

"His father's working in your country. He sends back money and brings presents when he visits. He hasn't forgotten about his family yet." Pedro stood up and walked away, to the steeper part of the mountain.

He threw a rock over by a wandering goat. It glanced up at him and moved closer. He threw another rock, harder this time, not to guide any goat, just to throw.

He picked up a huge rock, nearly the size of a watermelon, and lifted it with two hands over his head. His face was red and straining. He hurled it over the cliff. It bounced from boulder to boulder. Pieces chipped off here and there, flying away. He breathed hard.

"You'll probably start hanging out with Felipe now," he said, "watching TV with him, maybe taking him back to your country to see his father. . . ."

"Pedro, that's not true." I saw the silvery thread between our souls stretching, getting thin and weak again.

"He has three pairs of Nikes," Pedro said. "Seven baseball caps. He doesn't have to work. He doesn't smell like goats." He picked up another big rock and hurled it over the cliff. It split like thunder on the rocks below.

My chest felt tight, and I felt things falling apart, felt him moving away, as if he were already just a red dot on the next mountain over.

"Pedro." I stood up, tossed my sketchbook onto the bank, and waded across the stream. The hem of my shorts got wet, but I didn't care. And I didn't even wince at the sharp stones that poked the soles of my feet while I walked to him. I was determined. One hundred percent determined. *You can do anything, Clara.*

He watched me and his hands shook at his sides.

I reached out and took his hand and held it steady. Now that I had his hand in mine, I wasn't sure what to say. So I just whispered, "You're going to knock out one of your goats with those rocks." I whispered this in the voice I'd used with Felipe's baby sister to calm her down.

This was the first time we'd touched except for when I'd let my ponytail brush against his arm when we sat together playing guitar. "Pedro, I like the smell of goats. I like being with them. I like being with you."

"Really?" he asked. His mouth moved into a guarded smile.

"Yes. And now *I* smell like goats every day too. That's what Abuelo told me yesterday." I was very aware of the way Pedro's hand felt in mine, at first cool, but now warm.

He put his other hand over mine. My hand rested carefully between his like a little bird. He explored my hand, looking at every finger like it was something he'd never seen before. I wondered if he was going to look into my face and then what would happen.

He put my hand down and picked up his guitar. "I'll teach you a new song."

We sat on a fallen log, close, so that the whole sides of our bodies were touching. As he sang he turned his face toward me. I strummed and he did the fingers.

The melody sounded sad and happy at once. The refrain was *Gracias a la Vida,* and the last verse went:

Thanks to Life, that has given me so much.
It's given me laughter and tears
to tell happiness from sorrow,
the two materials that form my song.
And the song of all of you is the same song,
and the song of all of you is my own song.

Abuelita noticed my hands too. That night, as I was stirring the hot chocolate, she took my hand in her own and examined the palm and the fingers, and then turned it over and traced my knuckles.

"You have hands that heal," she told me. She set the spoon back in my hand. "How good that you are using them!"

"But I'll be with you only a few more weeks, Abuelita."

"Spirits can teach. My body will not be with you, but my spirit will."

I kept stirring. "How?"

"You see, Clara, my grandfather taught me after his death. And it was then that my powers truly blossomed. . . ."

Helena

SPRING 1938–SUMMER 1939

Whenever Ta'nu visited me in dreams, he arrived in a cloud of sweet copal smoke. In the mornings, I'd lie on my *petate* with my eyes closed, trying to keep the scent from fading. In the dreams, Ta'nu and the spirits showed me which herbs to use, where to find them, how to prepare them. Oh, I was glad of their help! After his funeral, you see, patients began coming to me. At first they came in trickles, then in waves.

At times a crowd of people waited outside the door to my hut, comforting crying babies, rubbing children's stomachs, wiping feverish foreheads. Other times there were no patients for days, and I spent that time working in my garden, weeding, tending to plants. Sometimes I collected wild herbs in the mountains. Deep in the forests, I left offerings for the spirits, for my spirit animal. And there I gathered strength, letting the mountain become part of me.

Once I was sipping water at a stream when I looked up and saw a jaguar on the other bank, staring at me. Water dripped from our mouths. We stared at each other the way you might stare at your own reflection. After that, I began leaving him gifts at the stream, wrapped in banana leaves. Gifts of cocoa beans, turkey eggs, green feathers.

A few months after Ta'nu's death, Aunt Teresa discovered she was with child. Five times before, she had been with child, and all but one of those had ended with her losing the baby. María was the only baby who had seen the light of day. Aunt always said that María's birth had been a miracle. So it was no surprise to us that the midwife instructed Aunt not to do any hard work or lift anything heavy until the baby was born. That extra work fell on my shoulders. But how could I mind it? A baby cousin would be a beautiful gift.

In Aunt's eighth month, traders from Oaxaca City began talking about a sickness that had come to the region. A sickness that killed the weak, the very old, and the very young. In our village there was no sign of the sickness. Yet I stayed alert, like a mother deer watching for danger. You see, if people fell ill, they would come to me for help. I had to be ready. I gathered heaps of herbs in the mountains, basket after basket, until I knew I'd have enough to settle stomachs, cool fevers, clear lungs.

One morning, while the women were washing breakfast dishes, after the men had gone to collect firewood, we heard the *clip-clop* of horseshoes. It was a stranger. We knew this, of course, because no one in the village had horses, only burros. Who could it be? María and I left our dishes half washed to find out. Even Aunt, holding her enormous stomach, struggled out of her chair and waddled like a duck with us. A short distance from the road, we stopped under a tree, where we could watch the stranger.

The man on the horse wore an official uniform. It looked as if it once had been crisp and black, but now it was wrinkled and dulled with dust. He had trouble getting off his horse and half fell onto the ground. When he tried to brush himself off, the dust spread around more. He limped in a circle around his horse, shaking out his right leg. Then, there he stood, looking lost. Poor man. I knew how it felt to be a stranger.

María looked at me and laughed. "Helena," she whispered. "Go talk to him."

"Why me?"

"You're the only one who speaks Spanish here. All the men are off in the woods."

True, the only man in sight was don Norberto. And he was drunk and passed out under a tree at the roadside, as usual. He was too drunk to speak his own language—imagine him trying Spanish!

"Find out what he wants," María urged, pushing me toward the man. How she loved strangers, excitement, new things! She should have gone to Oaxaca instead of me. Oh, she would have loved it.

"Probably bad news," Aunt Teresa murmured. Her hands circled her belly protectively. "Always is with people in uniforms."

After my run-in with the police, of course I agreed with Aunt. But María was bouncing up and down like an eager puppy. "I'll come with you, Helena!"

The man was tying his horse to a tree, looking around,

most likely searching for a man to talk to. He spotted don Norberto, limped over to him, and said something. Norberto blinked open his eyes for a moment. He swatted at the air, as though the man were a pesky fly. Then he let out a loud snore and dozed off again.

Startled, the stranger looked around. All he saw were us women, huddled in a small group, pointing, laughing, whispering. He threw his shoulders back and puffed out his chest like a rooster.

María and I clutched each other's hands, still wet from the dishwater. We walked right up to him. In polite Spanish, I greeted him. "Good morning, *señor,* how can we help you?"

Up close I saw that his face was burned red from the sun. It peeled off like snakeskin. Ayyy! How painful it must be to have skin so delicate, so fair. I had the urge to spread cool aloe juice over his skin to soothe it.

The man's eyes darted around. Why was he nervous? What did he think three women would do to him? "Where are the men?" he asked.

"Gathering firewood, *señor.*"

"When will they be back?"

"Not until lunch."

"I don't have time to wait." He rubbed his leg.

"What's the matter with your leg, *señor*?"

"Just a strain."

I wanted to ask him to roll up his pants so that I could look at his injury, but I held my tongue. How could I ask this of a stranger from the city? Of course, anyone here in the village would be grateful for my advice, but I had the feeling that a man from the city would not. Remember, whenever I'd offered my cures to the García López family, they'd accused me of working with the devil.

"You look thirsty and tired," I said. "Would you like some tea? Would you like to sit down?"

"No, thank you," he said, looking impatient. "You will pass a message on to the men?"

"Of course."

"What's he saying?" whispered María. She was nearly bursting with curiosity.

"Shhh . . . wait, María!"

The man cleared his throat. "You have heard of the sickness that is killing people?"

"Yes. It hasn't come here."

"Well, it will." He spoke with arrogance, the way men boasted to each other while drinking. "It will come, unless you follow these instructions. Do you have the *baños de temazcal* here?"

"Yes," I said. Oh, what relief. Maybe this sickness could be cured with the *baños de temazcal*—steambaths with special herbs. I gave *baños* to women after they'd given birth. And for men, sometimes, if they'd pulled a muscle. Perhaps it worked for this sickness, too.

"You may no longer do the *baños,*" he said.

"What?" Had I misunderstood?

"Anyone who does will be sent to jail. Doctors say the *baños* are filthy. They spread diseases like wildfire."

"But the *baños* are good. They cure."

He spoke to me with impatience, as though I were a small child. "Have you gone to school, *señorita*?"

I shook my head. There was no school in my village. I had heard that there was a school in a nearby town, but the girls didn't go. They had too much work to do at home.

"Can you read?"

Again, I shook my head. Now my throat was tightening up. Blood was rising to my face.

"Well, these doctors have books. Shelves and shelves of books. I've seen them myself. And the doctors have recommended that the *baños* be forbidden." He began walking away, showing me that he was done with the conversation.

I followed him. "Wait," I said. I was trying to stay calm, thinking about Aunt Teresa. She would have her baby any day now. It would be a hard birth. The midwife had felt the baby the wrong way inside her. And Aunt had nearly died after giving birth to María. She would need many steambaths to recover. This I felt sure of. "There is no sickness in our village, no need for this law."

"All you must do is pass the message on to the men, can you do that?"

To him I was an ignorant Indian girl, nothing more. María saw that he was on the edge of anger. And maybe worse, that *I* was on the edge of anger. She pulled my arm gently. "Let's go, Helena."

I stood like a tree rooted to that spot. I felt my face changing, my eyes narrowing. The hair on the back of my neck bristled.

"Come on," María said. She tugged at my arm.

At that moment the man turned away, toward his horse. He straightened his jacket, squared his shoulders, took three steps, and tripped over a tree root. This sent him stumbling into a chicken, which squawked and flew up against him in a rage. He staggered back with a cry and fell, just missing a pile of fresh burro droppings.

María let out a squeak of laughter and clapped her hand over her mouth. I felt the beginnings of a smile on my face. A guilty smile, because as a healer, I cannot laugh at other people's suffering. But my fury was fading, and I felt some compassion for the poor man.

Together María and I ran back to Aunt, under the tree. Her huge belly jiggled with her own laughter. In the shade, we watched the man struggle to climb back onto his horse and ride off. Really, he was not to blame for bringing bad news. I decided that if he returned, I'd gather some herbs for a poultice for his leg, and a tea for the pain. What he truly needed was a *baño de temazcal.* But of course, he would never accept that, would he?

●

I was right about Aunt's delivery. All night, the midwife struggled with her. And all night, I worked. I made poultices to slow the bleeding. Brewed tea to ease the pain, ground up fresh herbs to help her push the baby out. Cup after cup of *ruda* with hot chocolate she drank. And yes, finally, the baby came out alive, healthy. A little girl with a perfectly round face and big moon eyes.

But afterward, Aunt was pale and wrung out as an old rag. Her bleeding wouldn't stop. Her belly ached. Her whole body ached. She wouldn't eat, and her breasts had just a trickle of milk for the baby. After a few days, both the baby girl and Aunt lay on the *petate,* limp, nearly lifeless.

"Helena, you must give your aunt *baños de temazcal* to heal her," the midwife told me. "To make milk for the baby."

"But the steambaths are forbidden now," I said. I thought of the prison, the dirt floor, the stale, sad smell. Doña Three Teeth, who had nothing left after ten years in there.

"She could die, Helena," the midwife warned. "If you don't give her the *baños,* she could die."

The midwife was right. And I was the only one in the

village who knew how to give the *baños* now. The *señora* who used to give them had died the year before.

"I will give her one *baño* every Sunday night," I said finally. "For five Sundays. I will do it at night, in secret."

●

After the first *baño,* Aunt Teresa's delight in food returned. Her breast milk began to flow. Her baby seemed more alert now. Soon the baby's moon eyes were following María and me around the kitchen. Still, Aunt felt weak, and still, pain lingered in her belly, but little by little her strength grew, while her pain faded.

On Sunday evenings, I walked to the stone *temazcal.* It was shaped like a small dome, just big enough to fit two people sitting or lying down. In the nook at one end of the dome I prepared the fire. Onto it I placed large rocks. For hours the rocks sat, growing hotter and hotter. Then, late at night, Aunt met me at the doorway of the *temazcal,* under a shelter of thatched palm. She came wrapped in wool blankets to keep off the chill. María stayed back in the hut with the baby.

The first four Sunday nights were peaceful. Pleasant, even. It was the beginning of the wet season, and the smell of rain filled the air. A sharp, clean smell. Soaked earth, damp leaves, new petals.

But the final night, oh, the final night was far from peaceful. As always, I prepared the *baño* alone, arranging the hot rocks, the *petates,* the blankets. Yet I felt myself jumping at every noise, flinching at every shadow. You see, Ta'nu had come to me in a dream the night before. He'd looked worried and warned me to be careful. But this was to be Aunt's last *baño,* I told him. I wanted to be sure her treatment was complete. Just one more night.

When she came to the *temazcal*, I greeted her quickly, then crawled inside. In the darkness, I felt the heat, a dry heat at first. Then I dipped a gourd into the clay pot and sprinkled water onto the rocks. *Sssssss!* The rocks spit up clouds of hot steam.

"Come in now, Aunt," I said, feeling the steam burn my throat and chest with every breath.

She crawled in and lay down on her stomach. I knelt beside her. I picked up my bundle of fresh *pirúl* and spiraled the herbs in the air above our heads. With little circles, I drew down the steam and swept her body with the leaves. As always, she tensed at first with the shock of the heat. Soon her body relaxed. Onto her back she turned, and I brushed over her stomach and chest and legs. Three times I brushed over her body, from head to toe. Then I told her to crawl out. Outside, she lay resting under her blankets beneath the palm shelter.

So far everything was going well. So far, no hint of danger. I lingered inside the *temazcal*, inside the wet heat, the ocean of steam. The heat surrounded me, pressed on me from all sides. Imagine the feeling: somewhere between a peaceful glow and burning suffocation. Oh, you could almost give in to the terror. The terror of feeling trapped in a small, dark place. For a moment I was back in that prison cell. Panic hit me. I crawled out as fast as I could.

Outside I breathed in the cool air. What relief. I stepped outside the shelter and saw the night sky stretched above me. Rain clouds held the light like pearls. I ducked back under the shelter and lay next to Aunt under a blanket. Our skin glistened with beads of sweat. Our chests rose and fell. Oh, how I dreaded going back in.

"Ready?" Aunt asked me.

Each night we went in and out of the bath three times,

resting in between. Two more times left tonight. The second time I entered, the panic came back. A sharp, burning fear. I threw water onto the rocks and brushed Aunt with the herbs, just as I'd done so many times before, only faster now. Much faster.

"Turn over," I told Aunt. I brushed her stomach quickly. The rocks and coals glowed red, like the hellfire that visiting priests always spoke of.

"You can go out now," I said.

"Already?"

"Yes," I said, nearly pushing her out.

We lay outside and rested. I thought of the story of the grandmother spirit of the *temazcal*. One day her evil sons put a stone over the entrance. They trapped her inside, in that terrible heat. She suffocated and died. What helplessness, what fear she must have felt! And that was what I felt, knowing I had to go back inside again. I took a deep breath and tried not to let Aunt see my trembling. But no matter how much I tried to ignore it, I knew. I knew that something bad was about to happen.

Back inside the *temazcal*, Aunt lay on her stomach, with me crouched next to her. I threw a gourdful of water onto the rocks. *Ssssssss!* The steam encircled us.

And when the hissing faded, I heard it. The *clip-clop* of horse hooves. I froze in the heat. My hand that held the herbs rested on Aunt's back.

"What's that?" whispered Aunt. Her back tensed under my hand.

The *clip-clop* stopped. We heard the sound of someone getting off the horse. Then squishy footsteps, coming through the mud, toward us. Should we try to hide? Squeeze ourselves against the back of the *temazcal*? But he must know we were inside because of the steam slipping around the blanket over the doorway.

Aunt reached her arm out and pulled in our blankets. She wrapped herself up, and handed a blanket to me. Then she crawled out.

"Helena!" she cried.

"Who is it?" I asked, already knowing. I felt about to faint in the heat.

"That man in the uniform. With the limp."

She spoke to me in Mixteco, of course, and the man couldn't understand her. I stayed in the *temazcal,* trying to decided what to do, remembering the spirit grandmother who died inside. Remembering the walls of the prison. Thinking *What to do, what to do*—when the blanket was raised. That man's face loomed in front of me. There I knelt in the *temazcal,* my body limp and drained. Cornered.

"Come out, señorita Helena," he ordered.

I crawled out with the blanket wrapped around me and stood up straight.

He held a lantern to my face. "You?" he said, surprised. "You are the famous healer?"

"I am Helena, and yes, I cure," I said. "*Señor,* please let my aunt go home. I am the one who gave her the steambath. I take the blame."

He nodded and flicked his wrist for Aunt to leave.

"Aunt, go back home now," I said. "And cover up well. Wrap the shawl around your head so a cold air won't strike you."

"But what did he say? What did you say? What—"

"Aunt, please, before he changes his mind."

Slowly, Aunt gathered her clothes and walked toward our house. Every few steps she looked back.

The man and I faced each other. I wrapped the blanket tightly around me. I breathed in the smoky scent of the wool, trying to steady myself.

"It is forbidden to do the *baños de temazcal,* as you know," he said.

"Yes. But my aunt was in danger of death."

"You're under arrest, señorita Helena. Dress yourself and come with me." He turned his back to let me dress.

Where was the jaguar now? If only he would leap from the shadows and pounce on this man. Or if only Ta'nu would appear. Oh, he would tell me what to do. I slowly picked up my *huipil* and pulled it over my head. Maybe I could run. The man might not be able to catch me, with his limp. But then what if he found Aunt and punished her instead?

I tucked my *huipil* into my skirt and took a deep breath. "I am ready," I said.

We walked toward the tree where his horse was tied up. We had to climb a slight hill, muddy and slippery from the rain. The man's limp threw off his balance, and he stumbled. His feet slid out from under him. He fell into the mud.

"Ayyy! My leg!" He clutched his leg, writhing in pain. His face tightened and the veins of his forehead stood out. His eyes were clenched and watering.

I picked up the fallen lantern and set it beside him. Then, without thinking, I began massaging his leg. This kind of injury happened to men in the fields sometimes, and they called on me for treatment. "Breathe," I told him. "Breathe." I whispered sounds we use to calm babies and animals. To calm any suffering creature.

"What's your name, *señor*?"

"Valerio Cruz Velasquez."

"Breathe, don Valerio, breathe." With my hands I drew out his pain and flicked it away into the night.

After a while, his face relaxed. "I thank you," he said. Mud covered his clothes, even his face.

I took his wrist and felt his pulse calming. "How did you hurt your leg the first time?" I asked.

He moved his gaze away, embarrassed. "I was getting on my horse a few weeks ago when I felt a pain. A terrible pain that shot down my leg like a bullet. For weeks, every step has been a knife stabbing into me." He blinked back tears. "And just now, when I slipped, the pain came back, stronger."

"You will rest here tonight," I said firmly, in what María called my mother's voice. The voice that no one could argue with. "Stay here, in the shelter of the *temazcal*. I have enough blankets."

I helped him up and led him toward the shelter. He leaned heavily into my shoulder. Under the palm roof, I set his lantern down and spread out a *petate*. He lay down, wincing, and I covered him with blankets.

"I'm going to fetch some hay and water for your horse," I said. Again, in my mother's voice.

Don Valerio nodded. Oh, he could barely move; he had to trust me. "Again, *señorita*, I thank you."

I walked to the house and fetched a bucket of water and an armful of hay from our burro's pen. When I was on the way back to the *temazcal*, it started drizzling. The sudden coldness, the sudden wetness, made me stop in my tracks. *What am I doing? Healing a man so that he can arrest me tomorrow? Healing a man who will throw me in prison?*

But I had no choice, you see. I am a healer. This was a decision I'd made years earlier, when I drank from the sweet cup of light. When I promised to use my powers for good. So you see, I had to help the man.

Back by the *temazcal,* I watered and fed the horse. Then I knelt in the circle of lantern light, beside don Valerio.

"You know, *señorita,*" he said. "My great-grandfather was a *huesero,* a bone doctor, in his village. I was remembering that once he cured me as a boy. I had forgotten it. He cured a shoulder strain I had. Your hands remind me of his."

"Did he teach you to cure?"

"Oh, no. I was a city boy, through and through. My grandfather moved to the city years ago, and my father was born there. We didn't want people to think we were backward country people. So no one learned my great-grandfather's skills. His knowledge died with him."

"It is sad, isn't it," I said, "that people move to the city and forget their customs? They deny the gifts of their ancestors."

"My grandfather meant well. He only wanted a better life for his children. He worked hard and grew wealthy so that he could attract a fair-skinned wife. He made all his children take fair-skinned husbands and wives. In this way, our family gained wealth and respect. But you are right, *señorita,* we sacrificed a part of ourselves."

We sat in silence and watched the flame of the lantern. I promised myself then that I would always keep my head high when I told people where I came from. And when I had nieces and nephews one day, I would teach them to be proud of our customs, our wisdom. And maybe one day, I would teach this to my own children, my grandchildren.

But as soon as the thought came to me, I pushed it out of my mind. I would never have children, because I would never marry.

Don Valerio groaned, and his face tightened. "The pain is coming again," he said.

"*Señor*," I said. "I can cure your leg."

"Could you?" he said, flustered. "How?"

I looked into his pale eyes, wet with tears. "The *temazcal*."

He laughed for the first time. A nervous but warm laugh. "The *temazcal*?"

I nodded, and smiled.

"Oh, life is strange." He chewed on his fingernail, looked at the *temazcal*, then at me, then back at the *temazcal*. "I would lose my job if anyone found out."

"You have my word. No one will know."

"Yes," he said finally. "I accept."

"Take off your clothes, *señor*, wrap yourself in the blanket, and crawl inside." I crawled inside with my clothes still on. As he came through the doorway on all fours, I caught a glimpse of his white body, skinny like a plucked chicken, and spotted with red. His bony shoulders curved into a sunken chest. Poor man, he looked like a sickly dog.

"You know," I told him in the darkness, "this steam bath will also help with your other problems. Your stomach cramps, your headaches, your troubles sleeping . . ."

"How do you know this about me?"

"I know many things," I replied. "As did your great-grandfather the bone doctor." And I couldn't resist adding, "Even though neither he nor I could read the books on those doctors' shelves in the city."

"My apologies, *señorita*," don Valerio said.

"Thank you, *señor*. Now lie on your stomach."

I threw a gourdful of water onto the rocks and smiled at the sharp *sssssssssssss*, the sudden cloud of steam. I brushed him with the herbs, focusing on his left hip and leg. During the first rest, he lay under the blanket breathing like a baby.

"*Señor*," I asked. "How did you know I was giving *baños*?"

"Oh, you're famous," he said. His voice sounded looser now. "Today, at the bar in town, men were talking about you, about how you saved your aunt's life with the *baños*. Your uncle boasted that the famed healer Helena was his niece, like a daughter to him."

"Really?" Uncle José had said I was like a daughter?

"Yes, and he said that he told you who you could cure and who you couldn't." Don Valerio smiled. "But I'm beginning to think that no one tells you what to do, señorita Helena."

I laughed, and along with my irritation at Uncle, I felt a bit of tenderness for him.

In and out we went two more times. Once we finished, don Valerio lay there under a blanket, all his muscles relaxed, his eyes closed. The wrinkles on his forehead had melted. He began breathing deeply.

When people are sleeping, they become as innocent as babies. Just look at the little pulse beating under their neck skin. You can't help feeling kindness toward them.

I pulled a blanket around my shoulders. I arranged another blanket up around don Valerio's neck, then walked out of the shelter, across the yard to my hut. Whispery spiderweb threads connected the leaves and raindrops and burros and chickens. Their spirits breathed together, interwoven like a *petate*, interwoven in peaceful, green, wet sleep.

The next morning as María and I were patting out tortillas, we watched don Valerio walk along the path from the *temazcal*. No trace of a limp. He came out from the patch of trees, stretched, and looked up at the sky. Smiling, he untied his horse and, without the slightest strain, threw one leg over its back and pulled himself up. He spotted us, took off his hat, and waved to us. We waved back. Whistling, he rode off. The morning light made his stray brown hairs glow in a crown. Then he disappeared around the bend in the road.

12

Clara

Copal smoke filled the kitchen. Sunshine came in through the slats of bamboo, making the smoke look solid. Stripes of light moved over Abuelita while she added more copal to the embers. Every once in a while her gold tooth would reflect the light at just the right angle and flash like a mirror. She was chanting in Mixteco, in a low, rhythmic voice. She was thanking the spirits, the saints, God—asking that they receive our gifts and continue to help us heal.

Next to her, I carefully arranged a green feather, an egg, and a pile of cocoa beans on a banana leaf. I tried to concentrate on being thankful, but what I kept thinking about was how normal it seemed to be doing this with her. And how strange it would be to go back to Walnut Hill with these new things inside me. How would I explain them to my friends? How could I make Samantha understand that the smell of copal smoke in a bamboo kitchen felt more real to me than the smell of new clothes on sale racks at the mall? Here in Yucuyoo my outside self finally fit together with my inside self, the way Abuelita's sandals had molded to my feet—or maybe it was my feet that had molded to her sandals.

I wrapped the banana leaf around the gifts and tied a string around it to form a neat package. Later that day, we carried the packages just past the edge of the cornfield, to the base of the mountain. We stopped at a shadowy nook, a kind of shelf formed by four stones. Three of the stones sat upright, leaning against each other, supporting the fourth stone, which came up to our waists. The top of the fourth stone was flat, an altar covered with white pools of hardened wax from old candles. Abuelita told me that the stones around it were darkened from years and years of candle smoke, from so many gifts left here, so many prayers and thanks.

With a match, she melted the bottom of the candle we'd brought along. Then she pressed it into the wax pool and lit the wick. I put the packages on the altar and whispered thanks to the white heron. Then I listed all the things and people I was thankful for. It took a really long time, longer than I'd expected. I was thankful for all kinds of things—that Dad had a job and could live with me and Mom. That in a few months Dad and I could go on fall hikes through yellow leaves under a blue sky. That I was beginning to like my squirrel cheeks. That my hands knew how to heal and how to make tortillas. That I'd discovered squash flower quesadillas, my new favorite food. That Pedro and I had held hands and it had felt good. Each thing I gave thanks for reminded me of another.

On the way back, Abuelita talked nearly the whole time. Maybe since I would be leaving next week, she felt the need to tell me everything all at once.

"Already, Clara, with my help, you healed the baby. The time will come when you must heal alone. When you are healing, stay focused. Stay calm. Never panic. Never let your mind confuse you. Listen to God, listen to your spirit. Let your spirit animal help you." And on and on she went, and I tried to make her words part of me, so that I'd be able to hear them even when I was far from here, back in Walnut Hill.

●

I didn't know that I would have to use her words so soon. But that night, lying in bed, I did have a feeling that something was going to happen. Something big, but I didn't know what. When I tried to think about it, it slipped away . . . but as I drifted off to sleep, the feeling came back, strong.

The next morning the feeling was still with me while I washed dishes and swept the kitchen floor and fed the chickens. Maybe that was why I ended up packing my backpack so carefully, to prepare for whatever was going to happen. My sketchbook, a pencil, a flashlight, an extra sweater, and the rain poncho were already in the backpack. In the kitchen I grabbed whatever looked good—some tortillas, cheese wrapped in a banana leaf, a big mango, a water bottle filled with lemonade, a chunk of chocolate, an avocado, and as always, the bundle of garlic heads to keep away poisonous creatures.

As I zipped up my full backpack, Loro screeched, "¡Adiós! ¡Adiós! ¡Adiós!" from the rafters above. Goodbye! Goodbye! Goodbye!

I nearly jumped out of my skin. Usually he'd just say, "¡Hasta luego!" See you later! His adiós sounded too final.

I walked out into the bright sunshine. "See you, Abuelita! See you, Abuelo!"

"Be careful," Abuelita called after me, watching me go.

Strange. She'd never said that to me before. Did she have a feeling too? *Maybe I should stay home today,* I thought . . . but Pedro was already waiting for me on the mountain, and we had less than a week together before I left.

By the time I reached our meeting spot by the stream, I'd forgotten about the warning feeling. Pedro sat there, cross-legged in his faded red pants, picking out notes on his guitar, looking comfortable. We spent the whole morning wading in the stream, making music, scrambling over rocks with the goats, weaving palm, looking for the waterfall.

Less than one week left before I had to go back—this thought buzzed in and out of my mind like a mosquito. I said nothing to Pedro about it, but knowing it made every moment with him precious.

A heavy heat had been building up all day—the kind of heat that usually ends in a crazy storm, Pedro told me. From the east the sky was gray-black; darkness was moving in.

We were just about to go back to our homes when one of the goats let out a squeal. We almost didn't hear its cry because the rushing sound of the waterfall was so loud here, like a washing machine. The goat's white fur flashed behind a tree, right between the vine-covered rock face and a pile of rocks. We ran over to it.

Its rear legs had fallen into a hole. It was whimpering and struggling to grip the ground with its front hooves.

Pedro grabbed the goat under its front legs and tugged. He looked like he was just about to tumble in after the goat, so with my right arm I grabbed Pedro around his waist and with my left hand held on to a tree branch to keep us from all falling down the hole. Pedro's face was red and straining, more than the time he'd held the watermelon rock over his head, and he pulled until he fell back against me with the goat in his lap. We sat sprawled in a pile, catching our breaths and letting our heartbeats settle down. Pedro moved his hands gently over the goat's stomach and legs, just like a vet, to check for injuries.

"The goat's fine," he said as it stood up and walked away, wobbly and dazed.

Then it dawned on us at the same time. I practically saw the lightbulb go on in his head and I said, "This is it, Pedro!" My excitement was growing by the second, the way it does on an airplane ride right before takeoff. This had to be it. The rushing sound was louder than ever, and sure enough, it grew louder as we crouched down and lowered our ears to the hole. We could see nothing but darkness inside.

"I wish we had candles," Pedro said.

"I have my flashlight!" I unzipped my backpack, rooted through my stuff, and pulled out the red plastic flashlight. Like I said, it pays to be prepared, even if it means dragging around a heavy backpack.

I shone the flashlight down into the hole, onto a big, triangular stone. The floor of the cave was a few feet down, just beneath the stone.

"Look, we don't even need a rope to get down there!" Pedro said.

He took the flashlight from me and started to drop into the hole. He lowered his body carefully. The hole seemed to swallow him up. Suddenly that warning feeling came back.

Before his head disappeared, I said, "Wait, Pedro!" I was

stalling, trying to think of a respectable reason not to go down there. "What about the goats?"

"They'll be all right. Just a few minutes, Clara, then to-morrow we can come back for longer."

I looked at the sky. The sun had disappeared, and dark clouds were blowing in fast overhead. There was a strange light, kind of orange-yellow, thick as squash soup. Everything glowed like a painting done in a palette of eerie colors. I picked up Pedro's abandoned guitar and put it in one of the deep cracks in the rock face, a little way down the hill. I didn't want his guitar getting ruined when the rain came, especially since I'd be leaving soon and he'd need it to keep the sadness—or maybe anger—from filling his heart, as Abuelita had said.

Back at the hole I knelt down. The rock face loomed above, about three stories high, with its curtain of vines dangling like growing-out bangs. On one of its jagged ledges, a white heron calmly watched us. I held perfectly still, watching the heron watching us. That was when I knew for sure that something big was happening.

"Come down, Clara!" shouted Pedro.

"Just for a minute," I called. I felt the heron watching me as I dropped my backpack to Pedro and lowered myself. I felt solid rock under my toe and let my weight come down onto it. I sat on the damp stone and then slid down onto the floor. While my eyes adjusted to the darkness, I put on my backpack.

We were in a small tunnel. Small enough that if I'd stood in the middle and stretched out my arms, my fingertips could have touched both sides. Water dripped down the rock walls. I reached my hands up and felt slick, wet stone just above my head. The sliminess made me pull my hands back quickly and wipe them on my jeans. A stream that looked about ankle-deep trickled down the middle of the tunnel.

We headed downstream, sticking to the sides, where the rock floor sloped higher than the water's surface. We made our way slowly along the edge of the tunnel with our sides pressed against the slimy walls. Pedro led with the light, and after a few steps, he reached back to take my hand. His hand was cold and wet. It didn't give me the same tingly hot feeling as the last time we'd held hands, but at least it made me feel braver. The rushing sound grew louder and louder until I felt surrounded by it, inside an ocean of sound.

Then the light went out. Absolute blackness.

"Shake the flashlight a little," I said. My stomach was already jumping around with panic. Hopefully the batteries had just lost contact for a moment.

"*What?*"

The sound of pounding water was so loud it swallowed up our words. "*Shake the flashlight!*" I yelled.

Still no light. He handed the flashlight to me. I had to fumble in the dark to open it. I pushed down the batteries, screwed the top back on, and tried it again. Nothing.

I moved closer to him and spoke right into his ear. "The batteries must be dead. Let's go back!" I started to turn and tugged on his hand. Now the bad feeling was taking shape, becoming clearer. It was a dark cave feeling, blackness closing in. I thought of the goddess trapped in the steam bath.

"Clara, wait! Do you see a light ahead?"

A faint light came from a curve in the tunnel. Something was glowing beneath the surface of the stream. As we moved closer, it became clearer. It was *sky*—bits of sky, and vines, and leaves! Had we entered a different dimension, an upside-down land?

Then I realized it was a reflection, moving on the surface of the water. It must be reflecting what was around the bend. I tightened my hand around Pedro's and we kept going, following the curve. Another thing I was thankful for came to mind—that Pedro and I were exploring this place together, that it wasn't *my* secret mission but *our* secret mission.

How can I explain to you what we saw when we turned that bend?

Imagine opening your closet one day, expecting the same dark, cramped space you see every day, and instead, being met with a humongous space full of light and water.

The tunnel opened up into a giant chamber, higher than three houses piled on top of each other. On the left side of the chamber, at the top of a steep embankment, there was an opening—a dazzling window to the outside, where vines were hanging, and behind them, that crazy orange sky. A rushing sound filled the chamber and echoed off the walls.

The stream emptied into a large pool in front of us. Other trickles of streams came out of the floor from under boulders and fed into the pool.

Everything seemed huge. It felt as though we had entered a realm of giants. We climbed onto one of the boulders, and from here, we could see past the pool, where the cave sloped down sharply toward the right and narrowed into another tunnel. Water tumbled over the rocks, and white foam churned wildly. Pedro and I didn't talk. We just tried to soak it all in, breathing in the spray and letting the mist coat our skin.

After a while, I stuck the useless flashlight in my backpack and pulled out the mango. I peeled it and bit into its orange sweetness. I passed it to Pedro and we alternated taking bites.

It felt enchanted here, and timeless, as though all the clocks in the world above could continue ticking and we'd sit here, forever. I looked at the vines whipping over the opening and remembered how it looked from the other side—the rock wall that rose like a skyscraper. From inside, the slope was gentler, but still steep—a slick embankment of rock and mud, dotted with a few shrubs and rocks. I wondered how high above the ground the opening appeared from the outside. The height of a house, maybe? It was the strangest feeling, seeing all this from the inside looking out. It made me wonder how many things I saw every day from the outside without knowing the inside.

Pedro was looking up toward the light too. "Clara."

I had to move my ear close to his mouth to hear his voice over the pounding water.

"Those are the same vines from that picture you sketched of me, aren't they?" he asked.

I nodded. "I had no idea what was behind them!"

Our faces were close. "Good thing we found this before you left," Pedro said.

I did not want to think about leaving.

"I had a dream last night that you left on the bus," he said. "The bus was growing smaller and smaller, and I was left behind here. Everything seemed so empty. I thought I'd feel better if I played guitar, but when I tried to play, I could only do the fingers. I couldn't strum. I couldn't make any music. I wandered all over the mountains, looking for you to help me, but I couldn't find you anywhere."

"I'm not leaving forever, Pedro," I said. I handed him the mango.

He took a bite and chewed slowly. A thin line of mango juice rolled down his chin and hung there.

I reached my hand up and caught the drop as it fell.

He held my hand there in midair, even though it was sticky with mango juice and slime from the tunnel. Like the last time, he began playing with my fingers, only now he looked up into my eyes.

I let my face move toward his, first touching my lips to the spot on his chin with the mango juice, and then to his lips. It felt like smelling a flower.

A crack of thunder made us jump. Lightning lit up the cavern.

"The goats!" Pedro said.

We pulled apart and I slung on my backpack while he lowered himself off the boulder. I slid off after him and we made our way back toward the tunnel. There was another boom of thunder, and then the rain began outside, whipping through the vines.

We stumbled around the edge of the pool. The water seemed higher now. When we reached the place where the chamber narrowed into a tunnel, the stream was no longer a trickle. It had risen and widened, so now there was barely any room to walk along the edge without getting our feet wet. This time I led. I held Pedro's hand behind me.

The stream seemed to be rising by the second. Soon it covered our feet and skimmed our ankles, even though we were walking close to the wall. Now water dripped every-where—down the walls, from overhead. I wished we could run, but with the stone beneath us so slippery, we had to take firm, careful steps. The darkness was so complete, I thought I would choke on it. I could barely tell the difference whether my eyes were open or closed.

When we were halfway through the tunnel, Pedro gasped and dropped my hand.

"What is it?" I groped around and found his shoulder.

"I just touched something sharp, like broken glass," he said.

I could barely hear him. "How could there be glass here?" I asked with my mouth at his ear.

"My arm!" He gasped again. "And my leg! Something's stinging me, Clara!"

It occurred to us at the same time. "Scorpions!" he yelled.

I pulled him ahead.

"There must be a nest of them, Clara!"

I dragged him along and tried not to slip on the slick stone. Now the water came up to our knees.

"How do you feel?" I called back.

"They stung me three times." His voice was tight and strained.

The flow of water felt stronger. It was pushing us back, and it became harder and harder to move against it. There was a flash of light ahead, followed by a crack of thunder.

"Almost there, Pedro!"

As we moved closer, I could make out the faint form of the triangular rock that we'd used as a stepladder. A few slivers of blue light shone down from above. I boosted Pedro onto the rock. I grabbed the top, found a crack to wedge my right foot into, and heaved myself up. Then I crouched on the rock and craned my neck and scanned the ceiling, trying to find the way out.

Something was wrong.

Where was the hole? It had been a big gap, at least two feet across.

"This was the place, right, Pedro?"

He didn't answer. His breathing was shallow and fast, coming in little gasps.

"Pedro!" I bent down and touched his face.

"Yes," he said, barely loud enough to hear.

Three stings. Was that enough to kill a person?

Suddenly I remembered the bundle of garlic and bars of chocolate in my backpack. My hands were shaking so much, it was hard to peel the garlic, but I did it and then gouged it with my fingernails to release the juice. I put it in his lap. "Rub this on your stings, Pedro." I handed him the chocolate. "And eat this, all of it, okay?" I put my hand to his cheek and felt him nod.

I stood up again, trying to feel the hole. I did feel a small gap, no wider than my hand, but something hard and rough scraped my fingers. The bark of a tree. It must have been knocked down by the wind, or maybe struck by lightning. I pushed and pushed, but it wouldn't budge. My feet nearly slipped out from under me as I tried to find something to brace myself against.

"Pedro! A tree fell over the hole!"

He didn't answer.

"How can we get out of here, Pedro?"

No answer.

I bent closer. I smelled the chocolate and the raw garlic. "Pedro!"

"If I die, my mother will be all alone." His voice was already far away, fading fast.

The water was churning and slapping against the top of the rock. I realized that if the water kept rising, it could fill the cave. We might drown, trapped in here.

"Just keep rubbing the garlic on." I prayed he wasn't allergic to scorpion stings, and pulled the sweater out of my bag and wrapped it around him. "Stay here." I eased off the rock. Now the water was up to my waist.

I'd have to go back to the big chamber, I decided, and try to climb up the steep mudbank and out the other opening. But even if I could climb to the top, how far would it be to the ground outside? Never mind, it was the only way. Then I'd have to run around to the other entrance—I hoped I could find it again—and somehow move the tree trunk.

Along the tunnel, the water was rising. At least it was flowing in the direction I was going. I gave up trying to walk and fell into the middle of the stream, letting it carry me down. I hoped the water had already washed all the scorpions downstream. Soon the current took hold of me with shocking force and threw me from rock to rock. I was a little insect being swept away, my legs and arms flying helplessly. I gasped for breath whenever my head came above the surface.

Terrible ways to die flashed through my mind. I prayed the rocks banging my body wouldn't knock me unconscious. I knew I'd have to somehow get out of the water fast when I reached the pool in the big chamber. If not, the waterfall would suck me down into the dark hole. Even if I somehow survived that fall, I would end up trapped in a deeper underground chamber. Meanwhile, Pedro might drown above me.

Just before I rounded the last curve, I saw the light, not as bright as before. Just the faintest blue-purple glow. I grabbed on to rocks to try to slow down, but I seemed to go faster and faster.

Once I reached the chamber, the sound was different, bigger, echoing off the rock walls. The stream led into the pool, and the current let up a little. Just ahead and to the right was the waterfall. I grasped more desperately at the rocks, trying to swim to the left, toward one of the big boulders at the edge of the pool. There, through the white foam, I saw the rock where Pedro and I had sat and shared the mango. Pedro's face, clenched in pain, came back to me. *Don't die. Please don't die.* Words for him and for me. I had to keep myself alive to save him.

My candle is still tall. Those were the other words that ran through my mind as the water and stones battered me—*my candle is still tall.* With all my strength, I threw my arms around the rock and clung to it with my arms and legs. My fingertips found a ridge in the top surface and dug in while my feet pushed against the side. Slowly, I raised myself up, lifted my left knee over the edge, dragged my right one after it. In one final burst of effort, I pulled myself up the rest of the way.

For a few seconds, I rested, soaking wet, shivering, coughing, gagging on the water I'd swallowed. I wanted to curl up here and sleep, and hope that someone would save us. I didn't feel strong enough to do this.

But when I closed my eyes, I saw Pedro's candle still tall.

Pulling myself up, I made my way across the rocks, toward the opening. The embankment was steep and muddy. I began to climb, grasping at shrubs and vines. Halfway there, I clutched a root that came right out of the mud. I lost my balance and slid all the way back down.

I lay curled in the mud for a moment, then forced myself to stand up. This time I used my feet more, bracing them against the bases of plants, so that when I had nothing to hold on to with my hands, I wouldn't slide down again. My fingers burned.

The ledge of the opening was right above me now. I grasped the ledge, pulled myself up, and threw my left leg and left arm over it, straddling it. Pushing up, I swung my right leg around and tucked my feet underneath me, so that I was crouched in the opening, looking out.

How strange to be perched here, like a bird, watching the storm. Vines whipped in front of me. I pressed my hands against the sides of the opening to steady myself. Looking down, I felt dizzy. I was too far up to jump—at least two stories high. And rain ran down the rock face, making it too slick to climb down.

I glanced back inside the cave. It looked strangely calm. From this bird's-eye view I scanned the chamber to see if there was any other way out.

No, this was it.

As I turned back around, a gust of wind struck me and nearly knocked me back into the cave. To try to catch my balance, I leaned forward. Another gust of wind caught me. My foot slipped. My arms shot out, clutching at anything. I began to fall.

My right hand grasped a thick vine. Now my other hand found it too, and then I was dangling, the bark burning my raw hands as I hung on, the wind pushing me this way and that. I couldn't fall. I had to stay strong to rescue Pedro.

I kicked the air with my legs until I was facing the rock. I stuck out my feet, pressing the soles against the wall. This took some of the strain off my hands. I let go with one hand and lowered it below the other, bouncing off the rock wall as I lowered myself. For the last ten feet my hands slid down the vine and I felt the top layer of skin on my palms rubbing right off.

My feet touched the ground. My legs gave way underneath me and I collapsed in the mud, my body shaking. For a moment I stayed curled up in a pile of broken twigs and wet leaves, feeling my rubbery legs and the fire in my hands.

Once again, I thought of Pedro, the water rising around him. Had it risen to his neck yet? I pushed myself back onto my feet. I steadied myself and wrapped my arms around a tree trunk and looked around to get my bearings. Branches were flying. Lightning was cracking. Chaos. I could barely tell which way was up. How could I find the entrance to the cave? Any of the fallen trees strewn around could be the one covering the hole.

Then I remembered Abuelita's words, as if she were right next to me, whispering them in my ear. *"Stay focused, calm. . . ."* The wind and rain and lightning seemed to fade, and I found a quiet spot inside myself.

I turned toward the rock face. I followed it farther down the slope of the mountain, looking for the pile of rocks that I remembered seeing by the entrance. As I walked, I pressed against the stone, protected from the wind.

Something bright white stood out through the sheets of rain. The heron. It stood on a freshly fallen pine. Its thin legs stayed steady in the wind. It stared right at me as I moved toward it. Just when I grew close enough to touch its feathers, it lifted its wings and rose up and over the treetops. Once it had disappeared, I looked down at the tree trunk where it had been standing. A small gap under the bark opened up into blackness.

"Pedro!" I yelled down the hole. "I'm here!"

I thought I heard a faint answer, but it could have been the wind.

His candle is still tall. I know it is. I wedged myself between the rock face and the tree trunk, pushing out with my legs. The trunk moved a little but then rolled right back into place. I took a deep breath and pushed. Again, it rolled partway but then rolled right back.

A thin voice pierced through all the wind and water. I moved my ear to the opening beside the trunk.

"Clara! The water's rising!"

He was alive. I braced my back against the rock face and pushed out with my legs. The tree rolled and then paused, as if it were trying to make up its mind. Finally, it rolled away, revealing the opening underneath. I clutched a sapling with one hand and lowered my other hand into the hole.

Pedro took hold.

I pulled up, making myself light as a heron rising, lifting him up with me. He fell against me in the mud. I held him for a moment and felt a wave of pure, deep thankfulness. Then I helped him stand.

With his good arm around my shoulder, he hopped along beside me. I led him to a protected spot beneath an overhang, where the goats were huddled against the rock wall. All ten of them. They'd survived.

"Look, the goats," I said.

But Pedro was in too much pain to notice. Walking this short distance had exhausted him. He leaned against the rock wall and sank to the ground.

"Pedro, come on. We have to get you to Abuelita."

His voice was slurred. "I can't walk now."

"Then I'll get help."

He grabbed my hand. "No! Stay with me!"

"But—"

"Please, Clara."

I looked at him closely. Color was coming back to his face.

"Listen," he creaked. "They say that with scorpion stings, if you survive the first fifteen minutes, you won't die. I'll be all right. Just sit with me."

That was exactly what I wanted to do. Just sit with him. I sat against the wall and put his head in my lap. I smoothed out the furrow between his eyebrows and moved my hands lightly over his body and tried to raise us out of the waves of throbbing and stinging and aching.

His breathing grew calm and deep and regular. I let my hand fall on his forehead. As he slept, I watched his eyelids flutter, his chest move up and down. The thunder and wind faded, leaving only a hard, steady downpour. We rested, safe and warm, under the giant wing of a white heron.

●

Drifting in and out of dreams, I remembered the next piece of Abuelita's life. It seemed like ages ago that she'd told it, although it had only been the night before. The furious storm she'd faced. Her scratches and bruises. Death so close she could feel its breath. Between raindrops, her words came back to me, with more meaning now that I had been there too.

Helena
WINTER 1939–SUMMER 1940

At the beginning of my fourteenth year, Clara, I was bloom-
ing like a lily during rainy season. Aunt Teresa told me,
"Helena, you look like a bird these days, just about to leap
into flight." Word was spreading about my curing powers.
Every time I found a patient's soul, or eased a child's belly-
ache, or cured someone's *mal aire,* word spread. People told
their aunts and uncles and in-laws and cousins and neighbors. Soon people from far-off villages were coming by foot
and by burro, looking for cures. Oh, it tired me, but it made
me feel more alive, too. Just as Ta'nu had said it would.
Through healing, you will learn what it means to be truly alive.
Sometimes I stayed up all night, for nights in a row. My

spirit journeyed far. It flew to thick forests and stark deserts. It flew to oceans, skimming the sparkling waves. And it swam deep beneath the sea's surface, inside the murky green.

In the mornings, of course, I couldn't rest. Too much work to do. That was another thing Ta'nu was right about. The life of a woman was work, work, work. Making tortillas, washing, grinding corn, cooking. But I did these chores with a glow around me, a glow that lit up the people and plants and animals nearby. A glow that let me see into them, see things I hadn't noticed before.

Aunt's baby, Lupita, staggered around the kitchen as we worked. How she loved it when I cured people! With her big eyes she watched me give *limpias*. María would say, "Lupita, show us how your cousin Helena cures." With a devilish smile, Lupita would take a deep breath, puff out her cheeks, and shower us with sprays of saliva. We'd back away, laughing.

It was the rainy season of that year when my first monthly blood came. That very day, as we were patting out tortillas in the dark kitchen, Aunt said to me, "You are a little woman now, Helena. You must start thinking of marriage."

Outside in the sunshine, María and Lupita were squealing and laughing, tossing grains of corn to the chickens. I felt a dull pain in my belly, a heavy ache in my thighs.

Sunlight came through the bamboo slats. Light sliced through the smoke and painted Aunt's *huipil* with stripes. Her face was in darkness, her hands in the light. Her hands patted out a tortilla and laid it carefully on the clay plate, just as they'd done thousands of times before. The hands flipped another tortilla and grabbed a new handful of dough.

"Aunt Teresa." I lowered my voice. "I will *not* marry."

"Well, I didn't want to marry either," she said.

"Why did you?"

"I will tell you. You're old enough to know. I was about your age, at the stream one day. I was filling a pot with water, crouching down to scoop the first gourdful of water into the pot. And that's when a young man walked up with his burro. He looked at me long and hard, as though I were a food he hungered for. He frightened me, so I stood up quickly and started walking back. When I heard him following me, I started to run. My pot fell and clanked against a rock. I left it behind, but I could not run fast enough."

Aunt's voice was shaking. She took a long breath and let it out slowly. "When I finally returned home, my mother saw my torn *huipil*. She saw the mud smeared all over my legs. She saw the handprint bruises on my arm, the dirt in my teeth, the tears on my face. 'Who was it?' she asked. I told her. 'The brother of the healer Ramón.' I didn't even know his name. Without another word, my mother marched straight to their house. She demanded to his father—to Ta'nu—that the young man marry me. And that is how I married your uncle José."

A shiver swept over me. I'd known Aunt had no love for Uncle, but I'd never imagined reasons so dark. "How can you stand it, Aunt?"

She wiped her eyes and shrugged. "That's how life is."

We patted out more tortillas in silence. My fury was growing.

Finally she said, "Helena, you must marry. What would you do as an old lady, without children to care for you? And until then, you need a man to protect you, to provide for you."

I laughed, a bitter laugh. Bitter as green fruit. How could Aunt say that? So many men we knew squandered their money. They spent it on liquor. They gambled. They bought any useless thing they stumbled over. And what man protects his woman? We knew how wives and children suffered when the men came home drunk. Men frustrated at their poor lives, angry at the world. Men who let their rage fly out at their families.

Oh, it was easy for Aunt to guess my thoughts, the way I was pounding my tortilla dough down on the *metate*. She smiled sadly. "But, Helena . . . what will people say if you don't marry?"

"That doesn't matter, Aunt. I cannot marry. It's forbidden to have relations with a man while I'm learning to cure. And who knows if my husband would let me cure at all."

People in my village told a story about a woman who had a calling to heal. This happened years ago, before I was born. Her husband was jealous of her powers. Jealous, too, of the men who came to her for cures. One day he forbade her to cure. He made her do only washing and tortilla-making with the other women. She warned him, "If I refuse my calling, I will die." That night she slipped out of the house. The next morning, at the foot of a cliff, they found her dead body.

"Women have no choice, Helena." Aunt's hands, sunlit, placed the tortilla on the clay plate. Flipped the other one. Grabbed more dough. I thought: *That's all she is, just a pair of hands for making tortillas, washing clothes, grinding corn.*

"Aunt, haven't you ever felt there was anything you *had* to do, even if people didn't want you to?"

"Perhaps, Helena. Perhaps when I was a little girl. But now, when I look in my mirror, you know what I see? A mixture of my mother's face and my daughters' faces. That is what I am. That is enough for me."

Oh, I must have had a terrible look on my own face because she patted my arm and said kindly, "Well, maybe you won't have to marry for a few years yet."

•

But it turned out to be soon, very soon. Two months later, our village had a weeklong fiesta for San Juan, our patron saint. Everyone was in the main square, eating *tamales* and drinking *mezcal*. Everyone except for me.

I was working in the kitchen, by the fire. I hung up some herbs to dry in the rafters and took down the ones that were already dried. I began grinding fresh *hierba amarga*—bitter herb—in *mezcal*. A tincture for stomachaches. In peace I worked, in near silence. No sounds but the fire sparking once in a while, the song of frogs outside. Loro moved softly above me in the rafters. There was no one else nearby except the pigs and chickens and goats sleeping in the yard.

Suddenly, the chickens let out a flurry of squawks, as if someone had kicked them out of the way. I jumped. Some *mezcal* spilled to the floor. I spun my head around.

There, blocking the door to the kitchen, was don Norberto. Don Norberto, the man who spent every evening sprawled under a tree in a drunken stupor. Whenever I walked by, he'd watch me with his small, half-closed eyes. There he would slouch, clutching a *mezcal* bottle. Slobbering on his filthy shirt. He was as old as Uncle José. His hair was turning silver, faster now, from loneliness, since his wife had died last year in childbirth. Oh, I remembered his wife well, poor thing. A frail woman, her skin always marked with bruises and scrapes. Wounds that appeared after don Norberto's angry drunken fits.

Swaying slightly, he moved closer to me in the kitchen. "I was looking for you at the fiesta," he said. His words slurred together.

"Leave this kitchen now," I told him.

An oily smile spread over his face. He took a step closer.

I took a few steps back and looked around. What could I defend myself with? I spotted the heavy grindstone to my right. Maybe I could aim that at his head.

Closer he wobbled. Now I could smell the liquor on his breath. A patch of dried vomit stained the front of his shirt.

Just when I was thinking that he was too drunk to see straight, he lunged at me. He grabbed my shoulders with force. Surprising force.

A moment of shock hung there, like a leaf held by a breeze. We looked at each other, our faces nearly touching.

Then a screech shot out of my mouth. A strange animal sound so loud it scared us both. My face felt like a jaguar's, my teeth sharp and ferocious. He loosened his grip and nearly fell backward.

I grasped the nearest thing I could reach. A piece of firewood, one end in flames. I held it there, out to my side. Now I was moving toward him as he was backing out. I heard myself screech again. That same wild scream. It wasn't a cry of fear. No, it was one of rage. And he knew that.

He stumbled toward the door, but another figure stopped him. Uncle José.

"Put down the firewood, girl," Uncle commanded.

I laid the wood back on the hearth.

"Norberto, what are you doing here with my niece?" Uncle José was drunk too, I realized. A mean, red-faced drunk. He staggered toward don Norberto and shoved him against the wall.

"I was going to ask the girl . . ." Don Norberto paused. He glanced at me with a yellow-toothed grin ". . . to marry me."

Uncle took a step back from don Norberto and looked at me.

I held my breath.

He looked back at don Norberto. Uncle's face broke into a smile. He gave don Norberto a friendly slap on the shoulder.

"Girl, go to sleep now," Uncle barked.

I left the kitchen, bewildered. Outside the hut I lingered, listening to their talk. They discovered the bottle of *mezcal* that I'd been using to make medicines. The two drank it together. They drank and drank until they passed out. When all was silent, I peeked into the kitchen and saw my uncle cradling the empty bottle like a baby. Don Norberto's head rested in my basket of dried herbs. A thin line of drool stretched from his mouth to the dirt floor. It glinted like a spiderweb in the firelight.

The following morning I found out I was engaged. The wedding date was set for a month later. No one had asked me if I wanted to marry don Norberto. For a week I tried to talk to Uncle José, to tell him I wanted no husband. Especially not a husband like don Norberto. I wanted to talk to Uncle when he was not drunk. But, you see, this was not easy during fiesta week.

One morning, when the men had just returned from collecting firewood, I decided to talk to Uncle. The men were sitting under the trees sharpening their machetes, waiting for the women to serve them food. I went up to Uncle José with his tortillas and beans.

"Uncle, I must talk to you," I whispered.

The two men next to Uncle laughed. Women never talked to men as they were serving food. They placed the steaming bowls down silently and scurried off as fast as they could.

Uncle scowled and set down his bowl. He stood up and grabbed my arm roughly. Then he led me a few steps away from the men. "What do you want?"

He was angry, yes, but at least he wasn't drunk.

"I can't marry that man."

"Doesn't matter if you like him or not. You feed him, wash for him, give him children. And he'll provide for you." He turned back to go to his food.

My hand reached out to stop him. "I want to cure, not marry."

"Then cure after he dies. When you're an old lady. When you can do what you want."

I thought of the healer who threw herself over a cliff. "But I *have* to cure. Just as I have to sleep and breathe." My voice grew louder, gathered strength. The other men were watching us, amused and curious. I lowered my voice now, but still, it trembled. *"I must cure. I have no choice."*

"Don't talk to me again. Not until you're married." Then he added, more loudly, so that the other men could hear, "Or else you'll regret it." But he could not meet my eyes as he said this.

He walked back to the men and sat down. He scooped up a tortilla full of beans and shoved it into his mouth. Spraying bits of beans, he shouted, "Now bring me more tortillas, girl."

As I walked toward the kitchen, my eyes met the men's. They looked away quickly.

In the kitchen, I piled tortillas into a basket. María

moved close and whispered, "Be careful, Helena. People fear your powers. They know that the powers could be used for good or bad."

"I'm not a witch, María. I'm a healer." But she was right. I could see how some people acted around me. They were cautious. They whispered and avoided my eyes. They feared I'd curse them if they angered me. Oh, yes, they brought their sick to me. They respected my healing powers. But it is true that respect can turn quickly into fear.

María folded the napkin over the steaming tortillas in my basket. Gently, she touched my arm. "Some people are re-lieved at your engagement. They say you're like a wild ani-mal, an animal that needs a master." A playful grin came over her face. "Do you know what your fiancé said about you?"

"What?"

She widened her eyes. "That you're a *nagual.* That you change into a jaguar at night and roam the forests!"

I laughed with María. But of course, I was thinking: *How close to the truth that is.*

The night before my wedding I couldn't sleep. The past month had felt like a bad dream. At first I'd felt anger, and then, only helplessness. As though I were drowning. As though my hands were tied and I was weighed down with a stone underwater. But now that the wedding was only a day away, the anger was returning. It started as a little pulsing ball un-der my belly. Out it spread through my body, gathering strength. That night I lay on my *petate* and felt my blood rag-ing, wild, under my skin. I could stand it no longer.

I slipped out of the house and ran into the forest. My

arms flailed, and my feet gathered speed. Right to the edge of the cliff I ran. The cliff that the healer had leaped off years earlier. I peered over the edge, dizzy. Dizzy but fearless. Breathing hard, I balanced there. I balanced, my toes off the edge, my heels on solid rock. Far below were dark forms of shrubs and stones.

I did not jump.

Instead, I turned and ran down the slope along the side of the cliff, down into a gully. I found myself in front of a cave. The cave where people left offerings to the spirits of thunder and lightning. I picked up a dead tree branch and slammed it against a tree trunk. Over and over I slammed it until I heard a crack. The branch split. I did the same with another and another. *Slam! Crack! Slam! Crack!* I was a storm myself. Sparks nearly flew off me. On and on I whirled until I was drenched in sweat, with bits of dead tree stuck to my skin.

The following morning Aunt woke me up to prepare for the wedding. I still had twigs in my hair. I still had mud under my fingernails. But what I didn't have was the crazy courage I'd had during the night. And I didn't have time to find that courage, because from the time I woke up, no one left me alone. Not for a second. My aunts and cousins, some who came from the next village over, washed my hair in water scented with flower petals. They dressed me in the new red *huipil* that Aunt Teresa had made for me. With don Norberto's family, we had hot chocolate and *tamales*. By the time we cleaned up, it was time to walk to the church.

Uncle José suspected I might try to run off, so he came to the kitchen himself to fetch me. He grasped me hard by my upper arm and led me to the church. During the Mass, he stood at my left side. Oh, how his fingers dug into my flesh. On my right side stood don Norberto, reeking of *mezcal*. A stench that turned my stomach. Yes, I might have run if I'd had the chance. But throughout the ceremony, Uncle kept his hand on my arm, squeezing the veins against the bone. My arm went numb, up to my fingertips. I thought, *That's what married life will do to me, turn me numb, like a scorpion sting. First my body will grow numb, and then my spirit.*

And I was married.

The feast afterward passed in a blur. I remember other people laughing and dancing as the band played. The light drizzle didn't stop their fun. They didn't notice the mud splattering their legs. Oh, but how I shivered. How cold my bones felt. I remember my new husband leaning against a tree with a *mezcal* bottle to his lips. Young girls watched the dancers with glittering eyes. Girls dreaming of their own weddings. I wanted to scream at them, *No! Run now!*

After the dance, the whole village led me and my staggering husband to our hut. Inside, we stood alone, staring at each other. I felt my eyes narrowing like a cat's. I didn't screech this time, but still, he backed away.

"You're a witch," he said. "And a *nagual*."

He backed out, clutching his bottle of *mezcal*. I heard his brothers arrive out front. Through the bamboo slats I saw them drinking and playing with their machetes. They were chopping firewood into small pieces. They were so drunk, so careless, I wouldn't have been surprised if they hit a leg instead of a log. Not noticing that blood, not sap came out. The image of don Norberto's dead wife came to my mind. Her empty eyes and bruised, tired body.

Someone snapped a branch. "That's what you'll do with your witch wife, Norberto. Break her."

I couldn't find enough saliva in my mouth to swallow. A heat prickled over my skin. I picked up a knife from the basket of tomatoes. It felt solid in my hands. I ran my fingers over the blade and began walking around the room. What could I do? After all the lives I'd saved, could I kill a person? Yes, I was desperate enough to do it. To plunge a knife into my new husband's chest. And that scared me even more.

Time passed. Finally, outside, slurred voices began to say, "I'm goin' home. G'night."

"Go tame your mountain-cat wife, Norberto," one said. He snorted and spit.

This was my last chance. I put Loro on my shoulder. Then I pushed the stool against the wall, climbed up, and cut the rope that tied the palm roof to the rafters. I lifted the roof and pulled myself over the wall. The bamboo's sharp ends stung my skin. Outside I tumbled, right into the mud behind the hut. Loro had let go. Gently he floated down next to me. He climbed back up my arm and found his place again on my shoulder. It wasn't until then that I realized my sandals were still inside. But I couldn't go back for them. I leaned against the back of the house, breathing hard. I heard my new husband open the door. I felt his confusion as he looked around the room for me. I heard him throwing things against the wall, cursing.

I ran.

All night I ran, in bare feet. Loro flew alongside me. Through coffee fields and forests I ran. Across streams and jagged rocks. Over fields of spiny cacti. And all night, thunder and lightning and rain came in waves. Again and again I slipped and fell in the mud. The wetness on my feet—how much of it was mud and how much was blood? I didn't know. And I didn't know if the men tried to come after me.

But I did feel something else behind me. Something kind. Something that smelled faintly of sweet copal incense. The spirit of Ta'nu, hovering behind me. A wispy, smoky form in the rain, urging me on gently.

At dawn I stopped running. I sat down on a mossy log by a stream. Loro perched on a low tree branch, grooming his feathers with his beak. The sky melted from black to deep blue to gray to pink. My heartbeat calmed, but my feet began to sting, to throb. Ayy! They were raw and bloody and riddled with thorns. I gathered herbs, limping around, crying out with every step. Then I carefully pulled out spine after spine. I washed my feet and wrapped them in the fresh herbs. *Carrizo, Santa María, sauco.* Finally I laid my head on the moss and slept. I dreamed of doña Three Teeth's village, even though I'd never seen it before. I dreamed of the green fields she'd spoken of, the thick forests, the sound of the waterfall.

Late that morning Loro woke me up with *"¡Buenos días buenos días!"* For a moment I lay there, content, feeling the warm sun over me like a lace shawl. Watching the light shine through the leaves, speckling my skin with jaguar spots. Breathing in the freshness of morning, the freshness of dew.

Then the pain came back. Ayy, how my feet throbbed! When I unwrapped the leaves from my feet, I gasped at how they looked in the bright daylight. So torn up, as though a dog had been gnawing on them. It would be days before I could walk on them.

But where would I go, anyway? I could not go back to my village. Uncle would be furious. Don Norberto and his family would be more furious. All that money spent on a wedding feast. Oh, the whole town would be furious. You see, people frowned at a disobedient girl. Especially at a disobedient wife. If I went back, Uncle would force me to live with my husband. And I had no doubt that my husband would punish me for humiliating him.

Never before had I felt this alone. The emptiness in my stomach spread over my body. The emptiness crept out to the forest around me, so *everything* looked empty. If a cliff had been nearby, I might have leaped off it this time. Just like that healer in my village. Yes, and if my feet hadn't hurt so much, I might have walked and walked until I *found* a cliff, and then jumped off.

Instead I lay on the fallen tree trunk. I lay with my eyes closed, blocking out the sunshine. There I dwelled in empty blackness. Everything seemed empty because I was empty. Because my soul had nearly given up. It had started drifting away from my body. The fire in my feet was crawling up my legs, filling my body with fever. My soul did nothing to stop it. My soul had nearly stopped caring.

Loro found little berries to eat. I ate nothing. "*¡Ánimo!*" he called to me. But I barely moved. Day faded into night and into day again. Rain fell on me sometimes. My body was almost too tired to shiver. Too hopeless to form goose bumps. In the mornings the sun dried my body, but in the afternoons rain poured on it again.

Faces from my past came and went. The faces drifted in

and out of my mind. Faces of people I might never see again. María laughing and touching my arm. Aunt Teresa flipping tortillas. Little Lupita pretending to do a *limpia*. Doña Three Teeth singing softly.

But wait. Doña Three Teeth's voice grew clearer and stronger, until it became too close to be only a dream. Her fingers held my wrist, felt my pulse. Her hands rested on my forehead, cool and dry. They gently lifted my head and dribbled water into my mouth.

I coughed and sputtered. When I opened my eyes, I saw her three rotten teeth, her worried eyes.

Soon there was woodsmoke. She'd built a fire. She disappeared and came back with armfuls of herbs. I watched her brew them in bubbling water, watched her blow on the tea to cool it. Sip by sip, I felt the pungent tea go down my throat. Little by little it began to fill the emptiness inside.

Was this a ghost? No, it couldn't be, because at night I felt her bony body. She pressed against me under a thick blanket, sharing her warmth. She sang to me. Thin wandering melodies she sang. Melodies that a mother might sing to her child. Little by little her voice pulled me out of my dark hole. She pulled me back out into the sunshine.

Then one morning—after she fed me milk with cinnamon and honey—the rusty words finally creaked out of my mouth. "*Nku ta'a vini.*" Thank you.

Her face lit up at my voice. "You'll live!" she chirped. She leaped up and danced. Around in the air she flailed her bird legs and twig arms.

Loro screeched and whistled along with her. "Helena Helena!" The first smile in ages came to my face. A few days later I was well enough to hear her story.

"Oh, Helena!" she said. "When the day came for me to

leave prison, I was terrified. Terrified! I walked outside and oh, I thought my knees would buckle under. And the sunshine! It was so bright I thought I'd go blind. All the colors, the noise, the people! And you know what I did? I ran straight back inside to the door of my cell. Ha! But the guard wouldn't let me back in! Imagine, locked *outside* my cell." She laughed, little squirrel noises. "I had nowhere to go. Of course, I couldn't face going back to my village. So I decided to drown myself in a river.

"Ah, but then I remembered the thirty pesos. The money you gave me, Helena! Well, what a waste to drown myself in the river without spending it first. Don't you think? After all, you were kind enough to give it to me. So I walked on my wobbly legs to the market. And here's what I did." She leaned closer. "I bought myself a chicken. And a pot to cook it in. And chiles and chocolate and nuts and tomatoes and sesame seeds and raisins and spices. And a little grindstone. You can guess my plan—to make chocolate-chile sauce for my chicken! Then I bought cherry pastries—a bag of them! One after one I ate them, leaving the city, leaving a trail of crumbs behind me. I walked until I found a forest with a stream where I could cook and eat in peace. My final meal.

"And you know, Helena, as I was cooking, I remembered things. I remembered how much I loved the feel of the grindstone under my hands. And the smell of roasting garlic. And oh, Helena, when I ate that chocolate-chile chicken, tears came to my eyes. Partly from the spiciness, yes, but partly from memories of village fiestas. Everyone would come to those fiestas and fill their bellies and dance and dance. Such fun! So you know what I did? Instead of throwing myself in the river, I danced. I danced and sang, and made a new decision. I told myself, *All right, Three Teeth, you can live as long as you can find food.* And I walked. Just walked. For two years I've been walking. I find fruit and nuts from trees. Sometimes people give me tortillas when they pass me on the road. Because, yes, there are still good people in this world, people who know we all eat from the same tortilla.

"And the odd thing is, Helena, that last week I found myself dreaming of you. Hearing your voice in the wind and the rain and the water. *Oh,* I told myself, *Three Teeth, you've finally gone crazy.* But I let your voice lead me here. A few days ago I was fetching water a little way up the stream. And all of a sudden that beautiful green bird of yours walked right up to me. 'Helena Helena!' he yelled. I knew it was Loro. I followed him downstream, and he brought me to you, love. You, lying here, a few breaths away from death."

●

Little by little my strength came back. I was a withered plant, slowly growing greener, growing stronger. Soaking up sunshine. Drinking up water. Feeling the rich soil beneath me and the blue sky above.

Once I gained back enough strength, I told doña Three Teeth my own story. I spoke of my curing, Aunt Teresa's *baños de temazcal,* my adorable baby cousin. But when I came to the part about the wedding, my voice turned bitter. "So, I am married now," I told her.

"Ha!" she laughed. She dipped a cloth into a pot of cool water steeped with herbs. "Of course you're not!" She squeezed the cloth and placed it gently on my foot. It felt refreshing and tingly.

"But I am," I insisted. "We had a ceremony in the church. We had the fiesta afterward. Everything."

"You didn't sign the government papers yet, did you?"

she asked. Her voice was confident. She pressed the wet cloth against the sole of my other foot.

"Well, no," I said. You see, an official from the city came once a year to our village. He brought papers for that year's weddings, and all the new couples signed at the same time. "No, the man with the papers hadn't come yet."

"So you're not married," she said with a wink. She dabbed the cloth over my ankles, over the scabs and swollen scratches.

"But the ceremony—" I began.

"That means nothing!" she cried. "Nothing!" She threw the cloth into the pot. Water splashed over the sides. "Your uncle forced you! I tell you, *you are not married, Helena!*"

"You think?" I asked, a smile spreading across my face. I felt lighter, as though I'd just shrugged a heavy bundle of firewood off my shoulders.

"Ha! I am certain! I married for love, Helena. And you will too someday."

"You sound like Ta'nu." I laughed.

●

Doña Three Teeth asked me to call her Nana. In Mixteco this means "mother." I called her Nana gladly. Sometimes, when we were cleaning dishes or fetching water, I would feel that in some way Nana *was* my mother.

One night we sat on a stone by the river. She combed my hair with her fingers. Softly, she sang the song about the rabbit in the moon. "Nana," I told her after the song had ended, "you are my mother because you gave me life."

She unwound the orange ribbon from her braids and carefully wove it into mine. She fastened the ends together.

When I woke up the next morning, there was Nana,

standing over me. Watching me. Waiting for my eyes to open. Oh, she was full of joy. Joy, spilling out all around her.

"Helena, you're well enough to travel now. Let's go!"

"Go where?" I mumbled. I was sleepy, yes, but already her joy had started seeping into me.

"To the village where I grew up!" she said. Her eyes blazed. "Together we'll find my children. Together we'll live by the sound of the waterfall. I dreamed this last night!"

"How will we live?" I asked. I sat up and stretched. "How will we eat?"

"Curing! We'll be the village's healers!"

I thought about this. She had learned to heal from her grandmother. And oh, how I longed to start curing again. Yes, we could do this together. We didn't need husbands. But what about Aunt, and María, and Lupita? Thinking about them made my chest tighten up. No, it was too late to go back to that path. My path now was leading me elsewhere, pulling me along like a river's current. Pulling me over the edge, like a waterfall. Over the edge to a new place, a different life. Oh, I would not live with my aunt and cousins again, but sparks from their souls flickered inside mine. And perhaps someday I would go back to see them.

"How far is your village?" I asked. I felt a flutter in my stomach, like the wings of a hummingbird.

"Oh, about three days' walk over those mountains." Nana pointed west. "It's called Yucuyoo."

Yucuyoo. The Hill of the Moon.

For three days we walked along paths, steep and rocky. We slipped and slid on the mud from afternoon rains. But the walking was good for me. Nana said that I was still too thin, but my cheeks were pink like rose petals. That my face glowed like a full moon. That my hair looked thick and shiny as a jaguar's fur.

And you know, Nana looked beautiful now too. How can a person be beautiful with three rotten teeth, you wonder. But she was! The fine structure of her face, strong like the old stone sculptures of gods that we came across in the cornfields. And I felt a warmth, a big light, that came from her little bird body. Oh, she was beautiful.

At the top of a tall mountain, late in the morning on the fourth day, we peered into the valley below. Smoke rose from houses. The women were making tortillas. How my stomach rumbled! We hadn't eaten tortillas for ages.

"We're home!" Nana yelled. She did a little dance, singing, "We're home, we're home. . . ."

Together we skipped, stumbled, tripped down the path. Of course, at the bottom we slowed down, because we couldn't have people in the village thinking we were crazy. No, they would need to trust us before they came to us for cures. In front of us, a young man led his burro, carrying bundles of firewood. We fell into step next to him.

"Good morning," he said in Mixteco.

"Good morning," we said. We were still breathless and smiling.

He was eating a quesadilla as he walked. He must have seen us staring at the food and breathing in the smell of melted cheese, because he offered us some. I chewed the quesadilla and savored every bite. As I ate, I looked sideways at the man. He walked with a limp, wincing at every step.

"How did you hurt your leg, *señor*?" I asked.

"Pulled a muscle last week hoeing the cornfields," he said.

Oh, I couldn't resist. "I can cure it with a *baño de temaz-cal*. To thank you for the food."

"Are you a healer?" he asked, surprised. "You're so young. You're not even my age."

"Helena's been curing since she was a little girl," Nana said proudly. "She's famous. People have come from far-off places to be cured by her. . . ."

Blushing, I squeezed Nana's arm to make her stop.

"Yes," he said, smiling. He tilted his hat up to see me more clearly. "I would be honored to be cured by you, señorita Helena."

And that's when I noticed the kindness in his eyes. One green and one brown.

Clara

When the storm ended, rays of orange evening light peeked out from behind the mountains. Even though broken branches and fallen trees dotted the mountainside, everything seemed fresh and sparkling—the shiny rocks, the leaves with water droplets clinging like diamonds. I ran my hands lightly over my bruises and scrapes. My skin had become a mosaic of purple and blue.

The goats began to stir. I looked down at Pedro. He lay perfectly still, his head in my lap, only the breeze moving his hair slightly. For a terrifying second I thought he might be dead.

"Pedro." I brushed my fingers over his forehead.

He smiled faintly.

"C'mon," I whispered, and picked up my backpack.

I helped him stand up and held my arm around him as we walked a few steps downhill.

"Wait," he mumbled. "My guitar."

"It's over here." I led him toward the crack in the rock where I'd stowed it. When I pulled it out, he gave me a relieved smile. I slung it over my back and let it rest against my backpack. Leaning on each other for support, we squished down the mountain. What I remember most about our walk were the butterflies dancing in the air above the uprooted trees, as though it were a day just like any other.

After dusk, we sat by the kitchen fire—my grandparents and Pedro and his mother and me, all drinking cinnamon coffee with lots of sugar. A couple of hours earlier, Abuelita and Abuelo had met Pedro and me at the base of the mountain and helped us walk home. Once we were back in the kitchen, Abuelita had placed cool cloths on my raw hands and made Pedro an herb tea for his scorpion stings. When his mother showed up, she hugged him over and over and settled her thin arm protectively around him.

"Ayyy, Pedro Victor!" she murmured, smoothing his hair. "Aren't you lucky Clara was with you!"

"Pedro *Victor*?" I asked. Where had I heard that name before?

"Victor's my middle name." Pedro took a sip of tea. "I was named after my great-grandfather."

"Pedro Victor, the romantic musician," Abuelo told me with a wink.

Slowly, the pieces were coming together. "Doña Three Teeth's husband?" I asked.

Abuelita nodded. "Nana lived long enough to see her great-grandson born," she said, motioning to Pedro.

Pedro's mother smiled. "She said he looked just like his great-grandfather."

The fire flickered in a way that lit up a perfectly formed spider's web in the corner. Thin, silvery threads stretched from a rafter to a basket of dried chiles to the wall. The threads joined with more threads and spiraled inward, meeting in the center. Only when the light was just right, only if you were paying attention, could you begin to see the connections. It occurred to me that hidden strands linked us all, through decades, over thousands of miles, across borders.

I glanced at Pedro and saw that he had followed my gaze to the spider's web. After a moment he looked back at me and smiled, and for some reason I felt sure he was thinking the same thing I was.

"Now," said Abuelo, "when will we hear about the spirit waterfall?"

Abuelita raised her eyebrow, curious.

"Yes, tell us!" Pedro's mother said, stroking his hand.

Pedro and I looked at each other. How to begin?

First we tried to explain the feeling that it was another world down there, how on the surface there's nothing more than a soft rushing sound, but once you go below you see its wild power. You know that it's always there, immense, existing right under the surface—whether you're sleeping or eating or working. You can ignore it, forget about it, until you let yourself really listen. And you get the feeling that everyone has a waterfall inside themselves, inside their deepest caves.

Maybe we each have to make this trip inside to really know who we are.

Pedro and I tried to tell them this, but the only words we found were "It's really big" and "It's really loud" and "The water was flowing really fast." Words felt too flimsy to explain that power.

●

The next day, I walked along the cornfield to Pedro's house for the first time. It looked a lot like my grandparents' place, a small cluster of shacks, only more run-down. Loose planks dangled by nails, shutters hung lopsided, and chunks of cement had fallen off the sink basin. His mother was washing clothes under a lime tree when she glanced up and smiled at me—the same wide smile as Pedro's, identical except for her two blackened teeth.

She wiped her hands on her apron and greeted me with a light handshake. "Ah, Clara! Pedro will be so happy to see you!" She motioned to the biggest shack. "Go in, Clara. Make yourself at home."

A sheet hung over the doorway. "Hi," I said, and pushed aside the sheet.

It was dark and cool inside.

"Welcome to my mansion, Clara." Pedro grinned. He was sitting propped on a narrow bed covered in a fuzzy beige blanket with a giant peacock design. Above the headboard was one small square window with clear plastic taped around the edges. The floor was made of packed dirt and the walls of logs. Sheets hanging from the ceiling divided the house into rooms. In the dining room were two dented folding chairs and a metal card table and not much else. In the other room, a bare mattress sat next to a wooden crate of folded flowered dresses and checked aprons—his mother's room, I guessed.

I moved close to his bed. "How do you feel?"

"Better now that you're here. All night and all morning half of my body felt strange. Like hundreds of little men were inside it, stabbing me with tiny swords."

"And now?"

"Now it just feels like ants crawling around in there."

"Good." I felt shy suddenly. I was used to spending time with him in the woods, not inside four walls.

"Have a seat." He motioned to two chairs in the room—wooden ones with green paint chipping off.

"Can I just sit next to you?" I asked.

He started scooting over to give me room.

"You don't have to move over," I said. I took off my sandals and sat down next to him, leaning my back against the headboard. The bed was creakier than the one I slept in, and even lumpier.

"I want to play you a song, Clara, but I need you to strum." He held up his right hand, which seemed a little swollen. "See? This hand is useless for a few days."

I rested the guitar on our laps. He moved his fingers over the guitar's neck while I strummed. It was the song about me coming out of the shadows in the middle of the night.

> . . . *I give you a song when you appear,*
> *The mystery of love . . .*

After the last note faded, I said, "Let's play another."

"How about a protest song?" he asked, smiling.

"Yes," I said, and I meant it. "A protest song." Over the past few days he'd explained the words of some protest songs

241

to me, and it seemed to me that they weren't too different from love songs. True, the songs talked about big life things like being poor and leaving home to find work and getting hurt by unfair government rules. But don't these things have a lot to do with love between two people? The thread of love between Dad and his parents was nearly broken because he left his village to make money. Same with the connection between Pedro's father and Pedro and his mother. Pedro and I had promised each other, after we'd made up from our fight, that our thread would stay strong no matter what.

A single framed picture hung on the wall across from the bed. It was a faded picture of three people in front of tall green cornstalks. The woman, a younger version of Pedro's mother, was holding hands with a little boy in a palm hat. On the other side, the boy held the hand of a man in a matching palm hat. The adults weren't smiling, but they had proud expressions. They looked hard at the camera, furrowing their eyebrows and pressing their lips together in concentration, as though they were trying to look into the future. The little boy had a huge white smile and was looking up and off to the side, toward the mountains. A single crack ran down the middle of the glass like a lightning bolt.

After we finished the protest song, I asked, "Is that your father?"

Pedro nodded and laid the guitar down at the side of the bed. "A few years ago I ripped that picture off the nail and threw it at the wall. Then I hid it in a box and refused to tell my mother where it was. 'I don't have a father,' I told her. Just this morning, I hung it back up."

"Why?"

"I wanted you to see me together with him." He ran his

fingers along the satin edge of the peacock blanket. "In the cave, when it looked like I might die, I thought of my father. I thought that I wanted to know him. I wanted him to know me."

I pushed my bangs behind my ears so I could take in every detail of Pedro's face as he talked, even though I knew his face pretty well already from sketching it so much. At least half of my sketchbook was filled with his different expressions, but no single one that captured who he was. He didn't look much like his father as far as I could tell, except for his strong cheekbones.

"Are you going to try to find him?" I asked.

"I'm thinking about it," he said. "What if he wants to see me but he's ashamed to? Maybe I need to make the first move."

"I could look up his phone number on the Internet and you could call him," I offered.

"Maybe," he said, and looked thoughtfully at the picture. He leaned over and picked up the guitar. We started playing another song, a song that was part love song and part protest song, woven together like a palm hat.

"Do you have any pictures of Marcos?" I asked.

He shook his head. "All that's left of Marcos is his music."

"And his ideas," I said.

I knew that back in Walnut Hill, I would hear Pedro's music, and it would remind me to search past the way things look on the outside to find their inside. His songs would make me think of all the threads of love in the world, and the ways they're all interconnected, like spiderwebs. Maybe that's what Abuelita meant about Marcos changing the world by changing Pedro. And through Pedro, changing me.

On the day Pedro could finally limp over to our house, we sat in the kitchen as Abuelita and I patted out tortillas and laid them on the clay *comal* over the fire. Abuelo took a deep breath and said quietly, "*M'hija,* you know what day tomorrow is."

Of course I knew, but I'd been trying hard to forget. I'd been changing the subject whenever he and Abuelita brought it up. I picked up a flattened circle of tortilla dough and placed it on the *comal.* My tortillas were perfect now. It had taken me all summer, but finally, they were just the right thickness.

Pedro sat massaging his leg in silence. The smoke was drifting into his eyes, making them shine.

"Clara, perhaps Pedro can help you pack after lunch," Abuelita said gently. "Tomorrow at sunrise we must leave to catch the bus."

I flipped the tortilla with my fingertips and watched it puff up in the center. My palms still had strips of white cloth around them where the top layer of skin had been scraped off. Somehow my fingertips had come through fine, probably because they'd gotten so tough after a summer of making tortillas. I picked the tortilla off the *comal* and quickly dropped it on top of the pile of tortillas in the basket. By the time I came back next summer, my fingers would be soft again. I wondered if I'd have to start all over to create the calluses.

"Is this enough tortillas, Abuelita?"

She gave me a long, thoughtful look. Then she nodded and sat down in her little chair. We ate lunch in silence— chocolate-chile chicken with tortillas and rice. Even though it was my second favorite, I barely touched it. My throat wasn't working right—the food seemed to take forever going down, and once it got into my stomach, it sat there like a stone.

Pedro wasn't eating either, I noticed. He watched the fire and didn't even blink when smoke drifted into his eyes again, making them watery and red. Finally Abuelita took our plates and said, "Why don't you start packing up now, *mi amor*? I'll wash the dishes."

Pedro walked outside with only a slight limp now, but instead of coming toward my room, he headed straight down the path toward his house.

"Pedro! Aren't you going to help me pack?"

He didn't turn around, just shook his head and limped down the path. "Pedro!" I shouted again, and started running after him. But he kept walking fast and wouldn't turn to look at me even when I'd caught up to him.

So I stopped and watched him go. I tried to memorize him, to take a picture of him with my mind as he disappeared through the tall cornstalks.

I didn't sleep that night. I lay in bed, trying to imagine Yucuyoo existing without me here—this musty room, the hidden waterfall, Pedro's music on the mountain. Back in Walnut Hill, Dad and Mom and Hector were probably asleep, and my room was sitting there empty. There was the mall just a mile away, with its giant parking lot lit up by fluorescent lights, and a mile farther, my school with the empty desks and clean blackboards and thin gray carpet. In two days I would be there, filling those spaces, and Yucuyoo would be far away—a jumble of sounds and smells and images—slowly fading.

At dawn Abuelita came into my room and placed her hand on my forehead. "Clara, *mi amor,* it's time," she said, stroking my face. I pretended to be asleep so that she would stay with her hand on my head and keep talking to me softly.

After a few minutes, she shook me gently. I dragged myself out of bed, put on jeans and my art sweatshirt, and tied my hair in a ponytail. Outside I splashed water onto my face and brushed my teeth in the blue half-light.

While we drank cinnamon coffee in the kitchen, Abuelo handed me my father's carved gourd. He'd filled it with roasted coffee beans and tucked it into a woven palm basket, along with a wooden stirrer and five chunks of cinnamon chocolate. "Now you can show your mother and brother how to make hot chocolate, *m'hija.* And the gourd and coffee beans are for Enrique. Tell him we hope the wind blows him our way again." His eyes were shining. One brown and one green.

Abuelita handed me a bag of seeds. "Who knows if these herbs will grow in your home?" she said.

"Oh, they'll grow," I said. "Dad will help me plant them. He can make anything grow." It was true. Mom always said he could make even a rock sprout roots and buds. And Dad would treat these seeds with more care than ever, I was sure. Some of the herbs he might not have smelled for twenty years. I could remind him of their names, even their names in Mixteco. After all the flowers and stones and seedpods he'd given me over the years, now I could give him something important back.

"Good, *mi vida.* You and your father plant these at your home, and every time you water them, think of us. Watch them grow and think of us. Know that they are alive, and that so are we, far away." She unbraided her hair and pulled out the faded orange ribbon, the one that Nana had given her. She stood behind me and carefully wove it into my ponytail, forming a single braid. She tied the ends firmly.

The ocean was welling up inside me again, only this time the tears were more sad than happy. "Thank you." I started walking out of the kitchen to get my bags before the tears could spill over.

Just then, when I was halfway through the door, Loro cried out, "*¡Hasta luego!*" See you later!

I'd almost forgotten to say goodbye to him. I stroked his green feathers and wiped my eyes and whispered, "*Hasta luego.*" One of his feathers had fallen to the floor, and I picked it up and stuck it in my braid.

"Ahh, he said *see you later*," Abuelo said. "He knows you will return next summer with the rains."

As I left the kitchen Loro called after me: "*¡Ánimo, Clara!*"

Everything looked blurry through my film of tears while we gathered the bags from my room and carried them down the dirt path. Every few minutes I looked back, thinking that Pedro might come limping through the wildflowers. Every time I heard a sound—*Is it Pedro?* The sky had begun growing lighter in the east. A few minutes after we crossed the stream, just at the edge of the patch of trees, we heard the faint rumbling of the bus. It was coming around the bend in the mountains above us.

We started running through the woods, the bags bouncing against our backs, slamming against our thighs. Maybe we would miss it! And there wouldn't be another bus until the next morning, and then I would miss my flight, and I could stay longer, and say goodbye to Pedro. But Abuelo sprinted ahead, waving his hat and whistling at the bus. The driver slammed on the brakes in a cloud of gray exhaust and waited for Abuelita and me to catch up.

I looked back again, to see if Pedro had come. I was squinting into rays of light through the branches. The sun had risen all the way.

Through the trees I caught a glimpse of red—his pants! He was running fast, only limping a little. By the time he reached us, all my bags were loaded. Abuelita and Abuelo had already settled in their seats, and the driver sat up front, wiping his forehead with a red bandanna.

Pedro was completely out of breath, and his cheeks were as pink as I'd ever seen them. He handed me a little package wrapped in a banana leaf. "It's for you. A tape of my music," he said. "Felipe let me use his tape deck. We stayed up all night recording it." Then he gave me an envelope. "This is for my father. If you find his address, could you send it to him?"

I nodded. I couldn't find words. Everything was rushed. I wanted to tell him so many things. Last night I'd imagined a long hug and a passionate kiss. But now, all the passengers were watching us and waiting, looking restless. The driver revved the engine.

"Don't disappear, Clara," Pedro said.

"I'll come back."

We touched hands.

Inside the bus I held the tape in my lap and watched Pedro grow smaller. Finally he turned and limped back into the woods, alone. Abuelo put his arm around me and Abuelita smoothed the orange ribbon in my braid and said, "You will see him again, *mi vida*. Next summer, in the full moon in June. When you come with your father."

I would play Pedro's tape hundreds of times over the fall and winter and spring. I would sit in the dark and watch the rabbit in the moon and let Pedro's music enter me. I would feel the mountains in my bones, the stream in my blood, the sound of the waterfall in my pulse. I would feel the fresh herbs dripping rainwater down my arms, the warmth of hot chocolate, the sweet copal smoke, the taste of mango juice, the color of his voice, the smell of goats.

15

Clara

Dad and I walked through a carpet of crisp fall leaves, up a mountainside in Maryland. Treetops rustled in the breeze, all reds and yellows against the blue sky. "*Espérate,* Dad," I said. "Let's sit for a minute. I want to sketch something." We sat on a rock by a small stream and sipped from our water bottles. Dad flipped through our *Medicinal and Edible Plants* book and examined wands of blue flowers growing at the stream's edge. I opened my sketchbook to a fresh page. I'd torn out the pictures from Yucuyoo and given them to Dad. The rest of the book was nearly filled with pictures for Pedro. The pages still smelled of woodsmoke from Abuelita's kitchen, and some were wavy from getting wet in afternoon rainstorms.

I looked around for something to draw and spotted, in the sunlight, a spider's web, stretching across the stream from a tree branch on one bank to a branch on the other. With the tip of my pencil, I drew the thin threads. I'd learned in biology class that spider's silk is stronger than steel of the same weight. I sketched the web, its circles widening, connected with spokes like those of a wheel.

I glanced at Dad. He had that excited, triumphant look in his eyes that meant he was close to figuring out the name of the wildflower. I studied his face, all lit up, and saw a piece of Abuelo shining through. And then I noticed Dad's comfortable silence, his steady breath, and I heard a piece of Abuelita.

Samantha had asked me to go over to her house that day, and when I told her I was going hiking with my dad, she said, "I wish my dad hung out with me." Over the summer, her parents had decided to divorce, and her father had moved out.

When I'd first gotten home from Mexico, Samantha had thrown her arms around me and cried, "I missed you!" and then she'd burst out sobbing. She talked and talked about how miserable and lonely she was. I held her hand and felt her fear, sharp as a scorpion sting, and her sadness, a deep ache. Then I felt the heron lifting her up, little by little, out of her pain. After a while, Samantha's gasps calmed into a long sigh. "I don't feel so bad now," she said. She wiped her tears and hugged me and whispered, "Thanks, Clara."

What she was really thanking me for was letting my soul touch hers. And it wasn't just mine. I thought of the bits of Abuelita's and Abuelo's and Pedro's spirits leaping around inside me like flames and sparking Samantha's soul.

I drew the final thread of the spider's web, closing the outer circle. "*Ya, vámonos*, Dad," I said. "Ready?"

"*Sí, m'hija.*" We headed down the trail, and he talked about the wildflower he'd identified, great blue lobelia, how its leaves cured headaches and coughs. Afternoon faded into evening, and the air smelled of earth and wood and fallen leaves. I felt the strength of the spiderweb's threads connecting me to people miles and years away, as real as the moon's force on the oceans. Then I felt my father's hand, warm and callused around mine. Then I noticed the breeze, light on my arms, through the holes in my favorite green sweater. Then I thought, *This is how it feels to be alive.*

Epilogue

The moon rises over a girl and her father as they walk on a path down a mountain. The girl points to the moon, and her father's eyes follow. Their heads tilt to the right. There, there it is, the girl says. The rabbit in the moon.

In Yucuyoo, an old woman with two long braids watches the sky, humming as she takes down clothes from the line. An old man in a palm hat walks to her and puts his arm to her back. He points to a tree branch where a heron, glowing white in the moonlight, is spreading its wings. It rises up and flies across the cornfield.

By a small house, the heron alights on a tree branch. It listens to the song of a boy who sits on the stoop, a guitar on his knees. He strums and sings and watches the heron watching him.

The moonlight bathes them all tonight, its invisible threads moving over them, moving between them, moving inside them.

GLOSSARY

¿A QUÉ HORA REGRESAS? *(ah KAY OH-rah rrray-GRES-ahs)* What
time will you be back?

ABUELITA *(ah-bway-LEE-tah)* Grandmother

ABUELO *(ah-BWAY-lo)* Grandfather

ADIÓS *(ah-dee-OHS)* Goodbye

ADOBE *(ah-DOH-bay)* A material for building houses, made of
clay, mud, straw, stones, and corncobs

¡ÁNIMO! *(AH-nee-moh)* Have courage! Cheer up!

BAÑO DE TEMAZCAL *(BAHN-yoh day tay-mahs-CAHL)* An herbal
steambath dating to pre-Hispanic times

BUENAS NOCHES *(BWAY-nahs NOH-chess)* Good night

BUENAS TARDES *(BWAY-nahs TAR-dess)* Hello/good afternoon

BUENOS DÍAS *(BWAY-nohs DEE-ahs)* Hello/good morning

BURRO *(BOO-rrro)* Donkey

CARRIZO *(ka-RRREE-soh)* A bamboo-like reed that is a
healing plant

Chile *(CHEE-lay)* Hot chile pepper

Chivo *(CHEE-voh)* Goat

Comal *(coh-MAHL)* Clay plate for cooking over a fire

Copal *(coh-PAHL)* Sacred incense made from tree sap

Domicilio Conocido *(doh-mee-SEE-lee-oh coh-noh-SEE-doh)*
"Address Known"—In some small villages, there are no street names or numbers. The mail carrier knows where everyone in the village lives.

Don *(Dohn)* Mr. (a title of respect)

Doña *(DOHN-yah)* Mrs. (a title of respect)

Espérate *(ay-SPAIR-ah-tay)* Wait

Fiesta *(fee-ESS-tah)* Party

Gracias *(GRAH-see-ahs)* Thank you

Guapa *(GWAH-pah)* Beautiful

Hasta luego *(AHS-tah loo-AY-goh)* See you later

Hierba amarga *(YAIR-bah ah-MAR-gah)* Bitter herb

Hierba buena *(YAIR-bah BWAY-nah)* Good herb (in the mint family)

Hola *(OH-lah)* Hi

Huele de Noche *(WAY-lay day NOH-chay)* "Smells at Night"—a tree with flowers that are fragrant at night

Huesero *(way-SAIR-o)* Bone doctor

Huipil *(wee-PEEL)* Traditional woven or embroidered shirt or dress

Limpia *(LEEM-pee-ah)* A spiritual cleaning with fresh herbs and flowers

Loro *(LOH-roh)* Parrot

Machete *(mah-CHEH-tay)* Long knife used for work in the fields

Mal aire *(mahl AH-ee-ray)* Evil air; a sickness

Metate *(meh-TAH-tay)* Grinding stone

Mezcal *(mess-KAHL)* Liquor made from maguey cactus

Mi amor *(mee ah-MORRR)* My love (affectionate term like "honey")

Mi vida *(mee VEE-dah)* My life (affectionate term like "honey")

Mira *(MEE-rah)* Look

M'hija *(MEE-ha)* My daughter (affectionate term)

Muchacha *(moo-CHAH-chah)* Maid, servant

Muy bien *(MOOY bee-EN)* Very good

Nagual *(NAH-wahl)* Someone who can transform into an animal

Oaxaca *(wah-HA-kah)* A city and state in southern Mexico

Petate *(peh-TAH-tay)* Woven palm mat

Pirúl *(pee-ROOL)* A healing plant

Pitaya *(pee-TY-ah)* A cactus fruit, red on the inside, with thorns on the skin

¿Qué decidiste? *(KAY deh-see-DEES-tay)* What did you decide?

Quesadilla *(kay-sah-DEE-yah)* Tortilla with melted cheese

Ruda *(RRROO-dah)* A strong-smelling herb used fresh in *limpias*

Sauco *(SAH-oo-koh)* A healing plant

Señora *(sen-YOH-rah)* Lady/Mrs.

Señorita *(sen-yor-EE-tah)* Miss

Sombrero *(som-BRAIR-oh)* Woven palm hat

Tamal *(tah-MAHL)* Cornmeal, chiles, cheese, and meat wrapped in a banana leaf or corn husk

Tortilla *(tor-TEE-yah)* Flat, circular bread made from cornmeal and water

Ya, vámonos *(YAH VAH-moh-nos)* Let's go

Yo solo y mi alma *(YOH SOH-loh ee mee AHL-mah)* Just me and my soul

People speak different kinds of Mixteco from region to region and even from village to village. So if you ever meet people who speak Mixteco, you'll notice that they might have different ways of saying things, depending on where they're from.

Mixteco is a tonal language. This means, for example, that a word can change meanings depending on whether your voice goes up or down or stays at a middle tone on each syllable. Here is a simplified pronunciation guide that doesn't indicate syllable accents or tones.

ITA *(ee-tah)* Flower

ITA TIKUVA *(ee-tah tee-koo-vah)* Butterfly flower

ITA TINDOO *(ee-tah teen-dohh)* A healing plant (*sauco* in Spanish)

IYO VA'A NII *(ee-zhoh vah-ah neee)* I'm fine

NAJA IYO NUU? *(nah-hah ee-zhoh noooo)* How are you?

NA KA'AN NO'O ÑUU SAVI? *(na kah-ahn noh-oh nyoooo sah-vee)* Do you speak Mixteco?

NANA *(nah-nah)* Mother

NKU TA'A VINI *(nkoo tah-ah vee-nee)* Thank you

ÑUU SAVI *(nyoooo sah-vee)* Mixteco (literally, "the Place of Water")

TA'NU *(tah-noo)* Grandfather

TON KUAA *(ton kwaah)* Good evening

YUKU NUXI *(yoo-koo noo-she)* Sap herb

YUKU KUAA *(yoo-koo kwaah)* Night herb

YUKU TAXINI *(yoo-koo tah-shee-nee)* A healing herb (*pericón* in Spanish)

YUKU TUCHI *(yoo-koo too-chee)* Bitter herb (*hierba amarga* in Spanish)

YUCUYOO *(yoo-koo yohoh)* Hill of the moon

Laura Resau lived in the Mixtec region of Oaxaca, Mexico, for two years as an English teacher and anthropologist. She now lives with her husband and her dog in Colorado, where she teaches cultural anthropology and ESL (English as a Second Language). This is her first novel.